To f.

Hope you enjoy it.

best wishes !

# Escape From Rindorn

Bart A. Eriksson

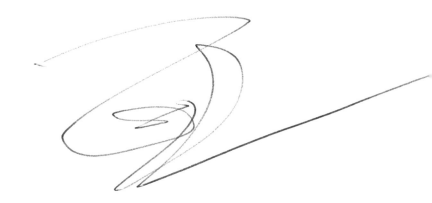

Knight and ninja images, Shutterstock.com.
Book cover designer: Miladinka Milic.
http://www.milagraphicartist.com

# DEDICATION

To my late sister Margaret and her daughter Carmen, who of all people are responsible for encouraging the creation of this book and its sequels.

# CONTENTS

# ACKNOWLEDGMENTS

Much of the credit for this book's existence should go to my late sister Margaret. She relentlessly kept showering me with books and articles on how to write, until I just had to give in and try. My parents, brother Jon, Mike Wellunscheg and other family members and friends also deserve thanks for reading through the earlier drafts and offering helpful suggestions. Betty Keller did the editing. Thanks again! Thanks also go to my niece Carmen, nephew Philip and the members of Unity Lutheran in Medicine Hat back in 2008, for their encouragement to get it published and to produce a sequel. And thanks need to be offered to Rick Bergh, Kobus Genis, and especially to my wife Darina for their help and encouragement with the final push.

# ESCAPE FROM RINDORN

## PROLOGUE

From his vantage point on the North West Tower, Hubert, sentry for the evening, yawned, gazed westward and thought about his tiresome work. On this night, as on all the other nights he had stood watch, nothing unusual was stirring beyond the walls. For the past two hundred years, the only real dangers to the city's safety had come from within. Thieves, bandits and the occasional corrupt city councillor, were the real threats. Yet due to ancient law, sentries like Hubert still stood watch over Rindorn every night. He grumbled as he contemplated the absurdity of his job and longed to be asleep like sensible folk below.

Turning his attention from the outside world, he looked inside over the houses, shops, church and the city's castle all packed densely together. Rindorn's five thousand people lived in a space that could comfortably hold only three-quarters that many. If by chance invaders should arrive, there would be little room for the country-folk who lived beyond the walls.

Hubert's nighttime reflections were abruptly disturbed by a clatter of stones off to the right. He moved to the tower's south side from where the sound had originated. Nothing in sight. *An owl has probably knocked some gravel off the top of the wall*, he thought. He returned his gaze to the city.

A few minutes later his eyelids drooped. He wished that the night was colder, making it easier to stay alert, but it had been a warm spring. There was no wind, and the thick woollen coat covering his chain mail kept out the chill too well. Somewhere in the distance a farm dog howled. Several moments passed. Hubert shuffled his feet.

There it was again—the sound of falling gravel just south of the tower. Curious, Hubert moved again to that side and peered out across the wall into the darkness. He was looking for a large bird, but he saw nothing. He decided that it must have already flown away. Then he saw movement along the outer wall. Was it just a shadow cast by his lantern? Hubert rubbed his eyes. Then looking again, he was sure he saw something crouching on the wall behind one of the battlements.

"Who's there?" he shouted into the darkness.

No response.

Alarmed, he darted towards the trap door leading to the ladder below. Heaving it open he hastened down, leaping the last few rungs, before bursting through the tower door and out onto the wall.

Twang.

Something metallic hit the tower behind his

head. He glanced over his shoulder and saw a crossbow shaft lying on the cobblestones just in front of the tower.

Shocked, he gazed at it for half a moment before remembering to raise the alarm. "To arms! To arms!" he yelled. "Men of the tower, to arms. . ."

Twang.

Hubert fell, dead. a single crossbow shaft had pierced his helmet.

## 1 THE INN

Thud, Thud, Boom!

Room Twelve at the Scarlet Raven Inn resounded with heavy knocking. "Open up, Jonathan," called a harsh voice. "We know you're in there."

Jonathan, rascal and plague of the city watch, lay fast asleep in his bed, a blissful smile spread across his handsome, youthful face.

Again came the sound of knocking, louder this time. Boom! Boom! Boom!

"Jonathan, no one's amused. Open up!"

Still no response from the sleeping Jonathan. His bed stretched itself out into the room. Mid-morning sunlight streamed in through the sizable window on the east wall, reflected off a mirror and brightened a patch on the floor next to Jonathan's leather sandals.

BOOM, BOOM, BOOM.

More knocking caused the door to shudder with impact. "Jonathan, this is no joke! It's Vonich talking. Open the door!" The voice seethed with impatience.

Jonathan finally rolled over and groaned. He had just had an unpleasant dream about presiding over a sumptuous banquet where in the end the dessert had been spitefully removed.

"If you don't open it, we will break it down. We have our orders." Vonich now spoke with measured control.

This time the voice had Jonathan's attention. He sat bolt upright clutching the blankets around his half-clothed body. Patches of dirty blond hair stood upright in tufts. Sleep still befogged his brain—but he did not have long to ponder.

THUD!

They were breaking the door down!

He looked around wildly for a means of escape. The window! It was just large enough to squeeze through.

He stumbled to the window. *Yes, I can do it. I can leap out the window.* Then realizing that he would be too conspicuous if he ran through the streets in only underwear, he darted back to collect his shirt from the bedpost.

THUD!

The wooden door looked sturdy enough, yet Jonathan knew that it would not last forever. Quickly he pulled the ragged white cotton shirt over his head. Trying to control the tremble in his voice, he feigned indignation.

"Vonich! What's the meaning of this?" he said.

"Oh, so you are in there," said Vonich, after a moment's silence. "Open this door at once or you'll be in even worse trouble, if that's possible."

"And what have I done to deserve harassment at this time in the morning? If the innkeeper hears about this, he'll . . . ." He pulled on his roughly woven brown woollen trousers.

"He can't save you, you piece of filth. This time you've gone too far! The only chance you've got—and it's slim—is the mercy of our Lord Mayor. So what were you up to last night?" Apparently, since Vonich could not get through the door, he had decided to start his interrogation from outside of it.

For reasons of his own Jonathan wished to avoid this question. "Let me get some clothes on and I'll open the door." As he said this, Jonathan, finished strapping on his sandals, and now he crept over to the bedroom window, picking up his sword belt on the way.

"Listen, you offspring of rodents," bellowed Vonich, "will you let us in or do you need more time to comb your hair? Open the door before I break it down!"

Jonathan searched for a witty retort, but none came to mind. Finally in desperation he shouted, "Hold on, I'll come when I'm ready!" As soon as the words were out of his mouth he knew he had made a mistake. It was too defiant, almost sure to cause an unpleasant reaction. Vonich apparently agreed. The door resonated with the force of a fresh impact.

Fingers trembling, Jonathan struggled with the window latch. The stupid thing was rusted shut! He glanced back towards the door just as another blow struck.

THUD!

This impact produced a sound of splintering wood. The place where the deadbolt met the doorframe had cracked.

Jonathan's stomach tightened with fear. It was

not the first time he had got on the wrong side of Vonich and he knew that the man did not make idle threats. So far he had always managed to evade detection and punishment. No doubt, Vonich thought the current situation provided a prime opportunity for revenge.

Desperate, Jonathan heaved on the rusted latch with all his might. Miraculously it broke, coming loose in his hand! Astonished, he stared at it for a second. Then recovering himself, he dropped it and pushed the window outwards.

It opened easily. The curtains flapped with the incoming breeze. He was free!

He stuck his head outside for a quick scan of his surroundings, blinking a couple times as his blue eyes adjusted to the blinding sunlight. It was already ten o'clock and there was not a cloud in the sky. If he were not about to be arrested, he would have thought that it was a pleasant spring day.

His third storey window overlooked the narrow cobblestone alley at the building's backside. Two men in white shirts strolled south, and a woman in a shawl ambled north. All were oblivious to his presence.

Then he looked down. With a feeling of relief he saw that the inn's kitchen entrance was almost directly beneath him, just a foot or two to his left, and the thatched roof of the door canopy overhanging the entrance jutted out into the street. This was good news. Instead of falling the full three storeys when he jumped, he could land on a thatched roof only ten feet below!

CRACK!

From behind Jonathan heard the sickening sound of splintering wood. Startled, he yanked his head back inside the room, striking it on the raised window frame. The door's top half had given way. All that protected him against invasion was the partially intact bottom half, plus a row of dangerous looking wood splinters still obscuring the top opening. One more solid blow and Vonich would be through!

Mentally preparing for the jump, Jonathan reached again for the window frame, then he stopped. His sword was still on the floor next to his bed.

From the hallway came the hubbub of many voices and Vonich's voice booming over top of them, "Get back to your rooms. This doesn't concern you!"

Hoping that the crowd forming outside would delay the guards, Jonathan turned and dashed towards the far end of the bedframe where his sword lay. At the same moment, he heard a final THUD as the door's bottom half gave way. Two guards staggered into the room.

Crouching at his bedside, the sword almost in his grasp, Jonathan grabbed hold of the bedpost with his right hand and reached downwards for the sword with his left. With relief he felt his fingers close around the sheath.

Vonich, entered the room and glanced right and left, not immediately perceiving his quarry. Pushing upwards with his right hand on the bedpost, Jonathan sprang over to the window.

"Seize him!" barked Vonich.

With his left hand Jonathan tossed his sword and scabbard outside, down onto the thatched roof of the door canopy below. Quickly, he placed his left foot through the window frame and tried to bring the right up beside it, but even the usually agile Jonathan found this awkward. Unfortunately the guards were faster.

Two pairs of strong hands plucked him out of the frame and stood him on his feet.

"Escaping arrest, eh?" sneered Vonich, cuffing him across the face with the back of his right hand. "It won't help your case with the Mayor. I can't guess what you were thinking, trying to slip out. It's not that we couldn't find you once you got down to the street anyway."

"I don't know what this is about," said Jonathan, shaken by the blow, "but you've really overstepped yourself this time, Vonich." He knew that protesting was pointless, but he felt he had to say something.

"Have I now?" replied Vonich. "Perhaps this will finally teach you some respect for authority. Not that I expect you'll get another chance! Which reminds me, we still have a score to settle about the royal ball—where you replaced the rose bouquets with cauliflower and drew a picture on the coronation dress. I think you're *long* overdue for a lesson on respect. Ivan, hold him."

"Yes, Captain," said a nearly monotone voice from behind Jonathan.

Jonathan felt the grasp of the two guards on his shoulders shift so that a single person stood behind him, pinning both arms behind his back. Apparently this was Ivan.

Vonich raised his right fist. Jonathan closed his eyes just before it hit him broadside on his left cheek. He gasped in pain. The next blow landed above his right temple, knocking him sideways. It was followed by a punch striking his ribcage just below his heart. He felt sick.

Then his fortunes changed. As Vonich paused momentarily, Ivan adjusted his grip, loosening it to find a better hold. Snatching his opportunity, Jonathan struggled free!

Instinctively he ducked Vonich's next blow, which instead landed full on the face of the unsuspecting Ivan. He felt only a twinge of sympathy for Ivan, guessing that the man had helped Vonich in this kind of work before.

Darting around the reeling Ivan and over to the window, he planted his hands on the inside of the frame and vaulted both feet through the window in one motion. His body followed, and in the same instant he pushed off with his hands from the building and over to his left.

But the task of escaping had so preoccupied him that he had forgotten to prepare himself mentally for the jump, and he was transfixed by the sight of the canopy roof rushing up to greet him. A split-second later his feet landed, but his left leg sank into the roof thatch up to the kneecap. Struggling to keep his balance, he momentarily flapped his arms before tumbling onto his back with his leg bent at the knee, still sticking halfway into the thatch. His sword was dislodged by his fall and clattered on to the cobblestones below.

At the moment, his vulnerable position did not bother him as much as the indignity of his situation. After escaping capture by three armed guards, and leaping valiantly from a third storey window, here he was, flopped over on his backside on a porch roof!

He cast a quick glance upwards. One of the guards poked his head out the window, saw Jonathan, and pulled his head in again.

Then from above he heard Vonich yell, "Don't just stand there. Jump down after him!"

# 2 RINDORN

Jonathan's heart beat faster as he fought to pull his left foot free. The dry straw bristles and wattle sticks had scratched his leg on the way down. Pulling the leg back upwards did not make it any better, but in a moment he had leapt lightly down from the roof. Picking up his sword, he started down the alley.

Just in time! Behind him, there came a crashing sound, and glancing back, he saw the torso of a guard buried up to his waist in roof thatch. His armour had made him too heavy for the roof to support.

Jonathan smiled. It was gratifying to see his pursuer stuck in a similarly ridiculous position. He only hoped that the guard would remain trapped for a long while.

*Where do I go? . . . . Where do I go?* thought Jonathan as he sped down the alleyway, glancing back from time to time for any signs of pursuit. This alley was typical for Rindorn—narrow, paved with cobblestones, and flanked by three- and four-storeyed houses on either side. Occasionally he had to dart around some passer-by, but luckily this was one of the quieter streets.

His biggest advantage lay in the fact that he knew the city better than most of its inhabitants. As a child he had played on top of all the houses and in every nook where it was possible to hide. But the city was not large, and he could run only so far before bumping into a guard or the outside wall. He had never expected to be arrested over the execution of a simple prank. *Granted, I performed it rather well*, he thought proudly.

Finally, as he turned a corner to another alley, an idea struck him. A short distance away stood an abandoned house where he had hidden as a child. Its outside door was locked, but it contained an internal courtyard open to the sky. If he could get to that part of the city without being seen and somehow climb up on a rooftop, he would be able to drop down into the courtyard and wait for pursuit to quieten down. Then by nightfall he could steal his way over to the loft where he sometimes stayed, collect a few possessions and slip out of town until this whole thing had blown over.

He was already three alleyways over from where he had started. Likely then he was in no immediate danger. Still, he wanted to make sure. Slowing to a walk to avoid attention, he cautiously approached the junction with the next alley. Hugging the buildings on the north side of the street, he peered around the corner to the right and then stole a glance to the left. There were passers-by and a few merchants selling their goods but no guards. Exhaling heavily, he relaxed just a little. He glanced behind to make sure of no pursuit and then walked around the corner to his right.

His escape plan had one difficulty, but it could not be helped. In order to get to the house that he was thinking of, he would have to pass through the central square, which was always watched by guards in the daytime. Fortunately, the square was not far away. In fact, the street he was currently on went down a gradual slope and opened out onto it.

Rindorn's central square was irregularly shaped. The southern side, the one Jonathan wished to cross, extended almost a hundred yards, whereas the northern side spread across a mere eighty yards. The square functioned as a gathering area and as a place for local farmers or craftsmen to come and sell their wares. There were only two market days a week in Rindorn, Tuesdays and Fridays, and on those days the square and the surrounding streets were filled with the booths of eager merchants from the countryside. As Jonathan got closer, on this Friday morning, the streets became more crowded with vendors who had spilled out from the square and into the alleyways.

Most of Rindorn's important buildings gazed out onto the square. On its northwest corner stood the castle, used by Vonich and the Rindorn watch as their headquarters. Only the sidewall of the main castle keep bordered the square and for the most part the castle stretched westward along one of the side streets. But the grandest building overlooking the square was the mayor's residence—brick and stone, towering five storeys into the sky and dominating most of the square's northern portion. Ivy grew along its southern face, partly obscuring many of the windows. In front of its main doorway stood the twenty-five-foot statue of Morden the Magnificent, the city's founder. Morden's sword reached boldly out in front of him, protecting Rindorn from its enemies.

At that moment a burly guard was struggling to climb Morden's statue. He had nearly reached the statue's shoulders and was pausing for a rest before advancing up the neck. The guard's final aim was to arrive at the outstretched sword where a pair of trousers, tied to the sword's point, flapped merrily in the breeze. The trousers clearly displayed the mayor's insignia.

Jonathan knew the soldier. His name was Aiden. Jonathan also knew the basic route along the statue's arm that Aiden would need to take in order to reach the trousers. He knew it because he had been the one who had tied them there—with much less difficulty—the previous night.

But Jonathan was not the only person watching Aiden. A whole crowd of amused onlookers, nine hundred at least, ignored the merchants' bargains and instead were focussing on the unfolding drama. They shouted words of encouragement to Aiden, who took it all in good humour.

"Climbing up in the world, I see," called out one bystander.

"Only a bit farther," cried another.

"Aren't there better places to dry your laundry?" said a third.

"Aiden, did they get hooked on the sword as you were climbing up or jumping down?"

"What does the city watch do when you aren't busy retrieving the mayor's laundry?"

The soldier only snorted in response and kept climbing.

Jonathan worried whether he could force his way

through the mass of people before Vonich and company arrived. Yet despite the danger, he found himself almost transfixed by the scene. It was gratifying to see his handiwork receiving so much attention. He wondered why he had not provided entertainment like this for the Rindornites earlier.

With an effort he forced himself to continue walking, glancing up now and then to check Aiden's progress. Trying not to attract attention, he slowly wove his way through the crowd to the square's far side. When he finally reached Nimlat Street, down which he hoped to escape, he paused, stood on his toes and again surveyed the spectacle.

Aiden now straddled Morden's arm, nearly twenty feet above the ground. Someone had given him a spear, and with it he was attempting to push the trousers down and off the end of the sword.

Jonathan already knew that this would not work. Anticipating this very thing, he had tied the trousers so they would resist being pushed off the sword point. But even though Aiden was having only marginal success with his new ploy, he had a broad smile on his face and occasionally he threw a verbal dart back at his observers. This was probably the most attention he had received in years and he was determined to enjoy it.

Suddenly he halted his efforts and glanced left. There was a disturbance in the square's northeast corner. A voice on the crowd's far side was bellowing something.

Jonathan stood on the first step of some stairs leading to a shop in order to see better, but all he could determine was that Aiden was talking over the heads of the crowd to whomever had shouted. Was this Vonich?

As if to confirm Jonathan's fears, suddenly Aiden sat upright and peered intently out into the crowd as if searching for something. Jonathan decided it was time to retreat. Most of the rest of the crowd apparently agreed, and when a swell of people began drifting away from the statue and back to the merchants' stalls, Jonathan took the opportunity to step entirely away from the shop entrance way. He permitted himself one last look back to check if Vonich had actually arrived.

That glance was his undoing! At that moment Aiden's and Jonathan's eyes met. The guard yelled and pointed.

Jonathan dashed up Nimlat Street. *Fortunately Vonich and company will need to force their way through the crowd, giving me more time,* he reflected.

Immediately the street curved to the right, taking him out of sight of his pursuers. Except for one other person, luckily for him the street was deserted. It looked as if almost everyone had been in the square.

As he ran he worried about the practicality of his escape plan. In order to hide from his pursuers, he needed to find a location where he could access a roof, and from there run along the roof peaks until he reached the abandoned house. The only problem was the climbing. It would take time to swing himself up three storeys. Could he do it without being seen?

Then ahead he saw a possible solution. A large eighty-foot tall tree was growing right up out of the cobblestones on the edge of the road. Its network of branches stuck out from its trunk like spokes on a wheel, some of them overhanging the houses on the street. He had to risk it. Taking a running leap, he reached into the air trying desperately to get his fingers around the lowest branch. He failed, ran back and tried again. This time success! Still hanging onto the branch, he swung his feet up, planted them on the tree trunk and walked up the trunk until he was horizontal to the ground. From there he rolled his torso onto the branch, stood up, and quickly climbed into the higher branches.

Just in time! He was twenty feet up when the sound of clanking armour reached him. Clinging motionlessly to the trunk, he waited, hoping against hope that the leaves and branches would conceal him. As he watched, five men in chainmail came jogging around the corner. Vonich was not among them.

Unfortunately, not far behind came a crowd of curious onlookers. Rindorn had rarely had such excitement and many of the people who had watched Aiden climb the statue were determined not to miss any additional thrills.

As the guards approached his tree, Jonathan prayed that neither they nor the crowd would look up and spot him. He held his breath. The guards passed right underneath and kept on jogging.

When the immediate danger had passed, he breathed a sigh of relief. *Five city guards! What on earth do they fill their time with when they don't have me to chase after?*

Since the crowd was still below he could not afford to relax. He remained motionless, thinking about his next move when he felt vibrations up the length of the trunk. He peered down in concern.

What he saw made his heart race. Two young boys who had come with the crowd had started to shinny up his tree. If he stayed put they would discover him, but if he climbed further, the crowd beneath would see movement and discover him. He had just about decided that he had to risk climbing when he heard an adult voice from below order the children back to the ground.

He exhaled deeply. *Ouch! That was close. Now if I can only get rid of these stragglers beneath me, I'll be almost all right.*

The answer to this latest wish came a few minutes later when the remaining people lost interest in the chase and remembered the bargains they had left behind in the square. He was alone again in the street, thanking his good fortune. The tree had turned out to be a better hiding spot than he could have guessed.

He considered remaining concealed in the branches, but the risk of more people emerging from the square made him stay with his original plan. One of the thicker branches about five feet above his head stretched overtop of a nearby house. He left his hiding place and within seconds had struggled out along the branch and onto the house's thatched roof.

Carefully avoiding soft spots in the thatching, he climbed to the roof's crest. As he reached its peak he heard sounds from below, and risking only one quick look down, he saw that the same two small boys had returned. He flung himself over the peak and onto the other side of the roof, flattening his body against the thatch. He clutched handfuls of it to stop himself from sliding.

Shouting erupted from the street beneath him. Lying still, he listened to the street noises before glancing cautiously once more over the peak. Because of the roof overhang he could not see much immediately below him but he could tell from the sounds that a crowd had gathered. He must have been spotted. Fortunately, the crowd on the other side of the street could not see where he was.

He unclasped his hands from the nearby thatch and let himself slide down the roof a few feet. Then, standing up, and with one hand occasionally grasping something solid, he walked along the roof's edge.

Usually he found this kind of thing easy. His success in balancing while walking in high places was part of the reason that he had escaped the city watch many times before. But for some reason today was different. He sweated with anxiety.

He was not sure what he was more afraid of, slipping off the roof, falling through it, or being spotted by onlookers below. He could still hear shouts and cries from the street that he had just vacated, but to his relief there was no sound coming from the street underneath him to his left.

Alternately walking, sliding and grabbing the nearby roof thatch, he made his way toward the abandoned house. It was not far. Then, five dwellings ahead he spotted it—just as he remembered. Its older grey and weathered thatch contrasted with the newer yellower thatch of the roofs nearby. He made for it with quick steps, slipping once more before finally arriving, but he got there, as far as he could tell, undetected. The building was a large one, its four wings surrounding an inner courtyard. When it was new, it would have belonged to a wealthy family. He wondered why it had stayed vacant.

One tricky part remained. He still needed to find a way down and inside. His usual method as a boy had been to jump from the side of the roof, then break his fall by grabbing a crossbeam attached to an old post in the middle of the courtyard. Yet he had not done this for years, and the last time that he had tried it he had weighed eighty pounds less.

Gingerly he approached the edge of the roof overlooking the courtyard. He hesitated. He knew that he was better at jumping and climbing than most people, nevertheless dangerous leaps onto uncertain landing places still made him nervous. Yet he could not figure out any other way down, and he could not afford to wait. There was nothing for it but to jump.

Springing away like a frog from a lily pad, he lunged, reaching through the air and catching the crossbeam on his way down. Then a moment later he heard a sharp crack from above his head as the crossbeam gave way and he continued dropping, landing with a jolt that he felt everywhere.

He was caught off guard by what happened next. From behind his back a woman screamed. Jonathan started in surprise.

"Rolf, Rolf, get over here! Rolf!" she yelled.

Jonathan's stomach did a nervous somersault. Something was terribly wrong. The once vacant house was now inhabited! In his rush to arrive it had not even entered his mind that someone might have moved in since his last visit. Wildly, he searched for an escape.

Too late. From behind he was tackled to the ground, his arms pinned. Rolf—whoever he was—had arrived. Then a second man appeared, and between the two of them they forced him through the house towards its street door.

"Wait!" he protested. "I can explain." But they were not interested. The front door opened, and with one heave he fell out onto the street.

Picking himself up, he found he was staring into the face of the last man whom he wanted to see— Vonich. Two henchmen stood on either side of him.

"Hello, Jonathan," he said.

Something hard hit him on the head, and the world dissolved into greyness.

# 3 THE ROOM

As he floated back into consciousness, Jonathan felt a searing pain ripping through his skull.

He was cold.

Water dripped from somewhere.

*Where am I?*

With an effort, he forced his eyes open. He might as well not have bothered because the room would not stop spinning. He put a hand to his face. It was wet. Someone must have recently splashed it with water.

When his vision cleared, he discovered that he did not know where he was. He could see that he was in a five foot by ten-foot room. There was one wooden bunk on which he was now lying. The walls were coated with a pale whitewash that covered both stones and mortar. The room's wooden door had two vertical bars defending its window and bars also secured the room's other window, six and a half feet off the floor.

Jonathan guessed that he must be in one of

Rindorn's jails, although he had never seen the inside of one before. *So this is what they look like. None too comfortable for the guests, unfortunately! Does anybody know that I'm here?* A wave of panic and loneliness took hold of him. He felt totally vulnerable and abandoned. He wanted to go home.

But where was that? He pictured the old widow's loft where he had grown up. Although she was no relation, he had always called her Aunt. And then he thought about his real home, where he had not been for a very long time.

He had only a few dim memories of his true home and real parents. They were not pleasant recollections, and he did not like to muse on them often. Consequently, he could occasionally almost forget all about them, though his parents were not the source of the bad memories. It was the way in which he had been separated from them that he did not like to think about much. The other disconcerting thing was that the memories he had were so odd that they made no sense. Because of this, he sometimes wondered if they were invented or partly delusional.

For instance, he remembered several large, long buildings near some mountains—and there were no mountains close to Rindorn. These buildings had lots of people living in them—people who looked like monks, except that they wore black robes instead of the long grey ones that the St. Swithun monks in Rindorn wore. He also remembered spending a lot of time around horses in a stable. He had liked hiding in the straw piles.

Beyond that, his memories became more bizarre. He had an image of his father in one of the black robes, which again made no sense because everyone knows that monks don't get married and have children. It was not just his father—his mother too wore a monk's robe, as did everyone else.

One more piece of his past puzzled him. Once when he was six years old and living in Rindorn, he had gone swimming in the river with two friends about the same age, Rannulf and Olaf. Olaf had pointed out something that he had never noticed before—a tattoo of the sun in the hollow of the bottom of his foot.

He had wondered for days what this meant and where the tattoo came from. Yet he had no answers. He thought about asking others for advice, but something always held him back. Growing up on the streets of Rindorn he had learned not to trust anyone, except his friends, particularly Olaf and Rannulf.

As he pondered these and other scraps of memories, he tried hard to recall more, but to no avail. Eventually, he let his aching head sink back onto the bare boards beneath him, and he slipped into a fitful sleep.

The next day began with a guard shaking him roughly by the shoulder. It was one of the older guards whom Jonathan had not seen much of before. A scruffy white beard poked its way out from beneath the man's helmet chinstrap.

Jonathan was hungry and he noticed that the soldier carried food on a tray. At least they were going to feed him.

The man did not go through any pleasantries. "What's your name, age, and occupation?" he barked as he put the tray on the floor.

"What?" replied Jonathan. He had not expected these questions.

"Your name," the guard repeated, "I need to know it—your age and occupation, too—that is when you're not busy doing pranks."

"Other than odd jobs, I play in two musical groups—lute in the Falconers and the sackbut for the Dragon Hunters. I'm sure you've heard of them," said Jonathan. "And if it matters, I'm seventeen years old." In fact, he did not know his exact age. Seventeen was a rough guess. "As for my name, it's Jonathan. Everybody in town knows that."

"No, your real name."

"What?" asked Jonathan again, confused.

"Is there anything more than just Jonathan?"

He finally saw what the guard meant—his full name. His mind flashed back to one of his possible childhood recollections where he was in the stable as usual. The blurred image of his father's face bent over him. "Jonathan," he had said, urgency in his voice, "remember, if anything ever happens to you or me, your name is Jonathan Makarios Crispin. This is the name you are to go by. Remember this, Jonathan. It's important." Then his father made him repeat it a couple times until he was satisfied that Jonathan remembered.

It was a confusing memory. For one thing, he did not really know that it had happened. As well, it made no sense. Why would his father tell him, "This is the name you are to go by," if it was his real name? It almost sounded as if his father was giving him a false name, a made-up name. As to why he would do that, Jonathan had no idea. All of this flashed through his head in a moment and still the guard waited for an answer.

"Why do you need to know my name?" he asked.

An expression of impatience crossed the man's face. "Well, you know what's going to happen to you. We need to post your name. It's the law."

A shudder went through Jonathan at these words. Yes, he knew. He had not dared consider it before, but he had realized somewhere in the back of his mind that the penalty for his prank—for someone of his class to publicly mock one of the nobility—would be execution.

He had deeply offended the honour of a noble house. Had he been a noble himself he would have been challenged to a duel, but being a peasant that was not an option. He would merely be executed as an example to the lower classes. Still, by law, they were required to post a notice and date for the execution, and they needed his name for the notice. It was the way things were done in Rindorn.

"If you really want to know, my full name is Jonathan Makarios Crispin," he said with some pride in his voice.

The guard smirked. "Pretty fancy name for a street urchin. But it'll do." And turning, he left the cell.

Time passed slowly. By day Jonathan listened to the noises from the street, the shouts of voices, the creaking of carts' wheels, the occasional bark of laughter. At night when the outside noises died down, he would hear the noises from inside his cell: the constant drip of water, the squeaking of rats, and the occasional buzz of crickets. But always, daylight brought with it the same prison cell, the same stench, the same paltry food. Typically the guards came in pairs to bring him meals at the same time each day. The door at the top of the steps outside his cell would open, light beamed down, and through the bars in his cell door he would watch them approach. They always left quickly without answering any of his questions.

On the fourth night he heard a voice at the outer window, "Jonathan?"

For a moment he was too surprised to answer. The past four days had left him in a kind of stupor. He reflected on what the voice might mean. It seemed pleasant to imagine that someone might be interested in him.

The voice repeated its question, "Jonathan?"

Suddenly he realized that he was not dreaming and that he had better respond before whoever it was went away. "Yes. Wait! It's me, Jonathan."

"Jonathan!" the voice responded in a happier tone. "I didn't think I'd find you. Olaf and I have been looking for you for two days, ever since they posted the notice."

By now he recognized the voice. It belonged to his friend Rannulf. "The notice?" Jonathan asked.

"Oh, you haven't been told," and here Rannulf's voice faltered. "You're . . . you're to be executed."

"I know that," Jonathan snapped back, feeling annoyed with Rannulf for thinking he was ignorant. It was not the appropriate response, he knew, but being scheduled for execution made him just a bit touchy. "Tell me about this notice."

"It appeared two days ago, posted several places around Rindorn and in some surrounding villages. Hey, I never knew that Makarios Crispin was your full name. You didn't make that up by chance, did you?"

Not waiting for an answer, Rannulf continued in a more sombre tone. "And then it gives the execution date eleven days from now. Oh yes, and a note that you will be set free if the sum of five hundred gold crowns can be paid to the justice of the peace before that date."

Jonathan was puzzled. He and his friends had seen a number of execution notices. They appeared three or four times a year as crimes punishable by death were common, but he had never before seen a notice with the option of a fine in place of the punishment. It was strange.

"I'm sure that you and Olaf would have no problem coming up with five hundred crowns!" Jonathan spoke sarcastically. Five hundred crowns was the equivalent of about fifteen years' salary for most Rindornites.

"I'm afraid not," said Rannulf after a brief pause. "We've already explored several possibilities. We looked into stealing. Unfortunately, if that amount of money suddenly went missing and showed up in your pocket or the pockets of your friends, they wouldn't believe it was ours. They'd likely keep the five hundred crowns and execute you for theft anyhow."

"And the rest of you, too," added Jonathan.

"We also thought about breaking you out," said Rannulf. "And if you had been in one of the city's other jails, we might have been able to pull it off. But you're in the castle dungeons. We can't break you out of here."

Jonathan now knew exactly where he was. Several decades ago, one of the castle's walls had been removed to make more space in the crowded city of Rindorn. With this wall gone, the back and side of the castle's central tower had been exposed to the street behind it where Rannulf now stood—a street which originated from the northwest corner of the town square. The tower had been made part of a newer shorter wall linking the existing walls on either side, and Jonathan's cell was partly underground, in the north side of this tower. Rannulf was correct. He was in the city's most secure prison with the thickest bars and walls.

The two of them could think of no more solutions that night. After discussing these and other matters, Rannulf passed some food to his friend through the bars. He then left, promising to return the following evening.

The next few days passed in similar fashion. Several friends, mostly from the musical ensembles in which he played, visited him at night when they would not be seen. But the friends he saw most often were Olaf and Rannulf. Both were apprenticed to local tradesmen, although in the past they had also occasionally joined Jonathan on his musical ventures.

Twice Rannulf came during the daytime. When this happened, he took out his tin whistle and played.

"You know," said Jonathan during one of these sessions. "It's not that I don't appreciate your music, but aren't rollicking melodies better suited to a dance than a prison cell?"

"If I pretend that I'm a street performer, the fact that I'm sitting outside your cell window won't look suspicious," explained Rannulf. "So I have to play the kind of music that street performers play."

Whenever there was no crowd nearby, the friends discussed Jonathan's release, and though they could not arrive at a plan for his escape, he found these visits encouraging. He had never appreciated his friends as much as he did during this period of his life. He felt badly now for teasing Olaf in the past about being clumsy and slow-witted. He viewed him differently now.

Even the rather aloof Sonja came to see him once or twice—which intrigued Jonathan. She often sang or played violin at their performances, and she spent the majority of her free time with Jonathan's friends, preferring their company, it seemed, to that of her female companions. Still, he and Sonja had never been terribly close. Her exceptional calmness, poise and seeming lack of concern about the opinions of others had always unnerved him.

The only one who did not come to see him was Helena. And that bothered him. Helena was the girl he had maintained a secret interest in for years, though it had been unrequited all this time. He felt more than a little embarrassed now that he had pulled his prank all for the sake of impressing her. He was sure she would not have been impressed if she had seen him in his jail cell. "The mayor's trousers aren't worth that much," he said aloud.

Strangely enough, in that cell, with his life's end quickly approaching, he spent as much time brooding over her as over anything else, including his impending death. When one is about to be killed, one looks for even illusionary straws of comfort. And as the execution date steadily approached, he endeavoured hard not to think much about it at all. It just gave him butterflies in his stomach.

He tried praying a bit, too. He supposed that one should do that when one was close to death. He had never really been much for prayer or religion of any sort and so he had the nagging feeling that he was doing it wrong. But he kept hoping against hope that somehow the sentence would be deferred or that one of his friends would miraculously get some money.

The night before his scheduled execution he hardly slept. He was to be executed at noon—probably in front of a large crowd. A guillotine had been erected in the central square—ironically, the same square where he had hung the mayor's trousers.

From what he could tell through his small cell window, the morning of his execution dawned bright and fair. A priest came in to pray with him around ten o'clock—the same priest who had popped in a couple times earlier. He did not know much about the prayer stuff, but it was nice to have company anyway. To his credit the man stayed longer than Jonathan had expected. After the priest departed there was nothing left for him to do but wait. And he waited and waited.

At times he paced around the room. Occasionally he prayed. Now and then he cried or yelled. Once or twice he tried peering through the cell window to look out into the square. As far as he could see, a large crowd had gathered.

After a while he just sat down. He started thinking about his family, about those images of the valley in the snow-covered mountains. Were they real memories or just things that he had made up?

Then he got angry again. He decided to go down fighting. When they came to get him, he would grab the weapons of the nearest guard and battle his way to freedom. It might not work, but what did he have to lose?

The minutes went by and still there was no sign of guards to escort him. He wondered what was keeping them so long.

He could swear that he had been waiting more

than two hours since the priest's visit, but he knew that this day was not a normal day and that his sense of time might be distorted. He told himself that in his nervous condition everything would seem to take forever.

He paced the length of his cell repeatedly. The time passed. More time passed.

The guards carrying his noon meal—or more properly, noon scraps of food—arrived just as they always did and shoved the tray under the cell door. Jonathan shouted after them to explain what was going on, but he got no response. He became impatient. It's a horrible feeling preparing for a tragedy only to have it postponed yet still dramatically hanging over one's head.

The sun sank in the western sky. The voices of the crowd outside the window grew quieter then ceased altogether. As the sun moved into the northwest, shadows from the buildings on the far side of the street grew and eventually cast themselves across his narrow cell window.

Supper arrived. Darkness came.

Sometime later he heard a sound that he had been eagerly waiting for. "Jonathan, you still there?" It was Rannulf's voice.

"Yes, it's me. What's going on?"

"Thank God you're alive."

"Yeah, it's nice isn't it? Can you tell me what's happening? Why I wasn't taken away?"

"I don't know. I thought you'd know," said Rannulf.

"You mean they haven't told anyone out there?"

"No."

"Strange."

"Rumour has it that you were executed in your cell," said Rannulf after a pause.

"As you can hear, that's not the case," said Jonathan, grinning. "Can it be that they are just changing the schedule to wreck any chances of rescue?"

"It's possible, I guess."

"So what happened today in the square?"

"Everyone showed up, the crowds, the guards, the executioner, but not you. We waited for an hour or so, then eventually the crowds just melted away. The guards had no clue as to what was happening. Sonja, Olaf and I waited in the inn across the way. The guards left about an hour before sunset. The guillotine is still up, but there is no announcement about a new time. Anyhow, it looks as if you have at least another day left to you."

A wave of relief swept over Jonathan and a few rays of hope began to glimmer. Maybe, just maybe, the execution would not take place after all. "So there're no rumours circulating about the delay in the execution?" asked Jonathan.

"No. . . well, yes. You were supposed to be dead already, but as we can both see that hasn't happened."

They talked for a while longer. Then Rannulf said, "I have to go, Jonathan. I need to catch up on the work I missed today."

Jonathan suddenly appreciated all that Rannulf had done for him that day and in the last few days. "Thanks for coming, and thanks for all the visits," he said.

"Don't mention it. I'm sure you'd do the same and more for me if you had to."

Evening passed, and for some reason Jonathan

was able to temporarily put the execution out of his mind. He slept much better that night.

Still, when he woke the next morning, he had a nervous knot in his stomach. In some ways this day was much worse than the previous one. Yesterday's reprieve made him long all that much more to stay alive. As a result, instead of resigning himself to his fate, he spent the rest of the day waiting in awful anticipation for the sound of booted feet descending the prison stairway to take him away.

Jonathan was no hero that day nor was he able to accept his condition stoically. Every loud noise made him flinch. By mid-afternoon he had become nearly frantic with waiting and dreading.

He welcomed the arrival of evening. There had never been a nighttime execution in Rindorn that he knew of, and so the chances of one happening to him seemed very small. Yet again, the anxiety of what the morrow would bring gripped him. Later, when Rannulf stopped by Jonathan commented that, "he didn't know what was worse—having an execution date set or still facing execution but not knowing when it was going to be."

"It's not going to be," said Rannulf.

He hoped that Rannulf was right. But he wondered how Rannulf and his friends could carry off their planned rescue if they did not have ample warning of the time that he would be executed.

The next day passed similarly, and the next. Still they had not come for him. Still no word came from the guards. His guillotine still remained standing in the square. Jonathan began to loathe the inside of his cell intensely.

Finally on the fourteenth day after he was

supposed to have been executed, he heard the noise that he had dreaded for so long. It was mid-morning, not the normal time for a meal, when the door at the top of the steps outside his cell opened. The usual light beamed down through the window in his cell door, and then he heard a sound that made his heart sink even further. Voices, several of them were coming. He did not want to accept it, but somewhere inside he realized that this was almost certainly his doom. They were taking him at last.

He watched as down the steps they came. Four of them. Two guards, Vonich, and an official that he didn't recognize who held his nose at the stench.

Curious, Jonathan stared at the man. This official was taller than the guards. He had dark brown hair flecked with grey, which just stopped short of falling into his piercing green eyes. His face carried an intelligent yet stern expression. Jonathan guessed that he was in his mid-forties. He had an athletic build. From the shoulders down he was covered by a dark green cloak beneath, which could be seen, a chain mail tunic, a scabbard with sword attached to a belt with an elaborate buckle, brown trousers and dark brown riding boots.

As they approached, Jonathan backed against the far wall of his cell, determined to give them a fight. Vonich took the keys from his pocket and fumbled with the lock, while the two guards stood poised, ready to enter once it was open.

Jonathan's heart raced. He glanced around wildly, trying to figure out some last minute escape, but in vain. In the confined space the guards easily cornered him. Despite his struggles, they grabbed him and hauled him backwards up the stairs towards the tower's front door overlooking the castle courtyard. On the way he managed to kick one of them in the shoulder, but for all his trouble he just received a cuff on the head and soon was standing at the door's gaping mouth.

Outside, he immediately noticed the heat. He blinked in the light of the sun, which he had not seen for four weeks because his cell window faced north. The guards started walking him towards the centre of the courtyard. Then strangely they stopped. They shifted their grip so that together with Jonathan they now faced Vonich and the mysterious official who had followed them up the stairs.

"And you of all people," snarled Vonich at Jonathan. "I don't know where you get your friends, or why they'd waste a penny on the likes of you, but I want you to know that this is the last time. If and when it happens again, nothing and no one is going to get between you and what's rightly coming to you."

"You can go now," said Vonich, looking at the guards. "And so, unfortunately, can you," he said to Jonathan, "on condition that you leave town before nightfall and stay in the custody of your benefactor. Do you hear me? I don't want to see your face again." Vonich spat and walked away.

Jonathan felt confused, unsure of what was happening. The guards, sensing that he was ready to run off somewhere, gripped his shoulders a moment longer while the news sank in. He was being released? Why?

It must have something to do with the man in the dark green cloak standing in front of him.

# 4 RAGNAR

The guards left, and Jonathan was alone with the strange man in the middle of the castle courtyard. The expression on the man's face softened. He gestured in Vonich's direction and smiled. "Charming fellow," he said. "You're obviously old friends."

Jonathan made no answer but gazed at the stranger blankly. He felt stunned at the recent turn of events.

The man spoke again. "Jonathan, do you remember me?"

Before he could stop himself, Jonathan blurted out "No." A second later he wished that he had waited. *Maybe this man bought my way out of prison thinking I was a long lost relative or friend. If he discovers his mistake too quickly, he might ask for a refund and have me thrown back inside.* Yet Jonathan had answered truthfully. As far as he could tell, he had never actually met this newcomer before in his life.

There was a brief silence. A spasm of anxiety passed through Jonathan as he studied the man's face.

He could not see whether his answer had made any significant change in the man's expression—nothing that might indicate his future fate.

"That's to be expected, I suppose," the stranger finally said. "It's been a number of years since we last saw each other, but we can reminisce later. Now to matters at hand—I am called Ragnar, and I have paid for your release. And since I don't trust your dear friend"—he waved towards the retreating Vonich— "my guess is that we will need to leave immediately if we want to avoid him again."

Then he glanced at Jonathan's dishevelled appearance, "Hmm. A wash and a change of clothes might be nice, too. Follow me."

Feeling relieved that his fear about returning to jail was unfounded, Jonathan trotted after the stranger. As he walked he became even more curious. Why had Ragnar chosen to release him, and why did he think that the two of them had met before? He studied Ragnar's clothing and manner, trying to come up with some clue to these riddles, but the man's style of dress told him nothing.

In any case, he appeared to be strong and energetic, briskly striding through the courtyard. After being confined to a cell for four weeks, Jonathan found it hard to keep up. The blue sky dazzled his eyes, and the sun on his head felt hot. Soon they were striding through the castle gateway, past the portcullis and into the cobblestone street beyond, where they met two men-at-arms standing in the roadway. The men were dressed similarly to Ragnar with long dark green cloaks covering chain mail shirts, sword belts, brown trousers and boots. A younger blond-haired man-at-arms looked slightly taller than Ragnar's six feet while a dark brown-haired man at arms stood a few inches shorter. Together they held four horses by the reins. Ragnar had a quick conversation with them, after which the two new men took two of the horses and vanished into the crowd that was moving towards the town square.

Ragnar turned to Jonathan, "I hope to give you a proper meal once we get to an inn. In the meantime would you like something to tide you over?" He opened a saddlebag and pulled out a leather pouch with some dried fruits, bread and cheese. Until then Jonathan had not realized how hungry he was, and when he saw the food he gladly accepted Ragnar's offer.

Ragnar reached up and undid something else strapped to the saddle. "Oh, here's your sword. I recovered it earlier today from Vonich."

"Thank you," said Jonathan, and he meant it. He had not expected to see it again.

"Now, since we can't stay in Rindorn, do you know of any inns nearby that we could visit?"

Jonathan thought for a moment. "How about Ravenhall?" he said. "It's a village less than an hour's ride away. The Ravenhall Inn is often used by travellers arriving here after Rindorn's gates have closed."

"Just the place I was thinking of," replied Ragnar.

When Jonathan had finished eating, Ragnar mounted his horse and motioned to Jonathan to do the same. Jonathan had limited riding experience, and it obviously showed, since Ragnar commented, "We'll teach you how to do that properly before long." Then, oblivious to the stares of the guards and the people nearby—many of whom recognized

Jonathan—the two of them rounded the corner to the market place and took one of the main streets out of Rindorn. Jonathan's horse followed Ragnar's closely as they wormed their way through the press of people near the gate.

Slowly the crowd moved forward. It was just past noon and already many of the farmers who had brought their goods into Rindorn to sell in the morning were making their way back home for their evening chores.

Just then, to Jonathan's great pleasure, by chance they crossed paths with Rannulf. When Rannulf saw his friend who had recently been slated for execution now riding a horse, the expression on his face was so comical that Jonathan laughed. Then heedless of Ragnar's haste, Jonathan clumsily dismounted and pulled Rannulf and the horse off on to a side street out of the main flow of traffic. Quickly he embraced his friend and told him what had taken place. Rannulf's eyes grew wider as he heard the story.

"This is for real?" he asked at last.

"I don't know," replied Jonathan, "but in any case I have nowhere else to go, so I might as well go with this man until I figure out what to do. Things are uncomfortable for me in Rindorn at the moment."

A hand tugging on Jonathan's sleeve interrupted their conversation. Ragnar had dismounted and was urging him to leave.

"I have to go," said Jonathan. "But I'll return some day—hopefully soon." Another thought came to him. "Can you meet us at the Ravenhall Inn tonight? I could probably tell you more there."

"I'll try," said Rannulf.

The tugging on Jonathan's sleeve became

irresistible. He struggled onto his horse again and waved. Then Ragnar and he re-joined the press of people leaving through the south gate.

While passing under the gate's archway, Jonathan caught the eyes of a guard. He could not be sure, but he thought that the man was one of those who had beaten down his door a few weeks earlier. Since he was leaving, he thought that it would not hurt to annoy the man in a small way, just once more for the fun of it. Grinning broadly as he rode past, he caught the guard's eye and waved good-bye in an exaggerated manner.

The man suddenly went rigid and gripped his spear. Then he relaxed and scowled, or did he smile? Jonathan could not tell. A moment later they were through the gate and beyond the city wall.

For all his forced cheerfulness, Jonathan felt strange about passing through those gates this time. Although he had gone in and out of them dozens of times he had never been thrown out of town before, and despite his optimism with Rannulf, he knew that he would not likely be back for a long time, perhaps never. He gazed back at the walls and spires of the place where he had lived most of his life and tried to tell himself that it was not the last time that he would see them.

Rindorn had been founded by Duke Morden (now called Magnificent) about eight hundred years before. Morden had been fleeing from the Ahasaw Rebellion and had escaped through the mountains into the valley where Rindorn was now located. Many of his soldiers were sick or wounded, so instead of fleeing further as he had originally intended, Morden stopped to build a wooden stockade on an island in the river. From there he hoped to hold off any attack long enough for his men to heal.

His strategy worked. But the threat of more Ahasaw attacks did not cease for some years, so Morden eventually replaced the stockade with stone walls surrounding a stone castle. Then other refugees from the conflict fled over the mountains to take shelter there. When Morden's people were not interrupted by invasions, they grew crops and kept livestock, which could be herded into the fort during attacks. Overall his people prospered.

After peace came, the new king of Magelandorn, the large kingdom nearby, asked Morden for his allegiance. And in return for pledging his fealty, Morden was offered not just Rindorn, but the nearby Duchy of Dorinon as well. Morden agreed and moved his seat southeastward to Dorinon.

The political boundaries had remained the same ever since. Rindorn was part of the Duchy of Dorinon, which in turn was included in the larger kingdom of Magelandorn. To this day, Rindorn, governed by a mayor, had remained the largest settlement near the range of mountains on Magelandorn's northeastern border.

Jonathan's thoughts returned to the present. They were now out of bowshot from the city walls. Ragnar had stopped his horse by the side of the road and stared intently at the crowd drifting out from the city gate. His clothing flapped in the breeze revealing the chain mail armour that he wore under his cloak. Eventually his two other companions emerged from the crowd near the gate and rode over to join them. Ragnar introduced the younger blond-haired man as Philip and the shorter dark haired man as Hugh. Now that he had a closer look at them Jonathan guessed that Philip was in his late twenties or early thirties, while Hugh could have been ten years older. The two men referred to Ragnar as their "captain." Like Ragnar, both newcomers seemed in good physical condition. After the introductions the four of them turned and proceeded towards Ravenhall.

As they rode, Jonathan was not involved in the conversation. He was trying to grapple with the fact that an hour earlier he had been facing certain death, and now he was on his way to a new life with total strangers who claimed that they knew him. He also felt shy and awkward. Having grown up with the same people most of his life, he was not used to making friends with strangers. Furthermore, he sensed that Ragnar and company felt impatient with his poor riding skills. At times, he tried to pay attention to what the other three men were saying, but he could not make much sense of the subjects that they discussed.

Philip appeared to be the most jovial of the three. Hugh was the more serious, and perhaps the most dangerous. As they rode, he occasionally withdrew a dagger from his boot and made elaborate flips with it before catching it again. Jonathan was glad that Hugh was his protector and not his opponent.

After some time Hugh rode up beside him and asked, "What did you do to get yourself thrown into prison?"

Jonathan felt uncomfortable with the question but he felt he had to come up with an answer. "I was trying to impress a girl," he finally said. That was true enough.

Hugh smiled. "And that's a criminal offence in Rindorn?"

"No, not exactly."

"You know, I've tried to impress a number of women in my day, but it's never landed me in jail—not yet anyhow."

"Mmm," was Jonathan's response.

"So what exactly did you do to impress this girl?"

"Uh, I broke into the mayor's house and hung some of his trousers off a statue in the city square."

"Hmm," Hugh grunted.

Uncomfortable with the silence, Jonathan added. "At the time, Morden's statue seemed like an appropriate place for the mayor's trousers."

"I see," replied Hugh. "And was the girl suitably impressed?"

"I don't actually know," said Jonathan. "I haven't talked to her since. I've been kind of busy."

"It would be a pity if she wasn't after all that work."

"I guess," said Jonathan.

"So, tell me about this girl."

Ragnar interjected. "Knock it off, Hugh. We're just happy we've found him alive and that he's not in prison."

"True enough," said Hugh.

Then changing the subject, Philip and Ragnar made a few polite inquiries: asking where in Rindorn Jonathan had lived, how he had supported himself, what he did for amusement, and so on. Jonathan found these questions difficult. After all, what was he to say? That he played music for money when he had to, slept where he could, often at the inn where he had most recently played, and for amusement tried to annoy the city watch?

He attempted first to avoid their questions but then finally said, "Most of the time I play music. That's how I make a living."

"What's your instrument?" asked Philip.

"The lute and the sackbut," said Jonathan. "The sackbut I picked up on my own. The widow who housed me played a lute that her husband had given her. She in turn taught me and gave it to me shortly before she died."

"Where is it now?"

"Probably lost. I left it with the innkeeper at the inn I played at before I was captured. Foolishly, I forgot to ask my friends about it. I've had other things on my mind in the last four weeks."

After this, conversation died, and Jonathan's attention was distracted by his hunger and general weakness. The effects of his time in the Rindorn jail were catching up with him, so to keep his mind off his stomach he watched the sunlight glinting on the pond beside the road.

Some waterfowl were providing a display of airborne acrobatics, periodically rising from the pond and swooping around in figure eight-like patterns before finally settling again on the water. Jonathan watched the birds for a while and then figured that it was his turn to make small talk. Philip was riding closest to him on the left.

"Where are you from?" he asked.

"Oh, not that close to here," said Philip. There was an awkward pause while Jonathan waited for him to say something more. He did not.

"That's interesting," Jonathan found himself saying. "Did you always live there or have you moved around a bit?"

"I moved around."

Again silence. Then Jonathan asked, "So, do you have any family back home?"

"No family."

"Do you like where you are living now?"

"Yeah, it's fine."

"And where did you say it was?" asked Jonathan.

"Oh, not very close to here."

Since Philip offered no more, Jonathan just sat back in his saddle and kept to the rear of the group. He found Philip's reluctance to talk odd. Was he hiding something? For the first time Jonathan began to wonder about these strangers and their motives. Who were they?

The road climbed a hill now and the pond was hidden from view by a thin strip of forest. They were close to Ravenhall. Jonathan thought he would try another line of questioning before they reached the town. "You know," he began, "I must say, I am very obliged to you for your help in getting me out of prison, and for the food. However. . ."

Philip interrupted. "You wouldn't mind knowing how we found you."

"In a manner of speaking, yes," replied Jonathan, pretending to sound as dignified and in control of the situation as possible when he felt anything but.

"That's easy to answer, said Ragnar, "you tipped us off."

"Me!" exclaimed Jonathan, surprised. "How'd I do that?"

"Your ransom notice, of course."

"My ransom notice?" But just as he said this, Jonathan realized the answer to his own question.

"Oh, I used the old family name."

Ragnar nodded, "Actually not quite, but you might as well have."

"What do you mean by that?"

"The name you gave wasn't the real family name. It was just a name that was used by your family when they were in hiding."

"In hiding?"

"Yes, it was a made-up name that you used—an alias as it were."

Jonathan's mind flashed back to the memory of his father telling him this name, and the urgency in his voice. "An alias," he said. "Yes. That might make sense."

His voice trailed off and conversation paused as he considered this new information. They had now reached the hilltop. From there it was possible to see Rindorn in the distance and Jonathan strained around in his saddle for one last look at the city that he had called home for most of his life. But when he looked behind, he saw something strange. A most peculiarly dressed man was standing a little way away from a clump of trees near the side of the road. Close-fitting black garments covered him from head to toe and a strip of black cloth that covered all but his eyes stretched across his face. He was staring straight at them.

Jonathan turned and called to Ragnar. "Quick, look back!"

Ragnar turned. Jonathan did too. There was no one there.

# 5 RAVENHALL

"What did you see?" asked Ragnar.

For a moment Jonathan was unsure what to say. Would Ragnar and his friends think he was crazy? But he told the truth. "A man clothed all in black and looking our way," he told them. "But he isn't there now."

Ragnar, Philip and Hugh exchanged glances. Jonathan could not tell whether they thought the man was real or that he was seeing things. For a moment nobody moved or spoke.

Ragnar broke the silence. "We should keep going. Jonathan, we'll save our conversation about your family for later." They turned and resumed their journey, urging their horses to a trot. Eventually the road curved bringing the village of Ravenhall within sight.

Ravenhall was built on a hill at the foot of which ran a small river and a water mill used for grinding flour. Jonathan had visited there often. A few years before, when the Rindorn watch were on his trail for one of his less serious pranks, he had hidden in the woods near Ravenhall and done some work with the town blacksmith. Since then, he would go there and work whenever the music business was slow or when the blacksmith had special need of help.

In the distance the travellers saw the inn. Like many other local buildings, its oaken support beams were visible on its outside wall and plaster-covered boards filled up the spaces in between. When they reached it they dismounted at the front door.

Ragnar gave Jonathan his horse's reins to hold while he went inside. Nervous around horses, Jonathan was relieved to see that these just stood without making much movement. In a few moments Ragnar reappeared and beckoned to him. "This way," he said.

While Hugh led the horses to the stable, one of the servants held a door open, and Jonathan followed Ragnar up one flight of wooden stairs to their chamber. It was similar to most inn rooms he had seen—the usual furniture, four beds, a small chest with a mirror. There was also a side door and behind this door he heard the sounds of a bath being prepared. Presently another servant entered bearing a tray with four cups of grindle tea plus an ample amount of eggs, sausage and turnip mash. The travellers ate greedily.

By the time they had finished, the water was ready. Jonathan savoured the experience of a real bath. Baths in Rindorn for someone of his lineage were rare. He usually swam in the river.

Ragnar, Philip and Hugh were not in the room when he emerged, but he discovered that a new set of clothes had been laid out for him: a green cotton shirt, thick brown cotton trousers, woollen socks and brown soft-leather shoes. Not one to avoid gifts, he donned them with pleasure, examining their make at the same time. They were not by any means the most expensive variety of garments available, but they certainly were a stripe or two better than his old ones.

His curiosity about his new friends increased. Growing up on the streets of Rindorn, he had learned to be suspicious of everyone—especially strangers. That suspicious part of him was now vigilant. There had to be a catch somewhere, something expected of him in return, and this made him uncomfortable. For a moment he was tempted to find an unguarded window and escape as he had from the last inn.

Half acting out his thought, he approached the window. From the inn's third storey he saw the birds in the distance doing their acrobatics. He found himself wishing that he could be like one of those birds—effortlessly floating on the air currents. They seemed to have no cares. Once more the urge to escape seized him.

Yet something held him back. It might have been the simple fear of repeating his experience in Rindorn, but there was more than fear restraining him. These people were his only possible link to a past that he could barely remember. He needed to find out who they were and what they knew.

Despite his uncertainties, tiredness eventually overcame him and he slept. The next thing he was aware of, Ragnar and Philip were smiling down at the sight of him lying on the cot. "Feeling refreshed?" asked Philip.

Jonathan rolled over, smiled and nodded in reply. The two men pulled chairs up to the table and sat.

They looked tired.

Jonathan joined them at the table. It seemed like a good time to continue their earlier conversation. "You told me how you had found me Ragnar, but you didn't mention why my family had been in hiding or who had sent you to look for me."

"I have been sent here by your uncle who has paid for your release," said Ragnar. "He earnestly requests that you come to live with him."

"Uncle?" asked Jonathan.

"That's right."

"Live with him?"

"Yes," said Philip and Ragnar in unison.

"Can you . . . uh . . . tell me more about this uncle?" stammered Jonathan. "Who is he? What's his name?"

"His name is Gorwin," said Philip.

"Gorwin?"

Ragnar nodded. "He wants you to join him in his castle."

Jonathan perked up at this. Only very wealthy knights or lords had castles. Who was this uncle?

"My uncle has a castle?" said Jonathan aloud.

"That's right."

"So then, uh . . . what does he do? What does he occupy himself with when he's not rescuing people like me?"

"He does what any noble does," responded Philip, "farms, takes care of his estate, keeps off marauders—that kind of thing. The only difference is that he's not actually . . . what would you say . . . he's not working closely with other nobles nearby."

"No, no, he's not," agreed Ragnar.

No one said anything for a few moments. Other

than the clip-clop of horse hooves on the village street outside, there was no sound in the room. Ragnar seemed lost in thought.

Jonathan was unsure how to respond. It sounded almost too good to be true. Since he did not know who his parents were, it was distantly possible that he was the long lost nephew of a minor noble someplace. But realistically, the chances of him being nobility would be pretty small. *Couldn't there be some kind of mistake?* he thought. *What if this man—Gorwin, or whatever his name is, really isn't my uncle?*

Jonathan eventually broke the silence, "Gorwin?" he said. "I've never heard of him. How come he knows who I am?"

"To understand that, you would have to know something about your family," said Ragnar.

"Yes, what happened to my family?"

"They were betrayed," said Ragnar, "and most of them were killed. Your uncle escaped, and you did too apparently."

"I escaped? How?"

"I was hoping you could tell us that."

Jonathan tried to think back to his life before Rindorn, but nothing came to mind. There was silence in the room while they waited for him to answer, but all he said was, "If you live far away from here, how did you hear about my ransom notice?"

"There are people in Rindorn who let us know."

"Who?"

"I'm sorry," said Ragnar, "I can't tell you that."

Jonathan felt frustrated by this response. He tried a different question. "So what's the real name?"

"The real name?"

"Yes, my family's original name. Not the alias."

Ragnar smiled reluctantly, "Look, Jonathan, I mean no disrespect, but some of this is best discussed with your uncle when we get to his castle. This is for your own protection—and ours, too. For instance, if by any chance we do get separated, or—perish the thought—you encounter our enemies, the less they can torture out of you, the safer and more pleasant it is for you." He paused then added, "And there also are some matters that only your uncle knows."

Ragnar waited again, expecting Jonathan to respond but Jonathan was too busy with his own thoughts. He found himself torn between emotions. On the one hand, he was wildly hopeful. For his entire life he had wanted to learn about his family, his real family. At the same time a burning passion was rising up within him. Ragnar had said that many of his family had been murdered! He felt a strong desire to search out the people who had killed them and make them pay for their crimes!

When Philip thought the silence had grown awkward, he asked. "A lot to digest in one day?"

A number of questions were travelling through Jonathan's brain at top speed. Voicing his chief concern aloud, he said, "How can I know that you are for real, that you actually are from my uncle—if I even have an uncle?"

It was almost as if Ragnar expected the question, "Well, we paid your way out of prison, didn't we?"

That was not good enough for Jonathan. He wanted more information. "Look," he said, "I'm very grateful to you for all that you've done, but I'm finding this difficult to swallow."

Ragnar looked straight at him. "Yes, I suppose it would be. You'll just have to trust me for now, and trust that all of this will become clear shortly."

When Jonathan made no response, Ragnar continued, "Unfortunately things will soon become dangerous for us, even here in this inn. We'll be safe enough here for the moment, but we should travel again this evening. We have friends nearby who expect us. Why don't you get some more rest?" He rose from his chair.

"Where are we going?" asked Jonathan.

"For now, it's too dangerous for you to know."

Unsatisfied, Jonathan got up and moved towards the bed. Then he stopped. His earlier suspicions resurfaced. "If I had an uncle," he ventured, "it would only make sense for me to remember something about him. But I don't."

"What *do* you remember?" asked Ragnar.

There was silence in the room. Jonathan realized that he could not answer this question. If he told Ragnar what his memories actually were, then there would be no chance for him to test the truth of Ragnar's story.

"Look," Ragnar finally said, "by rights you should be dead today. In fact, you should've been guillotined over a week ago, but I just finished paying five hundred crowns for your release. You at least owe me the chance to prove the truth of what I'm saying. Besides, as I understand it, at the moment you have no choice. Your release was conditional upon you leaving the district and staying with me. Do you have anywhere else to go? Or would you rather be back inside your cell?"

When he put it that way, Jonathan realized the sense of his argument. While it was true that he could probably live nearby and avoid capture for a while, he could not avoid it forever. He realized that the people that he really missed were his friends, and he wondered whether any of them would come that night.

They left Jonathan alone in the room. He knew he should try to sleep more if they were to be travelling that night, but it was no use. The questions that had often kept him awake as a child plagued him again now. Could all that Ragnar was saying be true? A wild hope took hold of him. In any case it looked as if he would soon find out.

He decided to clear his head and go for a walk. Feeling it unnecessary to bring his sword, he left it on the bed. Then he went down the inn's back stairs and out into Ravenhall.

Standing in the inn's street entrance, he surveyed the town square. The church and the town hall bordered the square, but these were both smaller than Rindorn's. The square itself was also smaller, containing only a few merchants' booths. Instead of being paved entirely with cobblestones, it had an attractive patch in its centre reserved for grass and trees.

Leaving the inn, he ventured towards his old employer the blacksmith, but when he could not find him, he wandered the square, glancing idly into stalls. Since most people in Ravenhall recognized him, he felt conspicuous, but to his bewilderment no one made any jeering or encouraging remarks.

*What's the matter? Do they think I'm a ghost?*

In fact, the details of his release were not yet widely known, and the good people of Ravenhall were concerned that, by talking to him, they might be perceived as aiding an escaped convict.

When he returned to the inn, a perturbed Ragnar was waiting in the doorway. "You should never go outside without your sword," he said.

Jonathan found his concern irritating. "Don't worry, Ragnar. I know the people here. None of them are dangerous."

"It's not them I'm worried about," said Ragnar. He paused and looked right and left. "Remember that man in black that you noticed earlier today?"

Jonathan did not know what to say.

Ragnar continued, "Come let's get some supper. We have a long journey ahead of us."

Jonathan shrugged and followed him into the inn. The two of them went to the fireside room where inn guests and occasional Ravenhall townsfolk gathered to have their meals. Ragnar ordered supper and left Jonathan to eat while he conducted more business in town.

Jonathan was halfway through the meal when to his joy his friends arrived. Rannulf was the first through the door. He was probably Jonathan's closest friend and his constant visits in the last few weeks had certainly reinforced that status. Rannulf had always been a sharp dresser. Tonight a three cornered hat sporting a tall black feather sat on top of his curly brown hair and he wore a brown leather vest overtop a dark blue shirt. Finely woven woollen trousers descended almost to the floor and a sword in a well-polished scabbard clung to his left hip. The polished brass buckles on his belt and black shoes shone in the firelight.

Olaf entered next. No hat covered his curly blond hair but a well-worn cotton tunic draped itself over his powerful frame, the sleeves rolled up to just above the elbows, revealing large, muscular forearms. It was ripped at the neck and various stains darkened its originally white colour. Suspenders and a belt held up baggy trousers overtop of leather clogs on his feet.

To Jonathan's delight the third person through the door was Sonja. While she often spent time with him and his friends, he was surprised that she cared enough to come this far to see him off. She strode into the room, cool and confident as usual, a hat with a single red feather resting on top of her long straight brown hair. Like Rannulf, she also wore a brown leather vest over top of a dark shirt. Trousers made from black material tucked themselves into black boots. A thin rapier in a scabbard clung to her belt, a quiver with arrows hung from her shoulder, and she carried a bow in her hand. Jonathan could sense the keen intelligence in her glance as she scanned the room. When she saw him, she smiled.

Most men would have thought her pretty, and a number of male customers glanced up as she walked towards him. But Jonathan had known her since childhood, and he did not think of her in physical terms. To him she was simply Sonja.

Gladly he welcomed them to his table. Earlier he had resigned himself to never seeing them again and here they were speaking face to face!

After ordering for themselves they quizzed him about his change in circumstances.

"Who are these people who rescued you?" asked Olaf.

Jonathan told them the little he knew about Ragnar, Philip, and Hugh.

"Yet you are worried," said Sonja.

"It seems too good to be true," he responded.

"But you aren't in prison anymore are you?" said Rannulf.

"What if it's some kind of bizarre mistake, though?" said Jonathan. "After all, what are the chances of being a nobleman's son really? And if I'm welcomed into this family and it's later discovered that I'm an imposter, would they kill me for knowing their secrets? Besides, what sort of family is this? Are they criminals? What if I don't like them, or they don't like me?"

"I wouldn't worry about it," said Sonja.

"Why shouldn't he worry about it?" asked Olaf. "What if this is a trick—Vonich's last attempt to torment him before his real execution? After all, Vonich knows that Jonathan doesn't have any real family nearby."

Olaf's words made Jonathan consider Ragnar—if Ragnar really was his name—more warily.

"Oh, come on!" said Sonja. "Caution is one thing, but stupidity is another. If Ragnar is such a deceiver, why did he pay five hundred crowns for Jonathan's release?"

"Good point." said Rannulf. "I don't think you need to be so concerned, Jonathan. Give Ragnar a chance. He might be who he says he is."

The time flew by as they chatted. Jonathan found himself wishing that he could bring them along with him, but he did not feel brave enough to voice his desire aloud.

Olaf, who had not been speaking much, suddenly interrupted the conversation. "Oh Jonathan," he said, "we almost forgot the biggest news of all!"

"What?" said Jonathan. "Are the guards coming after me?" he asked warily.

"No, St. Swithun's Amulet has been stolen."

According to legend, Swithun had been a holy man and hermit who lived about the same time as Morden the Magnificent, eight centuries previously. Supposedly, Swithun could prophesy the future.

One day three years after Morden had first set up camp at Rindorn, he and his men were busy replacing their wooden stockade with a stone castle, when in the middle of their labours, St. Swithun unexpectedly appeared. Morden knew of Swithun but the two men had never met. Even though Morden wore no identifiable clothing to distinguish him as captain, Swithun strode right up to him.

"I have a gift for you, Morden," he said. Then he took out a strange piece of jewellery—an ordinary stone set in a silver necklace.

"What's this?" asked Morden.

"This blessed stone has helped our people through many trials. It has come down to us from another place in days long gone."

Morden was not impressed. All he could see was an ordinary rock, and the silver was not worth much either.

Swithun could tell what Morden was thinking. "This amulet is more important than you know," he said. "As long as it remains inside the town you are building, Rindorn will never be captured by its enemies." Then, just as suddenly as he had appeared, Swithun turned and left.

Morden was left puzzling over the gift. He was tempted to toss it aside, but out of politeness he kept it and put it in a little wooden box. And whether from coincidence or not, it was true that Rindorn had never been captured in battle since that day.

Despite its simple appearance it was regarded with great reverence by most Rindornites. Jonathan had seen the stone a few times. The mayor wore it around his neck on election day, and visiting nobility wore it for special ceremonies. Aside from these occasions it almost never left its container in one of the castle tower's upper rooms.

Jonathan, however, had never believed the stories about the amulet nor its supposed powers. "Oh, no. Rindorn's magic pebble is gone!" he scoffed, "such a tragedy! But you know, I think it says something about Rindorn that, while the nobles from other places force their subjects to make them expensive crowns and coronation jewellery, our town founders were clever enough to stick our mayor with a common rock. Now they'll have to raise taxes to get him a real hunk of gold. It's too bad. That lump of rock has kept him happy for so long!"

His friends laughed. One was not supposed to say such things about the famous amulet of Rindorn.

"I feel jealous," he continued, adopting the air of someone deeply offended. "I lose my position as town mischief-maker, and already someone has stolen my spot. You'd think they could have waited at least a week out of politeness. But no! That's what's wrong with this world. Nobody has respect anymore!"

"Well, Jonathan," said Sonja, "perhaps you've discovered your new calling. You could return to Rindorn and lecture the youth there on the meaning of respect. In the meantime, I don't feel that sorry for you. I seem to remember a certain individual who dangled the mayor's trousers from a statue."

"Who would do such a thing?" said Jonathan in a shocked tone.

At that moment, Jonathan noticed that Philip had entered the room and gone over to talk to the innkeeper. "Do they know who took the amulet?" asked Jonathan, continuing the conversation.

"There are all sorts of theories," said Rannulf. "Some people are saying that you or your new friends took it today as the castle guards were distracted by your release."

Jonathan buried his head in his hands. "Why do they *always* think it's me?"

Sonja turned to him, "Because it *always* is you."

"But why would I want *that* thing?" he said. "Anyway, in two weeks time they'll probably discover that some child accidentally put it in his rock collection."

The group laughed again.

"Actually there is another theory about who took it," said Olaf. "The city councillors tried to hush it up, but a guard was found killed by a bolt from a crossbow on one of the walls some weeks back, just before you were thrown into prison."

"Was that when the amulet was taken?" asked Jonathan.

"They only noticed that it was missing this afternoon, but if the guard's death was somehow connected to this, then it disappeared over a month ago."

At this point Philip approached their table, and Jonathan made the necessary introductions. He was surprised to see that Philip was now very talkative. Olaf, Rannulf and Sonja remained for a while, chatting, yet they eventually noticed that it was getting late.

Olaf rose. "Well, I guess, Jonathan." he began.

But he never finished his sentence.

The front door of the inn slammed open, crashing into the wall behind it. Eight men, cloaked and hooded in black, sprang through the door. Their faces were draped with black strips of cloth that left only their eyes uncovered.

Jonathan jumped to his feet, knocking his chair backwards. This was a mistake. The invaders, noting his sudden movement, made an immediate lunge towards him.

He felt betrayed. Ragnar had paid money for him to be let go. This should not be happening! His hand reached for his sword but, as he grasped empty air, he realized that it was still on the bed upstairs! He chided himself for his lack of preparedness.

Meanwhile, Sonja had taken out her rapier, Olaf and Rannulf had grabbed chairs for defence, and the three of them had formed a wall to protect him. Quickly Olaf downed one intruder with his chair. Another black figure slipped past the crowd aiming for Rannulf, who unsuccessfully kicked at his opponent's shoulder before downing him with his chair.

The crowd was in confusion. Some got up to run. Others ducked under tables and covered their hands with their arms. This worked to Jonathan's advantage because, for the moment there was such tumult that the intruders could not get near him. He knew he must climb the stairs to collect his sword, but then he discovered that the milling crowd was as much an obstacle for him as for his attackers. In desperation he also grabbed a chair, and with it raised above his head, he dodged and weaved his way through the crowd towards the door. Just as he was about to dash up the stairs he glanced back at the fray.

To his amazement one of the mysterious men in black had sprung up and grabbed at the rafters. From there the intruder crossed the room, alternately swinging from rafters and leaping on tables. Jonathan was so taken with admiration for this feat that he forgot to run. He had seen a lot of fistfights in his time but never a move like this. The stranger was graceful, yet quick. And when he landed in front of Jonathan a moment later he could not recall where the man had jumped from last. It seemed as if he had come out of nowhere.

The man drew a curved scimitar from his belt and Jonathan suddenly remembered himself. Blocking the stranger's first blow with the chair, he caught the scimitar between the chair legs. Thinking quickly, he gave the chair a spin.

The stranger's scimitar was knocked out of his hands but he did not bend down to pick it up as Jonathan had expected. Instead he grabbed the chair and kept it spinning, effectively wrenching it out of Jonathan's hands! The next moment it was being used as a weapon against him.

Jonathan ducked in time so that he received only a blow to his shoulder, but it knocked him sideways to the floor. Fortunately, he fell beside his opponent's scimitar and grabbing it he used it to deflect the stranger's next couple blows with the chair.

Jonathan was figuring out how to get off the floor when good fortune saved him. Some of the crowd had opened a window and fled through it, and in through the same window leapt Hugh, his sword already drawn.

Hugh speedily moved to attack Jonathan's assailant, but again Jonathan was surprised by how quickly their foe responded. As Hugh's sword moved through its arc, the stranger ducked and flattened himself against the floor.

Meanwhile Jonathan had seized the chance to stand upright, and now he jumped over the intruder's body to regain the door to the upstairs. But the man in black was on his feet in a flash. Abandoning Jonathan, he spun, using the chair to parry Hugh's next blow. Next he dropped the chair with his right hand and with his left in one swift motion pulled a dagger from his boot. Ducking under Hugh's sword arm, he darted forwards with his dagger.

Hugh only had time to bring his leg up for protection. Even so he was unable to completely avoid the dagger's thrust, and he gave a yell as the weapon pierced his leg armour.

"Run, Jonathan, run!" he shouted.

Jonathan needed no more urging. With the passage clear in front of him, he bounded up the stairs to retrieve the sword he had so foolishly left behind.

Just then he felt something sharp sting him. Reaching around, he discovered a small wire-like dart protruding from his shoulder. He brushed it off and at the same moment saw his assailant at the bottom of the stairs, loading another dart into a short tube.

*What are they attempting to do, prick me to death?*

Jonathan cleared the remaining stairs and found the bedroom door unlocked. Bursting into the room, he saw his sword lying on the bed just as he had left it.

He grabbed it. But something was wrong. It was

much too heavy. Pulling it from its sheath, he started running back to help his friends only to discover that there was fog in the room. Or was it just fogginess in his vision? He could not tell.

He was almost at the door but his knees did not respond the way he wanted them to. He forced one foot forward, then the next.

Suddenly he did not want to run downstairs. He just wanted to relax. The next moment he felt his very heavy sword falling from his grasp. That was fine. It was unfair that it was so heavy. It shouldn't have been—really.

Looking up, a strange sight met his eyes. The furniture around him was bending, free from its bondage to firmness. In fact, the whole room rejoiced—dancing to unheard strains of music.

The curtains swam into view—waving back and forth at him. The bed table chuckled to itself in the corner.

Like an ocean swell, the floor rose up, rippling, as it naturally should have done, he was sure, so long before.

It felt better now.

It must have.

And he—

# 6 THE DRAGIKOI

He was swimming through stinking water that was filled with floating garbage. He passed a large black thing with a number of holes in it on the left. The water gradually became greenish in colour. Not right.

At first he thought that if he could only manage to swim past the garbage, the water would improve. Yet it seemed that the more he swam the more garbage he encountered. A beige object approached on his right. A darker green substance lay beneath him.

It was becoming more difficult to swim. He could not stay afloat any longer. *I'm sinking, drowning in a sea of garbage.*

He woke up. It was dark and uncomfortably hot. A blanket lay on top of him. He tried to kick it off, but for some reason his legs felt constrained, and he removed the blanket with his hands.

*What an awful dream! I must have a fever,* he thought.

He moved a hand to his forehead. It was warm. But maybe that was its normal temperature.

He tried to sit up, but discovered that he was very weak.

*Where am I?*

It did not feel like the prison cell back in Rindorn. Besides, it had never been warm there, always cold. He sniffed the air. It smelt better than the Rindorn jail, too. It resembled the smell of the lakeshore near Ravenhall. He could also hear the sound of water close by.

The floor beside him felt bare and wooden. He slapped it twice—hollow, too. A dim light originated from a space above. Starlight, moonlight or some kind of light peered down through a hole.

*How did I get here?*

He tried to recall recent events. There had been someone named Ragnar. Almost certainly Ragnar had been real and not just part of a dream. Then there was the Ravenhall Inn, his friends, and, yes, the black-shrouded intruders.

He remembered!

He guessed that his current whereabouts were connected to the intruders. That did not make him feel better, but at least he had a notion of what could have happened.

*Why won't my legs move*

Sitting up he felt down his legs towards his feet. His socks and shoes had been removed. A metal bracelet encircled each ankle and chains went from them to someplace else—the wall possibly. Yes, he had definitely been captured.

He racked his brains to determine why someone like himself, a prisoner from Rindorn, would be of interest to these shadowy figures.

The only explanation was that they wanted ransom money. The uncle who sent Ragnar had paid five hundred crowns for his release. The intruders must have heard this and have figured that he would pay more. This realization made him feel somewhat better. By understanding his situation and the possible motives of his attackers, he was one step closer to outwitting them and getting away.

Then a sudden worry seized him. If he had been captured, what had happened to Sonja, Rannulf, and Olaf, not to mention Ragnar and the rest? Were they all right?

"Rannulf? Olaf?" he whispered. "Are you there?"

No answer.

He thought for a moment. During the fight at the inn, the men in black had only chased after him, not his friends. Olaf, Sonja and the rest might still be fine, he told himself. And what about Ragnar, Philip and Hugh? He had been suspicious when he had first met them, but now he would have given anything to see them.

Finally he again reflected on his own stark situation and was swept up in a wave of self-pity. *A month ago I was a carefree citizen of Rindorn. But now twice in that space of time I've been captured and confined. Why is life so unfair?*

Then he remembered Ruth, the old widow that he had stayed with in Rindorn, saying, "Self-pity never solves anything." And of course, she was right. Slowly the feeling subsided.

As time went on, the birds outside began to sing. Gradually the light of the dawn crept through the room's top window and allowed him to see his surroundings. This was probably the most peculiar room that he had ever beheld. It was perhaps fifteen feet wide and thirty feet long with two open doors, one in the corner close behind him and the other in the room's opposite corner. It was also remarkably clean and bare. Space in Rindorn was limited and most houses that Jonathan had visited were crammed with furniture, tools, cooking implements and the like. This room was nearly empty. There was no stove, nor even a fireplace or chimney.

Still, despite its barrenness, it did not resemble a poor person's house. Its interior was of a much finer quality than he had yet laid eyes on. The floor was made of wood, which was rare in Rindorn where most dwellings had floors of packed earth. Not only was it wooden, but polished, similar to the panelling on the walls in rich people's houses. The walls in this room were panelled as well, and shelves climbed part way up two of them. These shelves held tall slender pottery jars. Jonathan also spied several candles in one corner. Besides these items, the room's only visible furniture was a stack of mats in the opposite corner. Most interesting yet, lying on top of the mats was a person. As the light grew stronger Jonathan tried to guess who this might be. Like the intruders in the inn, this person wore a long black robe. A black hood covered his head.

Jonathan decided not to wake him. If by chance the man was one of his captors, then it was best that he stay asleep as long as possible.

Just then the man groaned and rolled over. Jonathan stared. By the sound of the groan he realized that it was a woman, not a man as he had first thought. Intrigued, he studied her form in the half-light. Now he noticed that her ankles had collars around them, too, and chains led from the collars to the wall. She was also barefoot. Clearly she was not one of his captors. He wondered what their purpose was in keeping her here.

Jonathan turned his attention to the jars on the shelves. Lifting up his chain, he held it taut as long as possible to keep it quiet while he moved towards the jars. The chain still clanked softly a couple times— though not enough to wake his companion—and he hoped that the birds' chirping would mask any extra noises. Reaching slowly, he managed to lay his fingers on one of the jars and roll it a little closer. Carefully, he removed its clay stopper and looked inside. It held a paper scroll, which removed and unrolled.

The scroll puzzled him. The lettering on it—if it was lettering—was totally different than anything he had seen before. It looked more like a collection of symbols than words. Since he could not decipher the scroll, he replaced it. He was just in the midst of stuffing it back into its jar when a soft thud from the far side of the room startled him.

He glanced up. A figure, dressed just like the intruders at the Ravenhall Inn, stood on tiptoe as if he had just landed from a jump. This was the first time he had seen one of the intruders without a cloth across his face. Back in Ravenhall he had even wondered if they were human, but he was relieved to see that this man displayed quite a normal human face.

When the man in black saw what Jonathan had been doing, he leapt through the air and landed beside him. The jar with its scroll was snatched from his hand. The man examined it, saw that it was undamaged and replaced it on the shelf, this time out of Jonathan's reach. Then he laughed. Jonathan wondered if the man realized that he could not read it.

The other prisoner had been wakened by the stranger's laughter and sat up. Jonathan could now see that she was indeed a young woman. She had deep-set blue eyes and long blond hair, high cheekbones and a somewhat prominent though not overly large nose. She probably would have had a pretty face had it not been so dirty and had she not looked so sad.

The man in black approached the woman. Taking a key from his pocket he did something to her chains. She stood up. She was slightly taller than most women of Jonathan's acquaintance. Although her feet were still chained to each other, they were no longer attached to the wall, and she followed the man to the doorway nearest to her where they both disappeared.

He was left puzzling about this, but about fifteen minutes later she reappeared. The man shoved her toward the mats before reattaching her chains to the wall. Then he approached Jonathan. He too was unchained and led towards the same door. From the doorway he saw some steep, ladder-like wooden steps leading down to a boat. Hello! This house was not built on land, but on stilts, with actual water beneath it!

He desperately wanted exercise so he followed his captor down to the boat. As his guard rowed the boat away from the prison building, Jonathan saw that they were on a river dotted with many small islands and surrounded by forest on all sides. Above him the leaves of tall maple trees formed a canopy that filtered the sunlight, causing the forest to be bathed in a pleasant, greenish-tinged light. Jonathan thought that the beauty of the scene stood in stark contrast to his present difficulties.

Glancing behind him, he examined his prison house. Its tall stilts lifted it five feet above the level of the river and he could see that it contained two parts. The prisoners' room was on the house's eastern end, and he assumed that the room on the west side housed some of his captors. It was a strange-looking building. Unlike the roofs in Rindorn, this roof was steep in the centre and flatter near the edges. There were no doors, only four openings where doors would normally have been. The girl's opening faced the island, whereas the opening nearest the place where he was chained faced out into the main part of the river.

*If we are prisoners, why aren't the girl and I in a room with secure and locking portals?* he wondered. *Perhaps our captors feel so confident in the ankle chains and their own ability to fight off any rescue attempts that they don't believe they need closed doors?*

His guard rowed against a slow moving current over to a large treed island where he ran the boat ashore. He made Jonathan get out and then followed him as far as the edge of the beach. Once they reached the trees, the guard drew his scimitar, but did not follow Jonathan. As far as Jonathan could tell, he was free to wander around the island. He guessed that his captor assumed that with heavy ankle chains attached to his feet he could not swim, and Jonathan was not about to try.

Within a few minutes the man strode towards him, waving the scimitar. Apparently his exercise time was completed. Obediently he accompanied the man back to the boat, and with Jonathan rowing they returned to the prison house.

Shortly after being re-chained to the wall, their guard brought Jonathan and the girl food and water and then disappeared. There was not much food on the tray, and to Jonathan it tasted strange—mostly flatbread with something spread on it that he wasn't sure he should eat. Seeing his female companion eating it he gathered the courage to do the same. It was salty—perhaps made from fish or some peculiar vegetable.

After washing down the last of his food with water, Jonathan turned toward the girl. "Hi," he said.

"Hi," she responded, before becoming silent again.

"Do you know where we are?" he asked.

"No."

"Who are these people?"

"The Dragikoi," she said.

*Dragikoi.* He thought about that word. "Do you know anything about them?"

"Not much. They aren't from here. The northwest, maybe?" Then she put her hand to her lips indicating that Jonathan should be silent. This gesture puzzled him since there were no guards in their room.

Jonathan waited perhaps an hour, and then in a quieter voice he tried talking again. "Do the Dragikoi dislike us talking together?"

She nodded her head in response.

"How long have you been here?" he asked.

"Two weeks."

"Two weeks! Why are you here?"

She shrugged.

"Do you mind me asking who you are?"

She cast a furtive glance at the doorway, apparently checking for guards. "Tell me who you are first."

"That's a good question," he said in a voice barely above a whisper. "My name's Jonathan. I was orphaned when I was a child, then somehow a nobleman decided that I was his long lost nephew, though I've never met him or any other relatives. My guess is that I'm being held for ransom."

"I'm probably here for the same reason," she said.

This time Jonathan fell silent. If she was being held for ransom, it meant that she was a daughter of a wealthy family. Her father then was either a nobleman or a merchant.

"Where's home for you?" he asked at last.

In response she put her finger to her lips again.

Conversation died after this and Jonathan quickly grew bored. He examined his surroundings for possible escape routes, and when he had exhausted that project, he passed the time counting the flies buzzing through the room. After a while his thoughts returned to their captors. He wondered where they came from, and how they moved with such grace and speed. He was sure that he could find out more from his cellmate if there just was a chance to talk without being interrupted.

While he had been gone on his walk, one of the stacked straw mats had been moved down for him to sleep on, and he lay back on it, but he had just dozed off when five of their captors entered the room. They were dressed as they had been in Ravenhall, except now he could see their faces. They chatted together in a language that he could not understand.

What happened next surprised him. They lined up and in unison began doing a series of graceful movements, similar to dance moves, yet without music. He also noticed that many of their dance steps appeared particularly aggressive in nature. High leg kicks preceded punches that were accompanied by resounding cries that made Jonathan's fellow captive flinch.

He had heard of war dances before. He wondered if this was such a dance. Maybe the musicians would show up later? But no musicians came, and the men repeated the same series of movements several times, each time finishing with a shout.

Eventually, because he was bored and had nothing else to do, Jonathan counted the different movements. There were sixty in total. Then a thought occurred to him. Perhaps they were so graceful in battle because they practised these movements? He remembered talking to an acrobat who had come through Rindorn with a travelling circus. The acrobat had told him that he had taken up folk dancing because it helped him move more smoothly.

After making the connection between their gracefulness and their dancing, Jonathan stared at these moves with greater interest. If he could memorize the sequence himself, he would try to mimic it as best he could the next time that he was let out for exercise on the island. Unfortunately, just then they quit that particular dance before he had a chance to memorize it and they started on another. This time he was more successful in committing it to memory.

After they finished their dances, they took

Jonathan and then the girl back to the island for another stroll. Two of the Dragikoi stood near the boat with drawn scimitars while Jonathan walked to the island's far side. Behind the partial cover of the trees, he attempted to replicate the dances that he had just seen.

He knew that his dance was not perfect—and the chains around his legs severely hampered his movement, but he thought that at least he had replicated the gist of it. Improvement would come with practice. This time he did not mind being taken back to the hut to be chained again, because he had something to do with his time. He could mentally review the dance moves.

In the early afternoon they were again left alone in the hut, and he tried to nap. The Dragikoi were not giving either Jonathan or his fellow captive much food, and he felt tired.

Later, after it began to rain, five of their captors entered the hut. This time they practised combat, for close to an hour making throws, moves, attacks and dodges. Once or twice Jonathan had to roll out of the way when a Dragikoi nearly landed on top of him. He found himself thinking that, although he did not enjoy being locked up, if he had to choose between the Dragikoi's prison or Rindorn's, he would much rather be where he was. In this place at least he had periodic entertainment.

The activities were the same for the next two days. Jonathan and the girl would be left alone for long periods, but a few times each day the team of black-clad warriors would return and practise either their dances or their combative moves. Otherwise, Jonathan's main concern was hunger, and he noted that the girl looked very weak and thin. Her reluctance to talk also frustrated him. She seemed to be the kind of person that he would have liked to talk with more, and he started hoping that she would not be ransomed and instead the two of them could escape together.

He tried to communicate with her as much as he could with gestures, but she appeared too discouraged to reply. She did not smile often and preferred to sleep. He wondered if this was because of the lack of food or because she missed home or because of some tragic event in her past. Nonetheless, Jonathan occasionally managed to coax her into brief exchanges. They only tried these when there was no one else in the room and when noises from outside covered the sound of their speech.

He noticed also that she felt better about talking if there were long pauses between their brief snatches of words. He did not mind waiting. He had nothing else to do anyhow.

"I didn't catch your name," he said once.

"Charissa."

That was all for a while.

"Do you know what's in these pottery jars?" he asked

"No," she said.

"Any guesses?"

"They might be directions how to do those dances, or even orders from their commander, whoever that person is."

Jonathan thought about the implications of what she had said. If Charissa was right, the Dragikoi were part of a larger group with a central chief elsewhere. This place might just be one of their outposts.

An hour or more later to his surprise he heard her say, "They don't like it when we talk."

Jonathan nodded in response.

"There used to be another prisoner here," she said a few minutes afterwards. "He tried to talk to me. They killed him."

Shocked, Jonathan nodded again sombrely. No wonder she was not eager to chat! He waited for nightfall before risking another few words. "Do you know what day it is?"

"No."

Two days later Jonathan noticed that thirty or more Dragikoi warriors had suddenly shown up. Was another mission being planned or a battle, perhaps? On his next exercise trip he saw that these newly arrived Dragikoi were staying in four freshly built huts. These too were placed on stilts, but unlike the prison cell which stood in the midst of the river, the new structures were built overtop of a nearby island.

The following day when Jonathan was taken to the island again, they handed him a spade and a pair of sandals. One of his feet was unshackled, while the other was chained to a tree. Then, by signs they showed him that they wanted all the earth in a certain area dug up and turned over. It looked like they were planting a garden. Jonathan wondered if they were creating a more permanent base.

He did the digging that they wanted, but whenever the guard was not looking he practised the dance steps that he had observed earlier. Now that one of his legs was unshackled they were much easier to perform. He was sure that he had seen at least seven different dance series, but he could only clearly remember three. Eventually they returned him to the hut, though not before he had to surrender the sandals.

That same evening, long after the two prisoners were once again chained to the wall and their guards had left, from beyond the doorway closest to him Jonathan heard scuffling and the sound of creaking wooden stairs.

He froze.

A voice whispered from the darkness, "Jonathan, are you there?"

"Who's there?" he asked.

"Philip."

Jonathan was so happy he could barely speak. He might just have a chance of escape!

"How have they tied you up?"

"Chains and locks," he said. He was going to add something more, but Philip, who must have heard a noise, had quickly vanished.

He feigned sleep in case a guard came to investigate, and sure enough, one of the Dragikoi returned carrying a lantern. Through almost closed eyelids Jonathan saw him glance around the hut, observe them sleeping and then leave. He anticipated hearing more from Philip later that night or the next day but there was nothing. He hoped Philip had got away safely.

It was not until after dark on the sixth day that he was in captivity that Jonathan finally heard from Philip again. This time he actually climbed into the hut through the doorway nearest Jonathan. "I've got something for you, Jonathan," he whispered. "Careful, they may make noise."

"What is it?" asked Jonathan.

"Keys," he said, "they might work."

Jonathan received the keys with gratitude and held them tightly in his fist so they would not clatter against each other.

"I'll be back later," said Philip. "If you manage to free yourself, swim downstream to the monastery on the left bank. We're waiting for you there." Then before Jonathan could say much more than thank you, Philip crawled backwards out of the hut, down the stairs and into the river.

Hope rose in Jonathan's heart. Perhaps he would be free soon! Very slowly, so that the keys made no sound, he found the keyholes in his shackles. He tried each key in turn, but nothing opened or moved. Bitter disappointment was replacing his earlier hope, but he moved over to the lock that attached him to the wall. Still no success.

Frustrated, Jonathan wanted to throw the keys against the wall. Yet he restrained himself. Any loud noise would have attracted the attention of the guards. Instead he put the keys underneath his sleeping mat and hoped that Philip would return to claim them before they were noticed.

Philip did return about an hour later. "They didn't work," Jonathan told him.

Soundlessly Philip took the keys back. "We'll still get you out," he said.

"Bring us food if you can," whispered Jonathan before Philip slipped out the door and back into the stream.

Philip had left just in time. Someone in the room next door must have heard a noise because a moment later a Dragikoi appeared with a lit lantern. This woke Charissa, and Jonathan pretended to wake up also. The Dragikoi looked tired, but after finding nothing unusual, he extinguished the lantern. Nevertheless, he remained in their room, crouched in a corner.

The next day Jonathan was shaken roughly awake. He had slept longer than usual due to Philip's nighttime visit and this morning a rather suspicious-looking guard had been posted to their room. Jonathan felt uncomfortable eating under his baleful gaze.

After breakfast, his captors again assigned him a shovel, and during his digging duties he had ample opportunity to reflect on the events of the night before. He was disheartened that his hopes for immediate freedom had been dashed, but at least some of his friends were alive and they knew where he was. That meant that he was in a much better situation now than what he had thought earlier. Still, he regretted that he had been so occupied with trying to escape that he had forgotten to ask Philip about Ragnar, Hugh and his friends.

His captors kept him working the entire day, and once when he paused for a rest, one of the guards came and shouted at him in their strange language. By evening he was dead tired and had changed his mind about which jail experience he preferred. At least in Rindorn he had not been worked to the point of exhaustion.

When he was returned to the hut, he was surprised to see a guard still posted there. Obviously something during the previous night had made the Dragikoi suspicious. Jonathan's heart sank. What chance of escape did they have if their captors were going to watch them all hours of the day?

He fell asleep fairly early that evening but soon found himself awake. Loud noises were coming from the direction of the huts where the newly arrived Dragikoi were staying, and their guard appeared to be gone. Jonathan could not see much more than that in the darkness, but he could tell by the sound of her breathing that Charissa was awake also. There was enough hubbub outside that he figured he could risk a word or two.

"What's going on?" he asked.

"They're having some sort of festival."

Normally the Dragikoi seemed to live a fairly silent and disciplined life, but clearly not always. He wondered what the occasion was. Listening more carefully, he could hear drums, music, talking, and even some singing. It was the most noise he had heard from their captors since arriving. A thin whiny instrument played an elaborately ornamented melody, but it resembled nothing that he had heard before.

"Have they done this previously?" he asked.

"No."

Shortly afterwards their guard returned. Outside the music and voices continued. After another half hour the voices got louder, and the guard in their room sat up and took notice. Soon a lit lantern entered the room with a figure clothed in black following it. Jonathan was surprised to see this new arrival stagger a couple times and brace himself against the wall as he walked. He talked in a loud voice.

The two men exchanged keys and a moment later Jonathan heard the sound of the oars in the water as the first guard rowed away. Once the former guard had left, the new man did not silently sit down in the guard's usual corner, instead he turned and stared at the prisoners. Eventually he began talking.

Initially he spoke quietly as if to no one in particular, but as he kept on, his voice gradually rose to the level of a shout. He was obviously drunk. Jonathan could not understand a word, but the guard was clearly frustrated about something. For a time, he moved closer to Jonathan and bellowed into his face, waving his arms. Then rather abruptly his rant subsided to a murmur and he strode back towards his corner.

Jonathan stole a quick glance at Charissa. Nervous, she was sitting with her knees pressed close to her chin.

A minute later the man returned to Jonathan, shouting and waving his arms again. Then once more he interrupted his rampage. He turned and stomped closer to Charissa's doorway and Jonathan heard him take out keys. For a while he fumbled with a small wooden chest sitting on a bookshelf. In his drunken state he seemed to have great difficulty opening it but eventually he managed.

Now his murmuring crescendoed to a triumphant roar. Jonathan saw him stuff the keys into his pocket before staggering back towards him. This time he had something in his hand. Dangling the object in front of Jonathan's face, he taunted him with it. Since the man's body blocked the lantern light, all that Jonathan could see was a chain or a necklace of some sort. Finally he stumbled to one side, allowing the light to shine fully on the object. Jonathan gasped in surprise. It was St. Swithun's Rock, the Amulet of Rindorn! So the Dragikoi had stolen it!

When his captor realized that he had succeeded in gaining a reaction, he let the amulet fall to the floor and laughed. Then, becoming more aggressive, he started kicking. As far as the length of his chains allowed, Jonathan tried to avoid the kicks, and since the guard was drunk, only a few of his blows actually landed. But seeing Jonathan dodge only infuriated the guard, making him kick with more vigour.

Eventually, in his fury, he drew back his leg for an even more powerful kick. But misjudging the distance, he lost his balance and fell backwards. His head struck the floor and he did not move after that.

Remembering the keys in the guard's pocket, Jonathan realized he would have only a brief time to obtain them before the guard woke or someone came to replace him. He stretched as far as his chains permitted, but he could not reach the guard's pocket. He could, however, grasp the man's ankles, and he realized that he might just possibly be able to pull the guard's entire body towards him. It was risky because he might wake the man by doing it, but he had to attempt it before their one chance to escape was gone forever.

He grabbed the cuffs of his captor's pants, yet the body did not move. He tugged even harder and very slowly the man's body began sliding along the polished floor towards him. So far the man had not stirred.

Jonathan, exhaled, let go for a moment and changed his grip. At that moment Charissa's chains clanked as she sat up. As loudly as she dared, she whispered, "Stop! Are you trying to get us killed?"

But he dared not listen. Once more he grabbed hold of the guard's pant cuffs and pulled, this time dragging him a greater distance. The man remained asleep. Jonathan could reach the pocket now. Carefully, so as not to make a sound, he inserted his hand to extract the key. It caught on something.

Growing impatient he wrenched with greater force. The keys broke free but clanged loudly together. Jonathan heard a sharp intake of breath from Charissa. But their luck seemed to hold. The guard did not wake up, and no one else came to investigate.

Now his hands shook so badly he could barely get the keys into the holes in the locks that bound the chains to his ankles. The first key did not work, nor the second, nor the third. Finally a key fit. It turned! One ankle was free! The same key worked on the other ankle. Quickly he crossed the floor to where Charissa was chained.

"I hope you are right about this," she said. They found the key for her chains and in a moment she was free as well.

Before leaving the hut, Jonathan picked up St. Swithun's Amulet and hung it around his neck. He had never revered the amulet as others had, but he certainly did not want the Dragikoi to have it. Somebody in Rindorn would be happy if it was returned.

They left through the door on Jonathan's side of the hut, it being the farthest away from the island with the festivities. He took Charissa's arms and helped her down the ladder-like stairs and into the river. "As long as no one spots us or notices that we're gone, we should be able to get away," he said.

Then just as he turned around to descend into the river, his worst fear came true. The guard woke up. Their eyes met just as Jonathan's toes touched the water. The man rose unsteadily to his feet, staggered to the other doorway and started shouting.

If they managed to escape now it would be a miracle.

# 7 THE RIVER

"Can you swim?" Jonathan whispered as he and Charissa clung to the lowest step.

"A little," she said.

Jonathan knew that "a little" was not good enough—what they needed was a boat. Gazing underneath the building and across the river, in the moonlight he could see one moored about thirty feet away.

"Stay here," he told Charissa. "I'll be back in a minute." He left her clinging to one of the stilts on which their prison was built while he swam underwater to the boat.

Slithering out of the water, he saw that it was tied to a small tree on the shore. He would have to stand upright in order to untie the boat, but that was not to be helped. Although the rope had a reasonable amount of slack in it, the knot gave him trouble, partly because he could not see it clearly in the darkness and partly because he was shaking again—

from cold or nervousness.

Then just as he released the knot, he looked up and to his horror saw a figure approaching. The man was a hundred yards away but closing fast.

Jonathan guessed that in the semi-darkness the guard could not tell that he was not a Dragikoi, so he resolved to remain calm. He pushed the boat off from the shore but at just that moment he realized that his hurry, he had forgotten about the river current, which now pulled him downstream. Worse, the recent rains had swollen the river and made the current stronger. Jonathan fumbled in the bottom of the boat for the paddle, but by the time he got it, he was already far off course and drifting away from the prison hut.

Paddling against the current, he tried to get nearer to Charissa but the best he could do was stop the boat from slipping further away.

"Swim to me," he called.

Charissa at first hesitated, but then floundered towards the boat. Yet Jonathan's call had alerted their captors. He glanced behind. The man who had been approaching him had turned and was sprinting back to the festivities, shouting as he ran. "Hurry, Charissa!" Jonathan called.

Finally she was close enough that he could toss her the boat's bow rope. Looking toward the shore he now saw a number of Dragikoi running towards them.

Charissa grabbed the rope's end and Jonathan pulled her closer. She was just climbing over the side of the boat when the first of their captors reached the shoreline sixty feet away. A dart whizzed past Jonathan's ear.

Charissa was in the boat now. "Get down," he

told her. She flattened herself into the bottom, and he ducked down beside her.

Fortunately they were now drifting downstream but the darts could still reach them. Worried that more Dragikoi might soon arrive, Jonathan risked sitting up and paddling—twice on the left side. Then as he ducked again a dart ricocheted off the edge of the boat. He estimated that they were ninety feet from the shore now, and he chanced sitting up again, this time stroking twice on the right. A second later a splatter of darts hit the water on that side. Another time he sat up and gave three more strokes on the left.

In his present state of stress he had to force himself to remember that a boat turns towards the opposite side that one paddles on. And with more strokes on the left than the right, they were veering right—towards their captors and land—not where they wanted to go! Jonathan risked another two strokes on the right to correct their course.

"Be careful," Charissa called.

Perhaps it was the darkness or perhaps it was the alcohol in the veins of their pursuers, but none of their darts struck either of them. Jonathan was relieved. Another involuntary nap would have been quite inconvenient just then.

On his right he could hear the Dragikoi trying to follow them along the shoreline, fighting their way through bushes and brambles, but soon the current took the boat from the slower moving water between the islands into the quicker moving main stream.

"Do you think they have another boat?" he asked.

"I don't know," she replied. "I've only seen this

one."

"Let's hope it's their only one."

Eventually the sounds of pursuit faded. After perhaps fifteen minutes without any signs of the Dragikoi, they began to relax. Soon however, a new thought consumed him. It was possible that they might miss the monastery in the darkness. Maybe they already had.

"We have a decision to make," he said, sharing the difficulty with Charissa. "There is a monastery somewhere along this river where friends of mine are waiting and where we can get help."

"All right."

"The problem is, I'm worried about passing it without noticing. If we stop to wait for morning, we risk being discovered by our captors. But if we keep going down the river, we might overshoot our rendezvous point with my friends. What do you think we should do?"

She did not answer for a few moments, and they continued to drift downstream. Eventually she said, "We should stop and hide the next chance we get. The risk of missing the monastery in the dark is too great."

Jonathan agreed. Their captivity had left them both hungry and weak, and they were in no shape to go on a long wilderness journey without food or the help of friends—especially since they were barefoot.

Since Philip had said that the monastery was on the left bank, he steered left towards the southern shore. As best as they could in the darkness, they searched for smaller rivulets and creeks that ran down to meet their river. These would be good places to hide the boat. Yet it was frustrating. For a while after making the decision to stop, they found no tributaries.

Finally they found one. Jonathan paddled the boat into the shallow bay created by the junction of the two rivers. Thankfully the rivulet's current was not strong, and without much trouble he was able to manoeuvre upstream and around a bend that was a couple of hundred yards from the river. He tied the boat to some branches overhanging the water which formed a cover over top of them and the boat. Then resting together inside the boat, they waited for the dawn.

"By the way," said Charissa, "thanks."

"For what?" he asked.

"For getting us out of there."

"Oh, it was just a lucky break, nothing more."

Charissa only grunted in reply and to his surprise she curled up against him and drifted into slumber. Despite all that they had been through, he was a bit taken aback by this gesture. The girl who had been refusing to talk to him for the last week was now showing affection.

*Oh, well,* he thought. *She's likely just using me as a temporary pillow. She'll probably be gone home soon and none of it will matter anyway.*

"The most important thing is to stay awake," he said aloud. "Stay awake. If I fall asleep, they may discover us. I have to stay awake."

He kept on repeating the words "stay awake," but before long he too had fallen asleep. The two of them were unconscious in a strange forest while being pursued by their enemies.

"Jonathan, Jonathan! Wake up!" He felt a sudden

shock of cold water on his face.

Spluttering, he wiped the water out of his eyes and opened them to see Charissa grinning down at him. He could tell by the dim light that it was close to dawn. "Good morning!" she said.

He groaned. There was a horrible pain in his back where it had rested against the boat's gunwale.

For a moment he could not remember who she was. He had been dreaming that he was back in Rindorn at the Scarlet Raven Inn, and her face did not fit into the collection of his friends. Then he remembered the Dragikoi, the prison hut and the river.

He and Charissa were likely still being hunted! How silly he had been to let himself sleep. He sat up suddenly with a jerk and banged his head against an overhanging willow branch.

"Ouch!" he said quite loudly.

"Shh," was her response.

"What's wrong? Are they close by?"

"Who can tell?" she said shrugging. "Probably not, though." She grinned again.

Jonathan nodded, and resolving to look around, he got out of the boat. He waded carefully to the rivulet's shore and made his way back to the bank of the larger river. From the cover of a willow tree he scanned the horizon for foes, but all that he could see was the flowing river, its waves lapping at his feet. He was uncertain of its name but thought that it might be the Naharoze—one of the largest rivers in Magelandorn, and had he not been worried about pursuit, he would have thought it was a beautiful sight. The sun was just below the horizon, and the orange and red glow in the eastern sky reflected back towards him in gentle waves on the river surface. Despite the danger, he allowed himself a few moments to admire the view. Dragikoi or no Dragikoi there was still beauty in the world. And the fact that there was beauty was a reminder that somehow something good must be behind it all.

He returned to where Charissa and he had spent the night. There was no breakfast. He shivered in the cool pre-dawn air. They debated whether to travel through the woods on foot or take the boat down the river. They both preferred the boat because it meant less walking, and as the Dragikoi had taken their shoes, any trip through the forest would mean walking barefoot. On the other hand, the boat would be an open target for anyone watching for them.

After some discussion they decided that the risks of the river were too great. They chose the more difficult route through the forest, hoping they could get to the monastery undetected.

They crossed the rivulet in the boat, then tried to haul it ashore and out of sight on the far bank, but it was too heavy. Instead, they tied it up and climbed to the top of the river valley, using the trunks of small trees as hand holds. With no food in their stomachs, they both felt light-headed by the time they made it to the crest. Fortunately, the dizziness subsided as they walked through the forest, quietly slipping from tree to tree.

Walking barefoot was easier than they had anticipated. It was an older forest without much undergrowth. Since the trees were well spaced apart it was easy to find pathways. In addition, the trees' leafy canopy blocked out most of the sunlight allowing a soft carpet of moss to cover the forest floor. Old men's beard, lichens and mosses also hung from the branches. One advantage of walking in bare feet, they discovered, was that while they were slower, they were also more careful about where they stepped and they travelled more quietly.

They journeyed for about three hours, going roughly west and parallel to the river. All this time they saw and heard nothing from their former captors and they hoped that they had eluded them.

Eventually they came to the top of a small rise overlooking the river and in the distance they saw a thin round stone tower with a conical cap rising, pencil-like into the sky. Towers like this were common in monasteries, their great height allowing the monks to see marauders at a distance. Yet to Jonathan's frustration, one more obstacle lay between them and their destination. Another rivulet crossed their path. This meant a steep bank to climb down, willow bushes to fight through at the water's edge, a widening stream to cross, and another steep climb on the far side. Three hours' journey through the forest, on top of several weeks of captivity in two prisons had left him feeling so tired that he only wanted to sit down. He sighed.

Seeing this new obstacle, Charissa too was crest-fallen. But all she said was, "I guess we get another chance to wash our clothes before meeting your friends."

Wearily they began the descent, but soon they found an old beaver trail leading to the water. It was smooth, straight and avoided some of the larger willow thickets, but it was slippery. And since they were larger than beavers, they had to crouch down to get past the bushes overhanging the path. Several times they lost their footing and slid part of the way, their feet and legs getting scraped by branches and thorns. As they approached the rivulet, they spied a number of boats docked against the far bank. The monks, it appeared, used this stream as a harbour for their vessels.

They were carefully picking their way through the last fringe of bushes before the water when they heard someone crashing through the forest to their left. Hastily glancing upwards, Jonathan saw a single figure clad in black sliding down into the same ravine.

Jonathan knew that their only chance of survival involved getting across the water and up the far bank to the monastery before their opponent could catch them. Knowing that they were pursued gave them extra energy to force their way through to the river's edge. As they plunged into the water, something sharp—a rock or a pointed stick—bit into Jonathan's calf, but he had no time examine the wound.

It was only a small river, but deep in the centre, so they were quickly over their heads in water. This, however, was a temporary gift: they were unlikely to be shot at while their bodies were below the surface. When Charissa started to flounder, Jonathan grabbed her arm and towed her over to shallow water. Then just as he was helping her onto the shore, a dart struck a tree right above his head. They had no time to lose.

Another beaver trail led up the valley's far side. It was very slippery, but as it was the straightest and smoothest way to the top, they set off along it, stumbling their way up the bank. Unfortunately for them, the beavers had cut down many of the trees that would have sheltered them from their enemy's darts and another dart just missed Jonathan and plunged into the ground at his feet. As he climbed, the world around him started going grey. He was not sure if this was from a dart or from his empty stomach, still he had no choice but to keep going. They were almost at the top when from behind he heard Charissa shout, "I've been hit!"

Jonathan knew that he would be able to carry her once they reached the flat ground at the top, but carrying her up the slippery bank would be almost impossible. Pulling out the dart from her shoulder, he grabbed her hand. "Keep going as long as you can." he told her, "I'll carry you after."

When they reached the top, a short stretch of open pasture lay between them and the monastery wall one hundred yards away, yet Charissa was now stumbling. He took her in his arms, and despite the pain from the cut on his leg, he ran towards the wall.

But where was the gate? It was not on the near side, and he realized with dismay that it was likely on the side of the monastery furthest from the river. He would have to run alongside the ravine, potentially within range of their opponent and his darts, in order to reach it.

Luck was with him. No shots were fired and he realized that the Dragikoi must be still climbing the bank behind them and be out of range.

By now, his muscles were burning with running and holding the unconscious Charissa at the same time. He slipped and fell to his knees, nearly letting her hit the ground. Getting up, he threw her over his shoulder and continued his stumbling run beside the wall.

When he passed the corner, he yelled, "Open the

gates, open the gates!"

He did not know if anyone heard him. It was tough to yell, run and carry someone at the same time.

As he met the path leading directly to the gate, he tried again, "Open the gates, open the gates!" Sixty yards to go. He glanced back at the line of trees marking the edge of the ravine three hundred yards behind him. Just as he did so, the man in black emerged from the forest, sprinting towards them with the speed of the wind.

"Open the gates!" he screamed. Thirty-five yards lay between him and the gate, then twenty. Again Jonathan stumbled to his knees and got up cursing himself. Picking up his burden, he laboured on until he was just yards from his goal.

But the gates remained shut! The man in black was charging up behind them.

"Open the gates! Open the gates!" he yelled, louder this time.

Nothing happened. He looked behind. Their enemy was only sixty yards away. In a moment he would be on top of them.

# 8 THE MONASTERY

Just then a bell rang from the tower. Slowly the portcullis rose and the gates creaked open. As an arrow flew down from the top of the wall towards their pursuer, he stopped running. Instead he took out his tube and fired darts at the soldiers on the wall.

Finally the door was open wide enough for Jonathan to enter. Still carrying Charissa, he stumbled inside. The gate closed behind them.

He could not clearly remember all that took place next. A quick scan of the courtyard showed him a number of ordinary-looking wooden huts plus a longer and larger building with a thatched roof.

Gently he laid Charissa down on the grass and exhausted, he collapsed facedown beside her. People rushed over, but for the moment he did not care. He and Charissa were safe—that was all that mattered.

From somewhere he heard Rannulf's voice, "You made it, fantastic!"

With an effort Jonathan rolled over. Above him clustered the smiling faces of Rannulf, Olaf, and Sonja—all safe. He smiled back.

"Where are Ragnar, Philip and Hugh?" he asked.

"Hugh, is recovering in one of the huts," said Sonja. "And Ragnar and Philip are out searching for you in the forest."

A stab of worry pierced Jonathan. The Dragikoi were out in the forest. He hoped that his two friends would return safe.

"Your leg's bleeding," Olaf announced.

His friends picked him up and carried him towards one of the huts.

"Charissa," he said. "Don't forget Charissa."

"Don't worry, we'll bring her, too," said Rannulf.

When they entered the hut he found himself in an infirmary where several cots lined the walls. Three monks began washing mud and dirt from his cuts. It stung.

A moment later his friends arrived with Charissa. They laid her on a bed near his, but while her cuts were also washed, she did not stir.

"Take good care of her. She's a nobleman's daughter," said Jonathan.

Once Charissa's cuts had been bathed, food was brought to him. He ate what he could, then fell asleep.

The tolling of the chapel bell woke him. There was light outside, but he could not tell if it was morning or evening. Beside him Charissa still slept. No one else was in the hut.

He rose slowly so as not to wake her and he tiptoed to the door. Someone was talking outside but he could not make out the words.

He was deciding whether he should get up or go back to sleep when absent-mindedly he reached around his neck. The amulet of Rindorn was gone!

*Where was it? Have I walked into a trap?*

He put his ear to the door in an attempt to overhear the conversation outside. The voices were now coming closer, and eventually he picked out Rannulf's voice. Suddenly he felt foolish for being so anxious. If Rannulf was involved, then obviously there was nothing to be suspicious about.

Then the door opened and Rannulf and a monk stepped inside. "Hello, sleepyhead. I came to wake you but I see you're already up. You'd better hurry over to the dining hall before supper's all gone. The others are there now."

"Are Ragnar and Philip back?" asked Jonathan.

"Safe and sound. You'll meet them in the dining hall," said the monk, gesturing towards a building near the corner of the compound. Smoke lazily trailed from its chimney. Jonathan nodded his thanks.

"By the way, we have footwear for you." Rannulf pointed to some leather clogs on the floor. "We noticed yours were gone."

Jonathan nodded his thanks again and slipped on the clogs. Then accompanied by Rannulf, he limped over to the dining hall. He had to duck to step through the low doorway—a common defensive feature—and when his eyes had adjusted to the dim light, he saw that he had entered a long room with low roof beams. The walls were made of rough-hewn logs. Two plain wooden tables with benches on either side ran down the length of the room. His friends were easy to spot as they sat together with nearly two hundred brown-robed monks. They were already part way through their evening meal—stew with barley bread served in wooden bowls with wooden spoons—but room was made for Jonathan on the bench between Sonja and Olaf.

"Hi," said Jonathan, almost shyly when he saw his friends.

"Don't give me, 'hi'" cried the powerful Olaf, jumping up from his seat and giving Jonathan a crushing embrace. Jonathan winced as his feet temporarily left the ground.

"How's the prisoner?" asked Sonja.

"Thinner," said Jonathan.

"Welcome to St. Anselm's," interrupted Ragnar, leaning across the table. "I hope you find the food and lodgings to your liking."

"Thanks," said Jonathan, smiling. Still feeling groggy, he was trying to muster enough energy to make polite conversation.

"By the way, you might be looking for this," Ragnar took out the amulet and placed it on the table between them. "We didn't want you choking on it in your sleep."

Jonathan received it gratefully. The amulet was not something that he had cared about terribly much, but he was glad at least that it had not been stolen.

"So it was you who took it after all!" exclaimed Olaf.

Jonathan shook his head.

"Where did you get it then?" asked Olaf. Sonja and Rannulf were listening too.

"The Dragikoi took it," said Jonathan. "When we escaped, I got it back."

"How?"

Sonja cut him off. "Let Jonathan eat," she said. "Stories can wait."

Jonathan was left to spoon up his meal, and to his surprise, he found meat in the stew. Meat was rare in Rindorn. Obviously there were some benefits to living close to the land. Afterwards Ragnar led Jonathan outside and helped him limp across the field.

"We can rest here for a few days at least," Ragnar told him. "But not much longer. I don't think that we are in any immediate danger, still we need to move to a safer place soon."

"Do you have any idea where we'll go next?" asked Jonathan.

"There are a number of possibilities, but probably Dorinon makes the most sense. From there it would be relatively easy to get over the mountains to your uncle's home."

Jonathan nodded. He had heard that the local Duke had a large castle in Dorinon.

He had many other questions that he wanted to ask, but before he could form them in his mind, Ragnar bid him goodnight and disappeared into one of the wooden huts. Jonathan sat on a nearby bench, and feeling revived by the food he paid closer attention to his surroundings. Fifteen-foot walls with occasional stone towers enclosed the entire monastery compound, and within this was an inner circle of walls surrounding the chapel and the abbot's residence. It was not the best type of defence, he knew, but it would deter most invaders, and he guessed that this was what it was basically designed for—a deterrent, not a real defence in case of siege. Most of the monastery's buildings were made of wood and had thatched roofs, but the tallest tower, the round thin one that he and Charissa had seen earlier was built of stone and rose some seventy feet above the plain.

At this moment one of the younger monks stopped in front of the bench. "Could I show you around?" he asked.

"Thank you," said Jonathan. Rising to his feet, he pointed to a group of beehive-shaped huts made entirely of stone. "What are those?"

The monk turned to look. "Those are some of our oldest buildings. They serve as cells for our younger monks."

As the monk strolled and Jonathan limped through the grounds, Jonathan admired the beauty and the discipline of this place. Then they stopped in briefly at the wood carver's hut to watch him work on ornate pieces for the altar screen.

The stone chapel particularly intrigued him. Stepping inside, he gazed at the stained glass windows and inhaled the residual smell of incense. Right next to the chapel stood a cloister: a square-shaped, roofed-over walkway. Ornately carved stone pillars supported its slate-shingle roof and a grassy courtyard lay within its borders.

Soon Jonathan's friends came to look for him and he was at last able to satisfy his desire for information. "I'm curious," he said. "What happened in the Ravenhall Inn after I was knocked unconscious? It seems like another lifetime now but I guess it was only just over a week ago."

Olaf answered. "After the fight died down, the four of us followed Philip upstairs to your room just in time to see you being taken out a back exit. We followed, and once we got outside, we met Ragnar. He was just returning from purchasing an extra packhorse for provisions. When he heard what had happened he told Rannulf and me to saddle up as quickly as possible."

Rannulf chimed in, "He asked Sonja to stay and take care of Hugh."

"And she was very annoyed at being asked to stay behind," added Sonja, frustration showing on her face. "I can hold my own against any man in combat, but Ragnar doesn't know that." Then she shrugged, "I guess it wasn't totally a bad thing, because I used the time to send messages back to our families and friends in Rindorn so they wouldn't worry about us."

"And then what?" asked Jonathan.

"We pursued the Dragikoi throughout the night, getting as far as this district," said Rannulf, "but once we reached the forest we lost them. They knew where they were going, and we didn't, so they got too far ahead. There was no point in trying to track them at night, but Philip said that he knew of a monastery where we could stay. We came here in the early hours of the morning—dog tired."

"After we woke up," interjected Olaf, "they told us about a group of foreigners who had arrived in the area about a year before. They didn't know much else about the place other than that it was several miles upstream. Ragnar and Philip figured that this was probably where you had been taken and later that day they started searching for it."

Then Rannulf added, "Ragnar sent a message back to Hugh and Sonja in Ravenhall and they arrived here only a day before you did."

"How is Hugh?" asked Jonathan. "I remember that he got wounded in the fight with the Dragikoi."

"His wound healed enough so that he could be moved," said Sonja. "But he still hasn't totally regained his strength. He's resting here in one of the huts. Hopefully he'll fully heal soon."

"What about you?" asked Sonja. "Tell us about your adventures."

Jonathan told them about the previous weeks' events. They particularly wanted to hear more about the nighttime river escape and the Dragikoi's strange dance moves.

"Keep practising the dance moves so that you don't forget," advised Sonja.

Jonathan nodded. "So what's going to happen now?"

"What do you think will happen?" replied Sonja.

There was a silence for a moment as Jonathan searched for the right words. "I am very much obliged for your help," he finally began. "But for your sakes I wish you hadn't, since, as you probably realize, you've put yourselves in danger too."

Olaf broke in, "What else were we to do? We couldn't sit back and watch you get dragged away again."

"I shouldn't have invited you to come to Ravenhall to visit," said Jonathan apologetically.

"Nonsense," said Rannulf. "You would have done the same for us."

Jonathan found himself hoping that if it came to risking himself for his friends, he would rise to the challenge and perform as well as they had, but he only nodded in response.

"And don't blame yourself," said Olaf. "You couldn't have guessed that you would be attacked that evening. We knew that you had been banished from Rindorn and there were risks involved in visiting you."

"Besides," added Rannulf, "this is more fun than

annoying city guards. Here we're actually doing something useful for a change."

The four of them laughed and Olaf slapped Jonathan on the back, nearly knocking him over. He was glad that they were taking this adventure so well and he felt lucky to have friends like these. They talked for a while longer, but soon they excused themselves and went off to bed.

Jonathan remained sitting there, the events of the last week still churning through his head. Finally he got up and practised the Dragikoi's dance moves as Sonja had suggested. His cut leg slowed his movements somewhat, but he still remembered most of them.

After a while his actions attracted the attention of a brown-haired monk. "That's an interesting attack pattern that you're doing," said the monk. "Where did you learn it?"

"Attack pattern? Is that what it is?" asked Jonathan.

"That's what I would call it. I've seen the Dragikoi doing such dances."

"Yes, that's where I learned them."

"Intriguing," said the Monk. "But come. Let me show you where you will sleep tonight."

Jonathan limped across the compound behind the monk. "And here is your hut," said the monk when they finally arrived.

Jonathan lay down on one of the beds inside and was asleep within moments.

It was another day and a half before Charissa woke, and even after she regained consciousness, she slept most of the time and did not venture much beyond the infirmary. In the meantime there were no further signs of the Dragikoi. Jonathan was relieved not to see them, but at the same time their absence bothered him. He was sure they had not given up and he wondered what they were plotting.

During their stay the travellers did their best not to disturb the daily monastic routine, which was chores, interrupted by five brief prayer services. Jonathan's friends also assisted with chores. Since most of the garden plots were just outside the walls, whenever they went out to tend the gardens, pasture the cattle or go fishing, two guards went with them. Jonathan's friends also disguised themselves as monks by putting on cowls before going outside. The hope was that the Dragikoi would be less willing to attack monks, but in case this assumption was incorrect, two bowmen on the tower were also told to keep extra careful watch over the labourers.

No one would allow Jonathan to go beyond the walls. In any case his leg had not yet healed enough to walk much. Instead, he was given a bucket of water and the job of washing the vegetables that the others dug from the monastery garden.

During this time, Olaf, Rannulf, Sonja and Jonathan had a few additional chats by themselves. Jonathan was pleasantly surprised to discover that his friends intended to come along with him on this journey.

"You know that it will be dangerous," he said.

"Bring 'em on!" said Olaf. "Men in black are no match for good Rindorn steel!" For emphasis, he flexed one of his large biceps, making Sonja snort with laughter.

"What about your trades, your livelihood?" said Jonathan ignoring both Sonja and Olaf. "Don't you become journeymen next year?"

"Yes," said Olaf, "but we already know all that we need to know. Our masters are just getting cheap labour from us at the moment. Besides, I know several journeymen who don't have enough work. I don't think that Rindorn can support us all."

"That's also how I see it," said Sonja. "And to be honest that was mainly why I decided to come out and visit you that night in Ravenhall. I wanted in on the adventure."

Jonathan looked at her in surprise. In all the time that he had known Sonja she had always seemed to be a person of the moment. He'd never once heard her give any indications that she was planning for a future at all. There was obviously more going on in her head than what he had assumed.

"She speaks for me, too," said Rannulf.

"What about family responsibilities?" asked Jonathan.

"Actually," said Sonja, "I think that Rannulf's older brothers suggested that he go."

"They did," said Rannulf.

"If I remember right," said Olaf chuckling, "their exact words were, 'Why don't you go off and find yourself, Rannulf? You never know, *you* might be out there.'"

"My brothers like to tease," said Rannulf glumly.

Jonathan knew this well. Many of their childhood games had involved futile attempts to exact revenge on Rannulf's older brothers for their pranks towards him.

"What about your mother, Olaf?"

"My brother can take care of her," he said. "Besides, if I can get work with your uncle, I might be able to occasionally get some money back to them—probably more than I could in Rindorn."

"And you, Sonja?"

"I'm free to go," she said without elaborating.

Jonathan realized that there was no dissuading them. He had been dreading saying goodbye. Ragnar and Philip seemed like fine people, but it would be much nicer to travel into strange territory with old friends. "But" he said, "I guess we will have to ask Ragnar."

He was worried that Ragnar and Philip would not allow their plan, but to his surprise both men seemed open to the idea.

"I just don't want to depopulate Rindorn," laughed Ragnar. Then he became more serious. "How far can you trust these friends of yours?"

"With my life," replied Jonathan.

Ragnar gazed at him intently for a moment. "Fine," he eventually said, "bring them along if they really want to come. They should know that Gorwin expects all members of his community to do their share of work, though it isn't excessive. We might actually be able to use an extra hand or two where we're going."

So it was settled. Rannulf, Olaf and Sonja were coming.

On the fourth day after arriving at the monastery, Charissa was sufficiently recovered to help Jonathan with his vegetable washing. She had discarded her old ragged clothes and now wore a monk's cowl that was too big for her. Now that she no longer had the threat of imprisonment or death hanging over her head, she was a completely different woman—much more cheerful and talkative.

Jonathan found that he did not mind being left alone with her while the others were in the garden, as they were able to catch up on the conversations that they had not had while in captivity. The sadness that he had seen on her face while in prison now seemed to be gone also, and he noticed that she was quite attractive, even in an oversized monk's cowl. She told him her home was in Janzilar, on Magelandorn's eastern coast. Her parents were probably quite worried about her, so she said that she had arranged that a message would be sent from the abbot to her father at the nearest opportunity. He also discovered that she had an imagination and a good sense of humour.

"Don't you think that this one looks a bit like the Baron of Westerham?" she said to him one morning as they were busy scrubbing carrots. "It has such a sad and mournful face." She held the carrot up in front of him in what Jonathan observed were long and elegant fingers.

By this time Jonathan had been introduced to a number of carrot castles, ocean rocks, the crescent moon, and two carrots tangled together that looked like a dog, but this was the first carrot-person that he had encountered.

"Who's the Baron of Westerham?" he asked.

"Just a nobleman," she said. "Now that you are going to be living with your uncle, you might actually meet him." She fell silent, then a moment later leaned over and said, "But wouldn't it be wonderful if we could stay here forever?"

This puzzled him. Washing vegetables in a monastery garden was not exactly what he hoped to be doing for the rest of his days. "Sure, it's a nice a place to rest," he said, "but would you really want to stay here forever?"

"Why not? It's a shame that we can't take a walk in the forest nor help the rest of your friends in the garden, but really, all that one could desire is right here inside these walls." She actually seemed serious.

Jonathan put down the carrot that he was scrubbing and looked closely at her. "Why don't you want to go home?"

"Of course, part of me does want to go home. My friends are there. My whole life's been there, but my father has promised me in marriage to the baron's son from a nearby estate—Baron Westerham's son actually."

For the first time a pang of jealousy crept into Jonathan's heart. He tried to conceal it. "Oh, so that's why you don't like Baron Westerham," he said.

"It's not that I don't like him," she responded, considering. "And I guess I shouldn't have compared him to a carrot just now. He's just doing what every other baron, duke or earl in Magelandorn usually does—arrange a marriage for his son or daughter."

Jonathan found this story disturbing, and for more reasons than Charissa's attractiveness. It made him realize that there was a lot that he had to learn about Magelandorn's noble classes. Staying with his uncle was going to involve more than just a change in living quarters. He would be expected to understand and work with a group of people that he currently knew almost nothing about. He felt very inadequate.

"I take it that you don't want to marry his son," he said, fishing for more information.

"No. My father's arranging it because it will be a good alliance for him. But I have no interest in this baron's son. If I go home, I will just be abandoning one kind of captivity for another."

"Why don't you come to my uncle's castle?" responded Jonathan. "Ragnar has allowed my other friends to come along, so you might be able to come, too. Who knows? My uncle might allow you to stay with us, perhaps indefinitely."

"Oh, thank you, Jonathan. You are so gallant. But I hope I won't need to stay with your uncle forever."

Jonathan saw no sign of Ragnar that evening, but he was able to share the story of Charissa's plight with Philip. Word must have reached Ragnar, since the next morning when Charissa and he were back scrubbing vegetables Ragnar came to visit. He said that Janzilar was not very far from their eventual destination, so it looked as if Charissa would be coming along with them, at least as far as Dorinon, before heading for her home. Jonathan was happy to hear the news, and he hoped that Charissa was glad to hear it, too.

Despite her wishes, the day was approaching when they would have to leave the monastery. It was also becoming obvious that the abbot was uncomfortable with their prolonged stay. Jonathan actually regretted leaving the place so soon. He did not want to stay forever, but since arriving at St. Anselm's, he had thought a great deal about that memory of his parents hiding in a monastery. If that memory was correct, then a monastic community would have been his first home, and he was curious to see more of this life. Just by being in a monastery, he thought, perhaps he could recapture some of his own past.

But the others had no wish to linger. Ragnar began making preparations for departure. He instructed all of their party who did not already have a correctly sized pair of riding boots to report to the monastery shoemaker for measuring. Ragnar was purchasing a pair for every party member who needed one. Then one morning he summoned them all for a conversation with the abbot.

"Had Jonathan not been captured," said Ragnar, "we would have gone straight east from Ravenhall and over the mountains. But it now appears that it isn't safe for us to go anywhere near Ravenhall or Rindorn. This being the case, I am thinking that we should try to make a detour south towards the city of Dorinon. Can you tell us the safest way to get from here to Dorinon without being detected?"

"The river would be the fastest way," said the abbot, "yet you would almost certainly be seen. However, shortly after it passes this monastery, the river takes a bend to the north before it goes south and west again. If you follow the road on the south side of the river, you will eventually reach the Dorinon River, a tributary of the Naharoze. This river will lead you back upstream to Dorinon, the city for which the river is named. By taking this road you might even be able to lose your pursuers. They are unlikely to have scouts that far downriver."

The abbot hesitated before continuing more slowly, "What's more, there is an ancient and secret hiding place that our order has recently learned about. It belonged to another group of monks before they were forced into exile. It lies about two days' journey southwest of here. Once you reach this refuge, you are virtually guaranteed to be safe from any attack."

He waited for someone to ask a question. When no one did, he spoke again. "Of course, you are welcome to stay here as long as you like, but I think it would be wise to leave soon. We don't know if the Dragikoi will respect the ancient tradition of sanctuary that this monastery offers. I will send a guide with you as far as the hidden refuge."

They thanked the abbot for his generous help, and since the bell was tolling for their noon meal, they left for the dining hall. Ragnar stayed behind for a last consultation with their host. When he joined them later, he announced that they would leave the following night under the cover of darkness.

The next day during their noon meal Ragnar approached each of them. "You are relieved of chores this afternoon," he said. "I would advise you to try and sleep."

Jonathan found this difficult. He remembered the Dragikoi too clearly and the thought of encountering them again made him anxious. Eventually he did drift off, and the next thing he knew he heard the supper bell. He slipped out of the dining hall early. If they were leaving within a few hours, he wanted to take one last look at the monastery. Far away from the hustle and bustle of Rindorn, it had probably been the most peaceful place he had ever lived, and even in the few days they had been there, it had begun to feel like home.

Jonathan noticed that Charissa had changed clothes. She still had the monks' hooded shirt like he did, but she no longer wore the full cowl and instead had brown trousers tucked into some newly obtained boots. Charissa saw him staring at her ankles, "They told me we'd be riding horses," she said. "Trousers and boots are better for that than cowls."

Sonja was waiting for him when he arrived back at his hut. She thrust a parcel wrapped in sacking into his hands. "I've been forgetting to tell you. While I was waiting for Hugh to heal in Ravenhall," she said, "I made a brief trip back to Rindorn. I got my violin and your crumhorn and lute."

"Thank you!" said Jonathan, genuinely grateful.

"You're lucky I went. The innkeeper didn't want to part with our musical instruments."

At that moment Olaf appeared. "Oh, Olaf," called Sonja, "I've been forgetting to give this to you. I couldn't get your drum, but your mother sent you this." Sonja gave him a large package that Olaf unwrapped to reveal cylinder of wax-covered cheese.

"Mom!" cried Olaf, gazing at the cheese with tenderness.

A moment later a silhouette appeared in the doorway. "Time to go," said a voice.

They filed out into the twilight. The monk who had spoken wore a hooded shirt and trousers, but the knapsack on his back looked as if he was going on a journey. This was the same monk who had given him a tour of the monastery some days earlier.

"My name is Brother Fredrick," he said when all the others had joined them outside. "Assuming that all goes well, I will be travelling with you for the next two days."

At this point Jonathan noticed that Hugh was sitting on a chair just outside the doorway, eying the rest of them somewhat wistfully.

Jonathan approached him, "You're not coming with us?"

"No," he responded. "My wound's not yet

healed. I'll rest here for now."

Jonathan felt badly, knowing that Hugh had received the wound while defending him. "I hope it gets better soon," he said awkwardly.

One by one the other travellers shook Hugh's hand and wished him a speedy recovery. "We'll see you in Caerathorn, when you can get there," said Ragnar. "Take care of the monks in the meantime."

To Jonathan's surprise, instead of leading them to the main gate, Fredrick took them into the chapel, horses and all. Jonathan wondered if they were having some kind of blessing service before their journey and indeed the abbot, wearing his ceremonial robes did perform a brief office for them. But Jonathan was surprised by what happened next. The abbot climbed a set of spiral stone steps into the pulpit and pulled on something before descending again to the main floor. Then two monks with lanterns approached and after setting their lanterns on the altar pushed on a section of the chapel's back wall. There was a sound of clanking metal and amazingly, the wall started to move.

Once they saw what was happening, Ragnar and Philip moved forward to help the monks. With the four of them pushing the wall soon retreated revealing a large gaping hole. A musty, earth-laden smell permeated the chapel. The two monks retrieved their lanterns from the altar and beckoned the travellers to follow them into the hole. Their lantern light displayed a gradually sloping tunnel, vanishing into the depths.

"It will be a bit of a squeeze," said the abbot, "but you and your horses should be able to make it down all right. It's been done before."

One of the monks went first, followed by Ragnar leading his horse. Then Fredrick distributed candles to each traveller before descending also. The biggest problem was the horses. Even with the lantern light they disliked the look of the hole, although once they saw humans going downwards, they were convinced to try it as well.

Jonathan had the most difficulty with his horse. The beast stood inside the chapel absolutely refusing to budge, perhaps sensing that his rider was not comfortable around horses. Fortunately at that point Charissa took the horse's lead rope and began petting and talking to him, and eventually, with Charissa in front, the horse was willing to descend. Jonathan felt foolish for needing help and tried to make up for it by carrying two lit candles.

On the way down, he could see wall paintings that reflected religious themes or the life of the monks. It surprised him that the monks had seen fit to do artwork even here in a closed tunnel.

His stomach tightened anxiously as he neared the end of the descent. This would be his first time outside the monastery walls in a week, and there was no guarantee, even with their secret exit, that they could avoid the Dragikoi. Jonathan looked at his friends and wondered if by tomorrow they would all be dead or held captive.

The slope flattened out into a landing, and another long tunnel followed, ending in a door. Just before the exit, Fredrick told them to extinguish their lanterns and candles. For a moment Jonathan smelled the odour of burning wax. Then he heard the door in front of them opening. They moved forward into the darkness.

# 9 ESCAPE THROUGH THE FOREST

The door opened into a cellar—the most cramped section of their underground journey so far—but they squeezed their way through and out into a moonlit night. Jonathan heard the soft voices of the two monks with the lanterns bid them farewell.

Philip, Ragnar, Jonathan and Fredrick, received their own mounts. Charissa rode behind Olaf, while Sonja shared a mount with Rannulf. Jonathan found himself wishing that he had been placed with Charissa, but he realized it would make things too awkward to request it. Still, he tried to keep his horse right behind hers. He did not want to miss any conversation.

He need not have bothered. The first thing Fredrick did was to forbid them to talk. He then led them along a path behind the shelter of some trees on the flat near the river's edge. Soon they were climbing the riverbank at an angle. Once they reached the top, the path continued through forest, and for a few hours they rode along it in the moonlight. After a while the country opened up revealing farm fields to their right and left.

Jonathan felt nervous now that they had left the cover of the trees. In the bright moonlight anyone watching could have spotted them. He only hoped that their brief excursion underground had fooled their enemies or that the Dragikoi were watching a different part of the forest.

Eventually, light grew on the eastern horizon. It was almost sunrise. Amazingly he could see that Sonja had fallen asleep with her arms wrapped around Rannulf's waist and was leaning forwards onto his back. Charissa, he noticed with some annoyance, was similarly positioned next to Olaf.

In the growing light Jonathan studied the pasturelands they were passing. A herd of cattle, watched over by two farm hands, grazed in the distance. He did not see any foes, although it would be possible for some of them to crouch behind the stone walls that shielded the farm fields from the road.

"So who are these enemies of ours anyhow?" he whispered to Ragnar who was riding beside him.

"Enemies?" said Ragnar. He seemed pre-occupied.

"The Dragikoi," said Jonathan.

"Oh, of course, those enemies, yes," responded Ragnar.

"Why are they pursuing us?"

"I don't know." Ragnar paused then added, "But I can guess." He chuckled. "You will understand it all when your uncle explains it to you. Suffice it to say for the present that, if you are your uncle's nephew— and all appearances point that way— then you are part of an ancient family. And as I told you in Ravenhall, while your family has many friends, it also has some enemies."

"So the Dragikoi are pursuing us because they are some of my family's old enemies?"

"There's a good chance of that," said Ragnar cheerfully. "Don't worry, though. As long as we are careful, we should be all right."

Jonathan had trouble believing this last assurance. "But who are they?" he asked again.

"They are too well organized to be just common bandits. Besides, bandits look for easy prey."

"Oh."

"Which means," continued Ragnar, "that they probably came from one of two sources. Either the Black Wizard, but I doubt that—which means that they probably came from the other source, which is more likely. . ."

Jonathan did not find out about the other source because Fredrick, from the front of the line, suddenly called a halt for breakfast and Ragnar was summoned to help distribute rations.

Jonathan was left to absorb the information that he had just heard. The fact that one of the possible sources for their enemies was the Black Wizard was making his head spin. Ragnar might as well have said that the Dragikoi had come from hell itself. This wizard was probably the most fearsome creature in existence. Children in Rindorn were frightened into good behaviour merely by mentioning his name. Yet, unlike mythical monsters, the Black Wizard actually existed. He lived to the north and had launched full-scale war on the Kingdom of Magelandorn several times in the past. Even now there were reports of occasional border skirmishes by his soldiers.

Furthermore, the Wizard had been a constant threat for a very long time—throughout the lives of many generations. No one was really sure if he was some kind of immortal superhuman or if the present Wizard was one of a long line of descendants to whom the original Wizard had passed the mantel of his wizardry.

A sudden stab of doubt entered Jonathan's mind concerning Ragnar's story. How could a single family, such as his own, earn the specific enmity of the Black Wizard? Was Ragnar joking or somehow misleading him? Jonathan glanced at his face to see if there was any humour in it, but he could see none.

After they received their breakfast rations, Philip and Ragnar donned the chainmail shirts stored in their saddlebags and put their dark green cloaks overtop. Then they continued riding as before, except now Jonathan found himself nervously studying every hillock and clump of trees, half expecting masked bandits or some other creature to emerge and chase them. If these Dragikoi were the same enemies who had pursued his parents, he could understand why his parents had been surprised and killed.

But Ragnar had said that the Black Wizard was only one possible source for these enemies. What was the other source? Jonathan had heard all sorts of stories about noble families who were little better than powerful thieves. He found himself hoping desperately that his was a family with an honourable history as opposed to one with a long tradition of something like cattle thieving. That would certainly explain its having enemies.

The sun had now risen, and for a brief space the

trees gave way to reveal a majestic view of a valley with mountains in the distance. The pastureland had changed to fields of tall maize-corn. Philip and Ragnar rode together at the rear of the line, and Jonathan slowed his horse until he rode parallel to the two men.

"Ragnar, what did my family do to attract so many enemies?"

Philip and Ragnar exchanged a glance. "Look, Ragnar," said Philip, "we need to tell him something. Hints and riddles aren't enough."

"All right," said Ragnar. "It's not what your family did, Jonathan. It's more what they represent."

"What do you mean?" Jonathan was confused.

Ragnar thought for a moment. "How much do you know about what's going on in Magelandorn? Can you tell me the name of the ruling family?"

"Yes, it's the House of Verdorben. Everyone knows that."

"And tell me also—for how long have the Verdorbens held power?"

"Not long at all. Three generations ago they fought a civil war and took the throne from the previous ruling family, the Haravanians. Everyone knows that, too."

"Good," Ragnar seemed pleased with Jonathan's knowledge. "You see, Jonathan, Philip, Hugh and I, and your uncle are all loyalists. We support the royal family—the family the Verdorbens wrongfully deposed all those years ago, and because of that we have enemies. As a result, until we are safely home, if you or any of the rest of us are captured, we might be tortured into revealing information. The less any of us know, the better it is for everyone. Right?"

"Yeah, the torture thing, you mentioned that," said Jonathan nodding. "But I thought that all the members of the old royal family had been killed off."

"No," said Ragnar. "That's not quite true. To the best of our knowledge, there yet exist some descendants of the old royal house. For that reason alone, it's important that we keep our operations as secret as possible."

Jonathan nodded again, but something still did not sit right. He searched for the proper words. "I mean no disrespect with this, but why would you want to support the old royal house? I mean, isn't one king just as good as another? None of them seem to care much about their people anyhow."

Philip and Ragnar looked at each other. Jonathan could see that his question had touched a nerve.

"There are a number of reasons why one should support the original monarch," said Philip. "To start with that's the monarch to whom the people of Magelandorn rightly owe their allegiance. But it's more important than that."

"What do you mean?"

"Our support for the old royal family is based on more than just sentiment. We support them because it is necessary for the preservation of our kingdom and life as we know it."

"How so?"

"To begin with, we know that there's some kind of link between the Black Wizard and the current royal house. In fact, the Wizard was likely behind the success of the Verdorbens in the civil war."

"You're not serious!" exclaimed Jonathan.

"We are," said Philip. "We've seen evidence that the Wizard helped pay for the insurrection that placed the Verdorbens on the throne. The Verdorbens had never previously been known for their wealth, yet suddenly, they had a tremendous amount of money for mercenaries and to bribe other nobles to join their cause. The only possible source for that would have been a strong and wealthy ally from outside the kingdom. But in addition, we have also seen transcripts of the messages sent by the Wizard to the Verdorben family."

Philip's speech was interrupted by his horse, which stopped to eat grass. It took Philip a moment to convince his horse to catch up. "In any case," he continued, "we know that the Wizard's spies operate freely within the royal palace. It was the logical thing for the Wizard to do—get rid of a strong ruler who was his enemy, and put in place someone who was more malleable."

Jonathan was stunned. It was disturbing to think that his own ruler might have been put into power by enemy agents.

"The Wizard realizes that he isn't powerful enough to attack Magelandorn directly," added Ragnar, "because doing that would create strong enough resistance that he would risk a defeat. Instead, he's making use of the current ruler's weakness to gradually whittle away the kingdom and extend his own power. He hopes that eventually there won't be much of Magelandorn left to resist him at all."

"But in addition to allegiances, there is another reason that the old royal family is important," said Philip.

"What's that?"

"Traditionally," said Philip, "Magelandorn's royal house had six special items handed down from generation to generation that have allowed our country to remain free from attacks by the Black Wizard. These gifts, if they are used by the right people and in the right ways, give victory to our side and keep our enemies at bay. It's those gifts that ultimately have allowed our kingdom to survive for so long. We call them the sacred gifts."

"The sacred gifts?"

"Yes."

"I've never heard of them."

"I'm not surprised. The Verdorbens don't want anyone to know about them. Tragically, they do not believe in using these ancient items and may, in fact, be unable to do so. It was only one special family—the original royal family—that had the ability to operate these objects safely. The current king is, of course, from the usurper's family, and he decided that, if he couldn't use them, no one else would. To make sure that there won't be any rivals to the throne, he scattered these sacred objects around his kingdom to try to prevent his enemies from discovering them and gathering them into one place."

"If the current king won't use the sacred objects," asked Jonathan, "then how is he defending us from the Black Wizard?" He waved his hand at the nearby land. Forests had taken the place of the cornfields.

"We don't think he is," said Ragnar. "He has deceived himself into believing that he can defend us by negotiating with the Wizard, and that by treaties alone the forces of evil will be kept at bay."

"But it's working, isn't it?"

"No. Already the border fiefs—our allies to the north—areas that used to be under the sway of

Magelandorn, have been swept into the Wizard's dominions. This has happened without even so much as an acknowledgement on the part of the Verdorbens, let alone an attempt to defend them. All of this makes the Wizard stronger and us weaker. It won't be long now I fear, before Magelandorn proper, and even peaceful Rindorn, will be attacked. And we don't have access to the sacred objects to defend ourselves."

Jonathan gazed ahead in silence as he absorbed this information. "This is horrible news," he said finally. "What can we do? Is there any real chance the old royal family could retake the throne?"

Ragnar smiled. "There is always a chance. But there is more chance now than there was even a few weeks ago. So take heart. It is possible. Still, that is why we need to keep our activities secret."

Jonathan's opinion of Ragnar and Philip had changed in the course of this conversation. He now knew that he could trust them more. They were not merely stern warriors, he realized, but people who had dedicated themselves sacrificially to a cause that they truly believed in. Nevertheless, the conversation had also made him uncomfortable. It now appeared that he was not just being rescued by an unknown wealthy relative. He was also being asked to join in a war, one that sounded as if it was being operated against far superior forces with little hope of success.

He was still pondering this new information as the road descended into a valley, when suddenly wind rushed past his ear. A split second later he saw a crossbow bolt protruding from a tree ahead and just off to his right. He was still staring at the bolt in amazement when someone yelled, "Duck," and he hunched down in his saddle. The feared attack had come.

Ragnar unslung his shield from his back, and drawing himself up to his full height, he grasped the horn dangling from his belt and blew a blast. "Let us pass or meet us in battle!" he cried.

As if in answer, with a sound of breaking branches, five men on horseback emerged from the forest to block their path, three behind the travellers and two on the track that led up the slope ahead of them. They were Dragikoi, dressed in black from head to toe with cloth wrapped across their faces.

Ragnar thought that the chances of escape were better ahead so he spurred his horse, galloping across the valley floor and up the next slope towards the two foes in front. The others followed closely as arrows whizzed among them. To his dismay, Jonathan even saw a few darts. Several times he found himself ducking instinctively, and at least twice he felt the wind from missiles that flew just above his head. Ragnar was in front now, his sword clenched in his right hand. His cloak, flying in the wind, revealed the chain mail beneath it. Meanwhile, their two enemies, scimitars drawn and ready, sped down the slope towards them.

Then, *clang! clash!* With swords flying, Ragnar and the first of their foes met halfway up the hill. At almost the same time Rannulf yelled in pain and clutched his right shoulder. His horse reared and went wild, charging up the slope with both Rannulf and Sonja on its back. Surprised at the horse's unexpected behaviour, their enemies let them slip through their line and reach the hilltop. Ragnar and his masked opponent kept on fighting fiercely, with Ragnar forcing the Dragikoi back a couple of yards.

Then just as Jonathan drew his sword to engage an enemy soldier, Philip intervened and started exchanging sword strokes with the man. Having two opponents to fight, the Dragikoi was confused. He backed up and half-turned to face Jonathan, leaving his left side partially open to Philip, who knocked him from his horse. Then with Ragnar's man also down, the travellers rode wildly up the hillside ignoring the arrows from the three Dragikoi behind them. Jonathan looked back to see more Dragikoi emerging from the bushes on foot, but their three remaining mounted opponents had temporarily halted and were shouting orders to these newly arrived comrades.

After Jonathan's friends gained the crest of the hill, they followed the road leading away from the forest and out onto a plain. Here they briefly paused while Fredrick bandaged Rannulf's wound and Sonja transferred to Philip's horse. Then they recommenced their flight—one hundred yards, two hundred yards, three hundred yards—as of yet there was no sign of pursuit. Jonathan wondered why their enemies did not follow. Had the travellers' small success made their foes more hesitant?

Soon, however, Rannulf fell behind, clutching his shoulder, Jonathan could see that he was not standing properly in his stirrups. Just over half a mile from the point where they had emerged from the valley, the road turned a sharp corner and entered another section of forest. Here they waited, and as Rannulf drew up beside them, Ragnar called out, "How goes it?"

Rannulf made no answer but the blood staining the lower part of his left arm told the story. Fredrick's hurried bandaging had obviously not succeeded.

Ragnar looked concerned. "Philip, give me a hand with this, and Jonathan," he said, "you, Olaf and Sonja stand guard. If they come out of that valley, shoot arrows at them." He pointed to a bow and a quiver that were strapped to the back of his saddle.

Jonathan wanted to protest that he did not know how to shoot very well, but he realized that this was not what Ragnar needed to hear just then. So wordlessly, he got the bow from Ragnar and the three friends plus Fredrick rode back down the road to the point where the forest started.

Ragnar and Philip quickly bandaged the wounded Rannulf. They were just remounting their horses, when from the valley behind them eleven figures on horseback emerged, riding hard.

*That explains the delay*, thought Jonathan. *The Dragikoi stopped to assemble more horsemen.* He shouted a warning to his friends. Then wanting to impress Ragnar, he drew the bowstring and launched an arrow back towards their foes. Sonja, who always carried her own bow, shot as well.

But Ragnar shouted, "Ride! Don't shoot now! Ride! Ride!"

When both their arrows landed short, Jonathan did not argue. His mount was turning to follow the others anyhow, and he tried to make his horse gallop. The eight travellers stormed down the roadway with their enemies in hot pursuit.

For someone with little experience Jonathan rode well. But the Dragikoi's horses were fresher and faster and as they galloped, Rannulf's horse began slowing again. Eventually it became obvious that they had to turn and fight.

With one hundred yards separating them from their enemies, Ragnar reined in his horse and shouted to Jonathan, "Give me the bow!"

As Jonathan fumbled the bow over to Ragnar he glanced back. His stomach tightened. Philip had already freed his bow and commenced shooting but his arrows had taken care of only one of their opponents. Ten tall figures still pursued them. Pulling his sword from its sheath, Jonathan turned his horse to face them.

Ragnar and Philip managed to shoot a few more times while their enemies reduced the gap, and two more arrows found their marks. Then, since their opponents were too close to shoot at, Ragnar tossed his bow and quiver to the ground. Charissa leapt off the mount she shared with Olaf to retrieve them. Seeing this, Sonja followed, sliding from Philip's horse with her own bow.

After that the battle became rather confused. When one of the Dragikoi rode straight towards Jonathan, his horse suddenly took fright and veered towards the bushes. Unable to slow the beast, Jonathan just managed to steer him away from the trees, but the horse kept on down the roadway and away from the battle.

As he looked back, he saw that his opponent had turned around to take another run at him. Again, the man charged towards Jonathan, who, finally able to control his mount, wheeled around to face him. Then before they met, the Dragikoi halted his horse. The cloth mask had fallen from his face, and Jonathan recognized him from his days in the prison hut. The man's lips curled into a snarl and, shouting a challenge, he brandished his scimitar.

Jonathan's pulse raced. But just as his adversary charged, the man suddenly yelled and fell from his horse. An arrow had come whizzing towards him from the side. Jonathan had forgotten about Sonja's prowess with her bow.

Scanning the battlefield, he saw that Philip and Ragnar had already downed two of the men attacking them and were finding new opponents. Rannulf had stayed in the rear, but where Charissa was Jonathan could not tell. Olaf was not winning the battle with his opponent and was slowly being backed towards the trees. Jonathan immediately rode over to help his friend.

But when the Dragikoi saw that he now had two enemies, he turned and galloped back the way that he had come. A moment later their remaining enemies did the same. Jonathan gazed in amazement at their retreating backs. Was this possible? The apparently invincible Dragikoi had been defeated. He was tempted to laugh. Although, he reflected more soberly, this was probably only a temporary respite. They would likely return.

"That wasn't so bad, was it?" said Philip, echoing Jonathan's thought. "We've beaten them now not once but twice."

"Sure, we won," said Olaf, "but more importantly, did we look good?"

"Very good," said Charissa who just then emerged from the bushes holding Ragnar's bow and arrows. She stopped beside Rannulf. "How are you doing?" she asked.

Rannulf grinned. "A little sorer than normal," he said, "but none the worse for wear. The new bandage is holding."

Two of the Dragikoi's horses whose riders had been downed had not fled with their former masters and Sonja grabbed their reins. The travellers now had enough mounts for everyone.

They all felt cheerful. They had just finished driving off a larger and probably more skilled group of enemies, and other than Rannulf's earlier wound, they had managed to escape unscathed. It appeared that none of their opponents had actually been killed in the fight. Most had escaped, yet three wounded had remained on the ground.

After checking on Rannulf, Ragnar, Philip and Fredrick tended to the wounds of their foes. Jonathan wondered at this but it was Olaf who voiced Jonathan's concern aloud. "Why are you helping them, Ragnar? They were going to kill us."

Philip responded, "A true knight is always merciful, even to his enemies. Besides, these are no longer a threat to us."

"Are you going to bring them with us?"

"No. Likely their friends will be back to pick them up. If they don't come, Fredrick will ask one of the nearby hermits to take them in."

After bandaging their wounds, the travellers carried their opponents to the side of the road and left them a day's rations of food and water. The group then remounted and Fredrick led them westward.

As he rode, Jonathan reflected on the battle. From what he had seen in the Ravenhall Inn, on foot their enemies were definitely their superiors. But on horseback the two groups seemed more evenly matched. Ragnar and Philip's combat skills had certainly been superior. In Rindorn he had witnessed a number of skirmishes between the city watchmen and others, yet he had never seen two warriors alone take care of so many opponents—especially ones as superbly trained as the Dragikoi. He turned in his saddle to gaze at the two of them with new respect and curiosity. Slowing his horse until Ragnar was even with him, he asked, "Where did you and Philip learn to fight like that?"

"The Knights of the White Rose do not forget their ancient traditions," responded Ragnar.

"Knights of the White Rose?" Jonathan was incredulous. "I thought they had died out long ago."

"Not all of them," said Ragnar.

Jonathan mused in silence. The Knights of the White Rose were an ancient order who had been the guardians of Magelandorn's Royal House. His adopted aunt, Ruth, had told him many tales concerning the adventures of the Order's famous members—like the warriors who had battled three days with the Dragon of Westmarch, saving the local town, although themselves perishing in the deed. Then there had been a knight named Richard, who had supposedly wounded the Black Wizard himself. Many people doubted the authenticity of this last story, although some argued that it explained why the Wizard had been less active in the recent past.

Jonathan also remembered the story of the maiden knight, Cecilia, who had disguised herself as a man so that she could be trained by the Order. Afterwards she became a mariner, exploring the Southern Seas and even riding on the back of the great monster of the deep, which she had tamed.

If Ragnar and Philip really were Knights of the White Rose, then this was impressive indeed, and for a moment Jonathan felt envious. From within his own heart a great desire arose to be part of this same Order.

"Would it be possible for you to teach me the same skills?" he asked.

"There is a school that your uncle hopes to send you to," responded Ragnar.

"A school?"

"Yes."

"What kind of school?"

"I guess you'd call it a school for knights."

"Since when do knights go to school?"

"Philip and I did."

"And it's run by the Knights of the White Rose?"

Ragnar made no answer. Instead he rode up to the front of the line to join Fredrick. Jonathan had the feeling that this was another of those subjects that he would learn more about once they reached his uncle's house.

They kept on riding through pastureland, interrupted by occasional patches of forest. This time Jonathan could see no cattle close by. Now that the excitement of the fight had worn off, he felt very tired. He realized that he had been awake since the previous afternoon. Riding up beside Fredrick, he asked, "How much farther?"

"There's a place where we can stop up ahead," said Fredrick.

After two more miles they re-entered forest. The road forked and Fredrick led them down a cart track on the left. They descended into another valley, and Jonathan, afraid that he would fall out of his saddle, forced himself to stay awake.

"Fortunately," said Olaf who was riding in front of him, "the ground here is rocky. It will be tough for our enemies to track us."

A couple of hundred yards later they entered a small clearing in the forest where the road forked again. In the middle of the fork a thirty-foot tall stone rose skyward. They stopped here, and Philip and Ragnar gazed at Fredrick expectantly as he checked the road behind them for pursuers. There was no sign of the Dragikoi, nor had they seen anything unusual since the battle at sunrise.

"Yes, this looks like the place," Fredrick announced.

To Jonathan's surprise, instead of taking either the left hand or the right hand fork, Fredrick steered his horse straight ahead, between the two forks past the stone marker and into the forest. The rest of them followed, with Jonathan coming last in line. He had difficulty convincing his horse to move through the trees, but when the beast realized that he could be left behind he finally did as Jonathan urged.

A few minutes later they came upon an open patch of ground where a fire had swept through some years before. Charred tree trunks rose from a grassy meadow. Here Fredrick allowed them to rest and let the horses graze.

By the time they climbed into their saddles again, it was late afternoon. This time they rode through a younger forest with thicker undergrowth. Jonathan could not avoid getting scratched by occasional branches that loomed up suddenly in front of him. Then, after nearly getting wrenched from his saddle when his horse elected to walk under a fallen tree, he saw that the others ahead had halted.

"There's a trail over here," called Ragnar.

Ragnar's trail was wider than their previous path

and easier to traverse. It initially followed a stream going downhill. After the trail flattened out, the woods ended and they found themselves in a valley. Below them, two other creeks tumbled down from the left and the right to enlarge the stream that they had followed. Farther on, in the midst of the now broader valley sat a small hill encircled by a ring of crumbling walls. As they rode closer, Jonathan saw that the walls surrounded the burned remains of what had once been a sizable collection of buildings.

"What is this place?" he asked.

Fredrick answered, "This was a monastery run by another order of monks, the Black Robes. When the current king's grandfather usurped the throne, the monks fell out of favour and were chased out of the district. Their monastery was burned, leaving only this ruin."

The path climbed the hill and brought them through the open front gate. Fredrick led them beside blackened old buildings and the ruins of a chapel. It had no windows or roof, but from the remaining stone outline Jonathan could imagine what it might have looked like when it had been used. Anger coursed through his veins at the thought of the king who had done this. He wished that he had the means to rebuild it.

Like the front gate, the back one had mostly fallen down and presented no obstacle to their exit. Once they were beyond it and outside, their path twisted into the tree-covered hills. They were climbing a rise when Fredrick halted, turned and pointed back through some oak trees. "Look!" he said.

Across the valley, three miles behind them, a

group of thirty or forty horsemen were descending the same path that the travellers had used.

"Hurry," called Fredrick.

They needed no encouragement. Urging their horses to a canter, they followed his lead. Half an hour later the woods gave way to fields again, and the forest path broadened out into a wagon track. There was no sign of the party that they had seen a few miles back.

As the skies were growing dark, they veered off to the right, and after going down a shallow hill into another small valley they saw the outline of a stone cottage near the bank of a small creek. A dim light shone from within the cottage. "This creek joins the stream near the ruined monastery," said Fredrick. "I have taken you by a shorter path over the hills."

In the twilight, Jonathan could see that the forest began again a hundred yards or so behind the cottage, surrounding them in a crescent shape from the left to the right.

"We'll rest here for the evening," said Fredrick. "A little ways ahead lives a hermit who is a member of our order. After tonight you will not need your horses, so as agreed we will stable them here and tomorrow I will lead them back to the monastery."

He dismounted beside a stone-lined well and knocked on the cottage door. A moment later the door opened and an old man with long flowing white beard, white hair and a dark brown robe with a black belt emerged. Leather sandals protected his otherwise bare feet. Frederick chatted with him privately for a moment.

"Come right this way," said the hermit when his conversation with Frederick had finished. The old man stepped inside for a moment and returned with a lit lantern. Then he led them behind the cottage and into the woods a short distance. In a forest hollow stood another stone building. Jonathan presumed that this was the stable. If he had not been guided to it he might never have known it was there. In the lantern light they dismounted and brought their horses inside where feed had been left for them.

Jonathan untied his lute from where he had strapped it to his saddle and then draped the saddle over a raised bench. He turned to their host. "Pardon me," he said, "with all the distractions earlier I don't think I got your name."

The old man chuckled. "We were never formally introduced. My name is Anastasis, although in these parts nobody remembers that. They just call me the Forest Hermit—or the Hermit for short."

While the others unpacked their saddlebags, Fredrick told the hermit about their encounters with the Dragikoi.

He responded, "Go you back to the cottage and make yourselves at home. I will go and learn how it fares with your pursuers. I'll return tomorrow." With that he walked off into the darkness.

The travellers returned to the cottage and Ragnar led them inside. One large square-shaped room occupied most of the main floor. The fireplace, in the centre of the back wall, contained a small fire. In its light Jonathan could see several cots around the outside walls and a table surrounded by some stools just to its left. A single bucket sat on top of the table.

Wooden shelves—raised above the floor—took up the majority of the wall-space next to the fireplace. The light was too dim for him to clearly identify their contents but it looked like cooking implements. A single door on the left hand wall behind the table led to another room. Further to the left a steep ladder climbed through a hole in the ceiling to a loft.

Rannulf's injury demanded attention. While he rested on one of the cots inside, Sonja and Jonathan took the bucket to get some water from the well. After washing Rannulf's wound, Ragnar called a meeting.

"We'll stay here until the hermit returns," he said, "but since we don't know if the men who followed us will be able to find this cottage, we'll need to set watches. Jonathan, you'll take the first watch. Olaf, you take the second. I'll take the third, Sonja, the fourth, Philip next, and Fredrick, the final watch. If there is anything suspicious—anything at all—wake me immediately."

There were nods of agreement around the room. Then, as his friends got ready for bed, Jonathan went outside.

He was glad to have the first watch. The cottage was warm from the fire the hermit had left on the hearth, and it would have taken him a while to get to sleep anyhow. He figured that nobody approaching the cottage could see him, but just in case, he found a seat on a stump hidden within the cover of some bushes. He could feel the cool early evening breeze against his skin. His fingers were itching to practise his lute, but he knew that the sound could attract unwanted attention. Instead, he whiled away the time alternately gazing at the farm field to the north of them and staring at the clouds in the bright moonlit sky.

But he did not relax for long. Very soon he heard

the bushes rustling faintly in the forest behind him. Cautiously, he got to his feet and tiptoed closer to discover the source of the noise.

For a moment he could see nothing, but the sounds from the forest continued. He was on the verge of rushing back into the cottage to wake Ragnar when a deer emerged and trotted boldly out into the field. Another followed it and then another.

Jonathan breathed a sigh of relief. He watched the forest for a few moments longer, but the noises had ceased. He returned to his seat.

Sometime later, seeing that the constellations had shifted position, he returned to the cottage to wake Olaf. Then tumbling onto his cot he fell asleep.

He woke to the sound of commotion in the hut. It was morning. Someone had spread breakfast on the table—bread, cheese and water.

"Are the horses still here?" he asked.

Ragnar nodded. "Fredrick will leave with them after breakfast."

Jonathan was partway through his meal when Fredrick poked his head in the door. "It's time for me to go," he said, "but I hope to see you all again."

The travellers shook his hand and thanked him for his help. As Jonathan waved good-bye he knew he would miss the company of the cheerful and resourceful monk.

After they had cleared away their breakfast and packed, there was nothing for them to do but wait for the hermit. They set watches again, with Philip taking the first one. Two hours later, he burst into the hut, shouting. "Someone running towards us!"

Ragnar immediately barked orders. "Jonathan, Olaf, get your weapons. Sonja, Charissa, your bows.

Rannulf, get ready to move. And everyone remember where your packs are. We may have to leave quickly."

Ragnar and Philip then grabbed their own bows from the wall and rushed outside. Jonathan joined them, strapping on his sword belt as he went. He stood behind the two knights who had taken cover behind nearby trees. Each had an arrow trained on the roadway in front of them.

Soon they heard someone crashing through the undergrowth to the west of the cottage and a man wearing a long robe emerged, running towards them. He had been wounded in one arm and with the other arm he waved at them frantically.

"Hold your fire," hissed Ragnar. "It's Anastasis. Philip, Jonathan, you stay here." Dropping his bow, he ran to meet the hermit.

Together the two men jogged back towards the cottage. Jonathan was amazed that a man as old as Anastasis could run as fast as he did.

"Hurry," the hermit panted when he had reached them. "Soldiers behind me. Get your belongings at once."

# 10 A SECRET PLACE

"How far behind you?" asked Philip.

"Five, ten minutes," said Anastasis.

As soon as his arm was bandaged and the travellers had gathered their few belongings, the group followed the hermit into the forest. But they had gone only a few feet when Anastasis said, "Stop. Olaf, come with me." He left them standing while he and Olaf rushed back to the cottage. The two of them re-emerged a moment later with a lit lantern. The hermit grinned apologetically, "Now we can go."

Jonathan glanced back. As yet there was no sign of pursuers.

They hurried along a pathway that led into the oak forest south of the cottage. After about ten minutes, the trees parted to reveal on a hillock the ruins of a small castle built of stones and now covered with moss and lichens. Ivy also climbed over much of the structure. As they approached, some crows arose protesting their presence.

Anastasis was distressed with the crows. "There's

a reason they call it a 'murder' of crows. That will probably give us away, but it can't be helped. Hurry, over here!"

He led them through the ruined castle gateway into a large room without a roof. Fallen stones carpeted-over by old leaves littered its floor. A staircase descended into the ground in one corner, and Anastasis strode towards it. Jonathan had been immediately behind him, but he hesitated, not certain if he should imitate the hermit or not.

"He knows what he's doing," called Ragnar. "Follow him."

Olaf passed Jonathan and clambered down the stairs after Anastasis. Jonathan and the others did likewise. When Jonathan reached the bottom he could still see Olaf ahead, but Anastasis had disappeared. Then a moment later he re-emerged from the shadows. Taking the lantern from Olaf, he said, "This way."

They followed Anastasis along an underground passage until they were halted by a wall. Anastasis gave the lantern back to Olaf and with some effort pulled open an old metal door. "This way," he said again. His voice echoed.

Behind them Ragnar clattered down the steps. "Quick, our enemies are coming."

Scrambling through the doorway they found themselves in a wide tunnel. Jonathan put out his hand to touch the wall beside him. It was stone.

Once they were all inside Anastasis shut the door firmly behind them. Then taking the lantern back from Olaf, he led them down the passage. Like the tower above it, the tunnel was obviously very old, and here and there the walls had crumbled, allowing stones and earth to pile up on the floor. In those spots they picked their way with care along one side of the passage, often ducking their heads to avoid scraping them against the roof.

Two hundred yards further the passage ended in another wall. For a while, Anastasis seemed at a loss. The travellers watched as he searched the walls, looking for something. His apparent confusion made them all nervous. Jonathan, however, figured that the hermit would eventually solve his puzzle, and he sat down to wait, pressing his back against a wall and stretching his legs out in front of him. As he rested, he became aware of a humming sound, which seemed to come from the ground. He also realized that he had been hearing it for a while, but it had been so faint before that he had not paid it attention.

A few minutes later there was an "Ah ha!" from up front. The hermit had discovered what he was looking for. But in the next instant the tunnel resonated with the sound of pounding from the door behind them.

"Our enemies have arrived," said Philip.

Anxiously Jonathan moved closer to the hermit. Apparently Anastasis had opened up a small cupboard in the wall and as Jonathan watched he fiddled with something inside. Suddenly the wall that faced them slid to the left. Light filtered into the tunnel.

This was far beyond Jonathan's experience. He did not know if he was more frightened by their pursuers or by the bizarre thing that he had just witnessed. If Anastasis had not been a member of a religious order, Jonathan would have assumed that he had just performed magic. He felt as if he had stepped into another world.

And when the travellers moved into the next room, he was absolutely sure they were in another world. Ahead was a small room with a door in the opposite wall. Yet what really absorbed his attention were the two lamps on the ceiling. They were square but completely flat. Even odder, they had no visible flame inside! Instead, it looked as if they were made from some bizarre glowing material. Eventually he had to look away because of their brightness.

Anastasis walked back to the door through which they had just entered. He put his hand up to the wall, struck it and the door sealed itself shut. Then he moved to the wall that faced them. He struck it in the same fashion and it too slid to the left, revealing a large hallway. A broad stairway, with a ceiling containing more of the mysterious square lights, ascended.

After Anastasis closed the door behind them, they silently climbed several flights. Other than Anastasis and perhaps Ragnar, everyone was as astonished as Jonathan. The strangeness of the experience made him almost forget about their enemies. Eventually they reached another door. Once more, Anastasis did something to the wall beside it and the door slid open. A large hall, wide and long, greeted them. Intricately carved stone pillars supported its roof. The ceiling itself stood only twelve feet above the floor, but it was beautiful—deep blue with yellow mosaic patterns painted on it. A thick layer of dust lay on the floor. Obviously, no one had been in this place for quite some time. There were no peculiar lamps in this room, but windows in two of the walls, some thirty yards away, gave the room its light. The strange humming noise that Jonathan had heard earlier was louder now and seemed to be coming from beyond the windows, but now it sounded more like roaring.

"Where are we?" he asked, breaking the silence.

"In a place that very few people know about," responded the hermit.

Jonathan thought that more could have been said, but he saw by the expression on Anastasis' face that he did not want to reveal more secrets at the moment.

"At least we are safe," the hermit continued. "Try as they might, our enemies will be unable to penetrate those doors below and you can all take some needed rest. But first we should go upstairs to collect firewood."

Rannulf, still recovering from his wound, sat down with his back to one of the walls while the rest of them followed the hermit. Anastasis moved towards one of the corners of the room and yet another door opened. Once more, Jonathan marvelled at the almost magical way that these doors operated. This door led to yet another, though narrower, staircase that climbed upwards for three flights before reaching a wooden trapdoor. The hermit pushed with one hand against the door, and Jonathan saw that this time he was actually trying to physically force it open. Seeing him struggle, Ragnar and Philip moved in to help.

With the three of them pushing, the trapdoor slowly gave way, allowing bright sunlight to pour down through the opening above. In addition to the sunlight, vines, bits of grass and a fern now dangled into the hole. Anastasis resumed his ascent and the rest of the travellers followed.

What they saw next nearly took their breath away. They emerged from the hole and found themselves standing on an island in the middle of a river. On the river's two sides stood sheer canyon walls, but the island's summit was even in height with the tops of the canyon's banks. The river itself bubbled and foamed against the steep cliffs perhaps a hundred yards beneath them. Gulls rose from their nests and squawked at them, circling overhead in the stiff breeze.

From a distance the island must have looked like a large flat pillar of rock in the midst of the river. It was longer than it was wide, but from tip to tip it would have only measured around four hundred yards and one hundred and fifty yards at its widest point. Grass covered most of its surface although a few trees and some ferns had taken root there as well.

A broken stone railing circled the island's outside perimeter but it was covered in lichens to such an extent that it was barely recognizable. Anyone looking at the top of the island from either bank would not initially notice that there had ever been a human presence there.

And now Jonathan finally understood the source of the roaring sound—about four hundred yards downstream the river suddenly dropped from sight and a large cloud of mist billowed into the air. Sonja noticed it also. She pointed at the cloud of spray and tried to keep the wind from blowing her long hair into her mouth at the same time. "Is that a waterfall down there?"

"Yes," said Anastasis, "and there is another half a mile upstream from us as well." The hermit pointed to their right, upstream and towards a bend in the canyon walls, where Jonathan could see another cloud of mist rising into the air several hundred yards away.

"So, if this is an island in the middle of a canyon in between two waterfalls," said Olaf, "then I can't imagine a safer place in the whole Kingdom of Magelandorn."

"You have it exactly," said the hermit. "The only way to arrive where we are now is underground, and only a very few people know the secret entrances or passwords."

"What river is this?" asked Jonathan.

"It's the Dorinon River," said Ragnar. "The abbot mentioned it."

Nobody said anything for a moment. They were trying to absorb it all.

The cities of Rindorn, Dorinon and the surrounding lands were all located on an extensive mountain plateau, with mountains peaks that rose yet higher. These waterfalls were one of several steps that the river took to find its way down to the lands below. To his knowledge Jonathan had never visited these lowlands, but a travelling merchant had once told him that they were at least three thousand feet lower than Rindorn, though he did not know how anyone could measure such a thing. According to the merchant, the climate became noticeably warmer and wetter the closer you got to the ocean.

"Now," said Anastasis, "we came here to get firewood. So look around for any deadfall and bring it back to the trapdoor."

Mechanically, Jonathan obeyed. The travellers had no need for axes or hatchets. Although there were no more than thirty trees on the island, there was an abundance of deadfall, and most was immediately useable for firewood. Some, especially wood gathered near the island's eastern end, was damp, presumably from the mist created by the waterfall upstream.

Nonetheless, the job was easier said than done. Jonathan battled feelings of vertigo whenever he approached the broken railing. At one point Olaf sank to his knees and crawled towards some fallen branches near the edge. The task was made more difficult by birds that dove at them if they got too close to their nests. Some of these nests were on rock projections on the cliffs' sides, but others sat amid the grass and ferns on the surface of the island itself. Jonathan had to duck more than once as large white gulls flew straight at his head.

After they had collected their wood, Anastasis led them down the stairway again. He stopped one floor above the room where they had left Rannulf. This room had fireplaces and a stove—an old kitchen perhaps—the tiles on the walls were red spotted with white. They piled the wet wood in a corner to dry and deposited most of the dry wood into the fire pits, where, with the help of the lantern's flame they set a fire. Philip then pulled two pots from his pack and Sonja found a fishnet in one of the cupboards.

Seeing the net, Anastasis said, "That reminds me, Olaf, could you go down to the river and get some water for us?"

Olaf started in surprise. Clearly he did not relish the idea.

The hermit laughed. "No, you don't have to climb down the cliffs," he said, guessing Olaf's thought. "There's an easier way. I'll show you."

Anastasis picked up Philip's pots and led Olaf towards a corner where he opened another door. Jonathan was curious, and since no one had asked him to do anything, he grabbed the fishnet and followed them down a spiral stairway that was much steeper and narrower than any thus far.

Eventually they reached a doorway and emerged onto a landing in the open air at the very base of the island's cliffs, just where the rock met the foaming river. Fortunately the island's walls jutted out on either side into the river, making a small bay in its current. Jonathan saw that the stairway continued descending past this landing into the water and far below its surface, and that next to the stairs were metal rungs attached to the cliff's side, presumably to be used as hand holds.

They went down as many steps as they could without getting their feet wet and filled their pots with water. These Olaf and Anastasis took back to the others while Jonathan stayed behind in the hope of catching some fish with the net—a sport he used to have some success with as a boy. At first he had no luck, but after waiting patiently he managed to get enough trout for both supper and breakfast. When he re-entered the kitchen, the fire was roaring merrily.

Meanwhile, Sonja, Philip and Charissa had returned to the island's summit to collect eggs. Jonathan did not envy their attempts to dodge the large birds that would be diving at them but eventually they too returned with their prizes and the group made a satisfying meal.

"No travelling tomorrow," said Ragnar once they had finished eating. "In fact, I expect that we will stay here for a couple days yet. We have to give Rannulf a chance to heal. In the meantime, we need more firewood. And since there is not enough on the top of the island Anastasis will take some of you outside to quickly gather in all the dead branches you can find."

While the rest of them cleaned pots, Anastasis led Olaf, Philip and Jonathan into the tunnels again. Instead of going north through those they had travelled through previously, they took passages leading south and emerged through a door into a small cave.

"It is important that we don't go far," said Anastasis. "When we leave the cave, you must stay within sight of this place and of one another. You must also be absolutely silent."

Outside the cave they found themselves surrounded by forest. Fortunately, a large amount of deadfall lay near the cave opening also and they got to work quickly moving it into the tunnels. However, the longer this task took the more agitated the hermit became. Every twig that snapped and every branch that they had to break to fit through the door made him nervous. It was only after they were safely inside and he had shut the door that he relaxed.

Over breakfast the next morning Sonja asked, "So what is this place anyway?" Jonathan listened carefully to see if she would obtain more information in response to her question than he had.

"I think I know where we are," said Charissa. "I've never been here before, but I believe I've heard about it. If I'm right this was an old library." She looked to Anastasis for confirmation, but when he gave no sign, she continued, "It was built during the Founders' Wars. They designed it like this for protection for all the books and for the people who lived and worked here. The only way in or out is the underground tunnels."

"Protection from whom?" asked Sonja.

"From the founders' enemies, I guess. It's ancient history now," said Charissa, "but this is one of the oldest buildings in Magelandorn—far older than the town of Rindorn or the royal palaces."

"If it's one of the oldest buildings in Magelandorn, then why isn't it more run-down and weathered by age?" asked Rannulf.

"It was lived in until just a few years ago," said Ragnar, speaking for the first time. "After it ceased to be a library, the black robed monks used it as a monastery for some generations until the Verdorben family took the throne. But the Verdorbens did not wish to encourage monasteries and monks—or at least certain varieties of them—and this monastic order was one that they succeeded in driving out. The monks eventually fled."

"Fled?" asked Jonathan, "but if this place is one of the strongest in Magelandorn, why weren't they able to stay?"

"Monks are not warriors," interjected Anastasis, "and if you haven't noticed, there isn't much room to grow food on the top of the island. They could easily withstand a short-term siege here, but it couldn't go on for years and years. It was easy for the Verdorbens to cut off the monks' food sources. They had to leave."

"Why didn't the Verdorbens try to get control of this place then? asked Sonja.

"I think they tried," said Ragnar. "They captured several monks and tortured them for the passwords, but the monks chose to die rather than relinquish the secrets. The rest of the order left soon afterwards."

There was silence for a moment. Jonathan tried to imagine dozens of monks living within these walls. "Then how do *you* know how to get in here?" he asked Anastasis.

Before Anastasis could answer Philip smiled and said, "Ah, now! That is a secret that is carefully guarded and known only to a few. That also is not the kind of thing about which it's permitted to speak."

"Are the monks we stayed with connected to the group who lived here before?" asked Jonathan.

"No," said Ragnar quickly. "The monks we stayed with were given a royal charter to move into this area only a few years ago. The Verdorbens wanted to take the land away from the black-robed monks and give it to the brown-robed monks who are a newer order that is friendlier to the current king."

Jonathan wondered if Ragnar was telling the whole truth. If Fredrick's monks had no connection with those who had lived on the island, then how did Fredrick know where to find the hermit who was able get in and out of this place? Jonathan glanced over at the hermit, but he said nothing.

When he opened his mouth to ask another question, Ragnar spoke again, "Come, we should have some fun for a while." He gathered Olaf, Charissa, Sonja and Jonathan into the large hall with the blue roof. For the rest of that day, Ragnar showed them ways to improve their sword techniques. They practised with the sticks that Jonathan and Olaf had hauled in from the forest the day before, while Rannulf, still recovering, watched from the side. After their sticks had splintered, they gathered up the pieces for firewood and Ragnar taught them simple defence patterns using their bare hands and feet.

Charissa clearly relished these skills. "The women of noble houses," she explained, "are normally taught how to use bows and arrows, but not other weapons."

That evening, as the group of them relaxed in the great hall they took out their musical instruments that Sonja had retrieved from Rindorn. Rannulf played a rollicking melody on his tin whistle, while Sonja joined in with her violin and Jonathan with his lute. Lacking his usual drum, the burly Olaf danced, kicking up his ankles in an exaggerated fashion and making the rest of them laugh. It was perhaps the least graceful dance that Jonathan had seen. It was good, he reflected, that despite their several narrow escapes, his friends still remained in high spirits.

"This is the first time I've seen you dance, Olaf," said Sonja when the song had finished. "If you do this more, you'll end up breaking the hearts of all the ladies in Magelandorn."

"How about another tune then, Rannulf?" suggested Olaf.

Rannulf resumed and Olaf did an especially capering version of a slow waltz usually reserved for formal occasions.

"Very good," said Charissa laughing and clapping at the end. "I'm sure you'd teach them a thing or two at the royal court."

Olaf bowed in response and sat down to wipe the sweat from his brow.

"Hey, I've lost my dancer," said Rannulf, playing a mournful funeral dirge. Olaf waited until he had finished, then started singing a new piece. Although the friends had played music many times together in

Rindorn, Olaf had rarely done the singing and Jonathan was surprised to hear how good he was. Then as the flames from the fire grew lower Olaf led them in folksong after folksong from the mountains near Rindorn.

The next two days continued in much the same pattern. When they were not preparing meals, practising sword skills or playing music, Jonathan rehearsed the battle patterns that he had learned from the Dragikoi. These attracted attention and amusement from his friends and to Jonathan's annoyance, Rannulf began accompanying his battle moves on his tin whistle.

"You know," said Jonathan turning to Rannulf, "I don't think the Dragikoi intended these movements to be folk dances."

"Fine," said Rannulf, "They must be courtship rituals then."

Although, it was nice to be in the safest place in Magelandorn, eventually Jonathan found himself longing for a change. He was getting tired of eating eggs and fish and was also concerned that their enemies had not been idle during their time of rest.

Sure enough, on the sixth morning, Jonathan awoke to a clattering noise. A moment later, Olaf, who had gone collecting eggs, came running through the doorway. "The Dragikoi have found us!" he said. "They're scaling down the cliffs on the north side."

The travellers quickly scrambled to the island's summit to see for themselves. Sure enough, a little further upstream on the river's north bank, two Dragikoi were slowly descending into the canyon below by ropes. A third rope was also visible, and Jonathan assumed that another Dragikoi, somehow attached to that one, was below their line of sight.

"That's impossible," said Anastasis, observing the scene in front of them. "No one can cross the river like that with ropes."

Jonathan felt no reassurance. "I don't know," he said. "I've seen these Dragikoi do impossible things."

Charissa nodded in agreement.

"The hermit's probably right, but perhaps we should be going, in any case," said Ragnar.

They packed their belongings and made ready to leave. But just before they went out the exit Ragnar stopped them and said, "We are departing this stronghold now and in the next few days we may meet strangers. Some might be friendly, and others hostile. There may be spies looking for Jonathan also, so on no account is his name to be mentioned. Is that clear?"

There were sober nods of assent from around the group.

Ragnar continued, "From now on, and until we meet with Gorwin, we will introduce Jonathan to strangers as Cedrik."

Jonathan felt uncomfortable. It was unfair, he thought, to have this extra attention showered on him. He wondered about his friends' opinion of the whole business.

Once Ragnar had finished his speech, they went down the stairway to the tunnels beneath the island, taking the same passage that Olaf, Philip and Jonathan had used to get their firewood a few days earlier. Anastasis explained that by following this tunnel they had now crossed under the river and were on its southern side.

They departed the cave and turned left, walking

parallel to the riverbank a few yards in from the shore. They moved eastward and upstream through an older forest without much undergrowth. The only place where the bushes grew thickly was right near the river's edge where there was more light. This, too, worked in their favour. Thick bushes meant that they were unlikely to be seen by anyone on the river's northern side.

Philip sniffed the air. "It's good to be among trees again after spending all that time on the island," he whispered to Jonathan. "Besides, it's easy to conceal oneself in a forest if one has to."

As they drew near to the eastern waterfall, Ragnar said that he wanted to check on their enemies, and he led the travellers towards the edge of the river. They chose a concealed spot behind some trees and rocks, but could see no Dragikoi nearby nor on the opposite bank. The falls were a spectacular sight! Jonathan had never seen quite so much water before. The river dropped at least one hundred yards straight over the cliff, creating a huge plume of mist-like spray that made all of the travellers and all the surrounding area damp. Their ears were ringing from the sound of it when they left.

About two hours after they left the waterfall, Jonathan's attention was distracted by a strange sound. Instinctively he paused to listen. Then he heard it again. It resembled a birdcall, but something sounded odd about it—almost as if it was a human imitation of a bird rather than the real thing.

"Ragnar," began Jonathan. But he did not finish his sentence.

Ragnar, who was at the front of the column, spun around and gestured for the travellers to hide.

Puzzled by their leader's actions, they ducked into some fern bushes. A moment later they understood. A troop of mail-clad soldiers wearing the Verdorben royal crest came marching through the forest towards their hiding place.

The column halted within earshot of the travellers. "Sir, there are tracks here," said a soldier. "Look at this!"

The soldiers milled about excitedly until their captain called them to attention. He then ordered them to march along the trail that the travellers had already taken through the forest.

"It won't take them long to notice that they are going in the wrong direction," said the hermit after the soldiers had gone. "They'll be back."

"We should split up," said Philip. "It's more difficult to track two smaller groups than one large group."

"But where do we meet?" said Ragnar. He looked at the hermit.

"I know a place," said Anastasis, "an old stopping station for pilgrims going to the monastery. If you go due south," he pointed through the trees, "you will soon encounter a rivulet that runs through the forest and joins the Dorinon River not far from here. Follow the rivulet upstream until it forks. Jonathan and I will meet you at the fork in two days."

"Good enough," said Ragnar. "Now let's go. We have no time to lose."

All of this happened quickly. Jonathan was still watching the backs of his companions disappear into the forest when he finally realized that he was parting from his friends, at least for a while. He suddenly felt quite lonely.

"Come. This way," said the hermit, rousing him.

They started walking east, but they had gone no more than two hundred yards when, with a snapping of branches, three armed figures stepped out from behind the trunks of nearby trees.

"Run!" yelled the hermit.

With Anastasis leading, the two of them sprinted away from their pursuers. They were making good progress until an enemy soldier stepped out from behind a large boulder in front of them and knocked the hermit to the ground.

Enraged at such a cowardly attack on an old man, Jonathan drew his sword in one swift motion and slammed the flat of it down onto his enemy's helmet. The man fell to the ground stunned.

Jonathan looked back, checking for enemies. Two soldiers with bows were taking cover behind tree trunks thirty yards away. Then he glanced down at Anastasis.

"Help me up," said the hermit, reaching out his hand. Jonathan grasped it, and to his amazement his friend quickly bounded up and set off at a brisk pace through the forest. "This way!" he called.

Jonathan jogged after him, marvelling that the man could still walk let alone stand. But two minutes later they were halted again. Another soldier stepped out from behind a tree to block their path.

The old man backed out of the way to allow Jonathan to draw his sword and exchange blows with their opponent. He was unsure if he could have beaten him in a fair fight, but he had no opportunity to find out. An arrow flew through the air, missing Jonathan, but piercing the sword hand of his enemy. With a yell the man dropped his weapon and retreated.

Anastasis wasted no time. "Come on," he yelled, jogging off again, and Jonathan pursued him through the trees.

They continued running through the forest. Two more arrows whizzed past—a reminder of the ever present threat. Yet eventually the sounds of pursuit died down. Then just when they thought they had seen the last of their enemies, two more soldiers abruptly emerged about fifteen yards in front of them.

The hermit darted off to the right to avoid the soldiers and Jonathan followed, again amazed at how fast the old man moved. Their two opponents chased them, but fortunately they were wearing heavy armour, allowing Anastasis and Jonathan to run around them and get back onto the path. For the moment at least, it looked as if they were free to escape.

After twenty minutes of running from tree to tree without spotting any pursuers, the two slowed to a walk. Jonathan did not know where they were going, but he assumed that Anastasis did. After all, the forest was his home, and he had helped them avoid capture so far.

Then out of the corner of his eye, Jonathan saw a flash of sun reflecting off metal. Instinctively he whirled around. Just in time! He felt the wind of a sword flying downward, barely missing his neck. An enemy soldier stepped out on his left and another on his right. Jonathan's back was against a tree. Flight was impossible now.

Quick as lightning he drew his sword. One blow came. He parried it—then another. Stroke after stroke, he blocked them all.

But it could not to continue. Suddenly he felt a sharp pain on the top of his skull. Everything grew grey and misty. Then there was nothing.

# 11 THE HOUSE

When Jonathan woke, he was in pitch darkness and had no idea where he was. For a moment he thought he was back in the hidden library between the waterfalls. Then he remembered. He had been running through the forest.

He sat up but dizziness and nausea quickly overwhelmed him and he had to lie down again.

*Am I in jail again,* he asked himself, *or perhaps I am dead and in some "other" place?*

A moment of panic took hold of him. The pitch darkness was more terrifying than anything he had yet endured, and he lay motionless, afraid to move. Then, attempting to discern his whereabouts, he tried to remember everything that had happened. He recalled leaving the monastery. The waterfalls. The attack. The hermit . . . yes, the hermit. Anastasis had been leading him someplace and they had been discovered. There had been a fight where he had tried to fend off two swordsmen at once. Obviously, he had failed.

He tried moving various limbs. At least he could

move his hand. That was good. Then he reached up towards his head. Something was strange there. Clothes of some type? A bandage? Yes, it had to be a bandage.

This was hopeful anyhow. It probably meant he was not dead. If he was in heaven, then there would be no reason for him to have a bandage.

It was cold. Groping around in the blackness he discovered some kind of animal skin blanket on the floor, and he pulled it over himself. The smell of wood mixed with an earthy smell emanated from somewhere. He stopped moving briefly to listen for noises.

Nothing.

How big was this room? "Hello?" he said aloud. Dead silence. No echo either. The walls of whatever place he was in had immediately absorbed the sound.

*But if I'm not dead, what am I doing here?*

No answer to that question. He rested for a few minutes longer. Soon the blanket made him too hot. He pulled it off again.

Then a horrible idea occurred to him. Maybe he had been captured by his enemies and buried alive? With that thought desperation seized him. Despite his nausea, he tried moving again. He felt the ground nearby, his pulse quickening all the time. Was there an exit anywhere? Or even windows?

He sat up, still feeling sick to the stomach, but he decided that he had to move somewhere, anywhere. Then just as he was about to begin crawling, suddenly a distant door or window opened and . . . oh joy! Light appeared. He could now dimly see that he was in a room with a dirt floor and rough-cut wooden walls. A bed stood against one wall. But all his attention was focussed on the light approaching from around a corner. He saw a hand—not the hand with the light, but the creature's other hand—then an arm covered by a brown sleeve, then finally, a lantern.

The light hurt his eyes and he was forced to look away. When they had adjusted enough for him to look up again he recognized the lantern bearer. It was the hermit. Jonathan breathed a sigh of relief and tried to disguise the panic on his face.

"What are you doing on the floor?" asked the hermit.

"The floor?" asked Jonathan. He propped himself up on one elbow and looked around in the light of the hermit's lantern. A cot stood against one of the walls. "I must have rolled off the bed," said Jonathan. "So tell me, what happened in the forest?"

"Two of the king's soldiers stepped out from behind a tree and surprised us," said the hermit. "You resisted them—doing an admirable job I might say—but one of the soldiers clubbed you on the head with a mace and left you for dead. I brought you here."

"What about the others? My friends?"

"They are supposed to meet us here tomorrow. We can only hope that they are fine." He took bread and cheese from a leather satchel and gave some to Jonathan who chewed very slowly, being careful not to renew his nausea.

"It's good to see you in one piece," said the hermit. "But now that you're awake, we should perhaps see if you are hurt anywhere besides your head." He brought the lamp closer to Jonathan. "Can you move at all?"

"You mean walk?"

"Hopefully, yes."

Slowly Jonathan sat up. After a moment the dizziness subsided.

"Perhaps we should get you up and have you walk around a little," said the Hermit. "It will be good for you."

Obediently, and with his stomach doing occasional flip-flops, Jonathan crawled towards the wall, with Anastasis making encouraging sounds behind him. Then with the help of his friend, he pulled himself up to the wall. Again he waited for the dizziness to pass before allowing Anastasis to guide him past a thick cloth curtain. Then he was in the outside air, where he could hear the sound of wind and of water nearby.

With the hermit supporting him, they walked a few paces. The movement together with the outside air began to clear Jonathan's head.

"Where are we?" he asked.

"One of my houses," said the hermit.

"*One* of your houses? How many houses to you have?"

"Just enough to keep me comfortable."

Jonathan looked at him, surprised. "Why would a forest hermit need multiple dwellings?"

"Well, obviously during the winter I have to pick a warmer site to live in—and in summer, cooler places. I also have to be prepared for floods and there's always the possibility of enemies. So I make do with what I have."

"Usually only the very wealthy can afford more than one house," said Jonathan, amazed.

"Most people are actually wealthier than they think," continued the hermit. "They only need to consider the outside world to be their own personal castle. After all, no tapestry can compare with this." He waved at a gap in the trees through which the stars shone brightly. "That's one of the best things about being a forest hermit. You have the world's greatest works of art in your living space. As a result, you're one of the wealthiest people in the world!"

Jonathan was impressed by this speech, and he made a mental note to think about it. But he was not convinced. Giving up the company of others was a fairly high price to pay for this kind of wealth, he thought, unless one could convince others to live in the same way. He thought about Helena, the girl in Rindorn with whom he had been in love, and he could not picture her trying to survive on berries and living in a forest hut. No, it was not for everyone.

They took a brief walk through the forest but soon Jonathan's head was spinning again. When the hermit saw that Jonathan's steps were faltering, he guided him back towards a door in a strange-looking treelike house.

"This is odd," said Jonathan. "Aren't we going back to your house?"

"You are confused by the darkness," said Anastasis. "This *is* my house." The hermit guided Jonathan's stumbling footsteps through the doorway and over to the place where he had been previously lying. Anastasis then lit a fire. As the wood caught fire and the light grew, Jonathan could see the shadows from the flames dancing on the rough-cut wooden walls. Then with the world rotating slowly around him, he drifted into sleep.

He woke some time later, no longer dizzy but thirsty. It was now morning. Rubbing his eyes, he looked around at his surroundings in a way that he had not been alert enough to do on the previous evening.

The fire had gone out but light now entered through the windows whose thick cloth curtains had been drawn aside. He found himself in a long, oval shaped room stretching fifteen feet from end to end. Its rough wooden walls bulged in several places. His bed took up the back third of the hut. A hammock stretched between two of the walls just above where his feet rested on the edge of the bed. The front third of the hut contained a small open space with a chair. Next to it stood a leather curtain that hung from a rod about five feet above the ground. Jonathan guessed that a doorway lay behind it. In addition to the pots and a fire-tongs, garlic and various herbs, all with their tops braided together, hung from hooks in the walls.

Looking up, Jonathan could see that the hut had a thatched roof supported by the usual wattle poles. Unlike most huts that were square in shape, these support poles were spread in a circle with their ends coming together to form three cones.

Hollowed out knots in the wood served as windows—not large ones, but round in shape—and with the windows now open and curtains drawn apart, noises from outside were audible. He could hear the creaking of trees, the occasional chirp of birds and the sound of running water. A brick chimney from a small clay stove also jutted up through one of these round holes and a patch of clay had been baked around the place where the chimney met the wall. It was here that the hermit had lit the fire last night. But what seemed most out of place in this hut were the bookshelves that rested on pegs pounded into the walls.

Jonathan decided to quench his thirst with the water that he heard bubbling outside the cottage. Standing up, he narrowly avoided a string of braided onions as he walked over to the doorway. He parted the curtain over the doorway and stooped to exit.

The sun shone bright and hot. Turning to look back at the curious hut, he now saw that what he had surmised during the previous night had been correct. He had been inside a tree—or tree stumps really. Three trees had grown together forming one long line and they had been hollowed out from the inside. A piece of the stump had been fashioned into a door and each of the stump's various windows also had miniature doors, which when closed would effectively disguise them. From the exterior it would be difficult to tell that this stump was a residence unless one knew where to look for the telltale signs. He marvelled at the hermit's ingenuity.

A pathway led away from the hut, which after about twenty feet split into two branches. One side went to the right, presumably into the forest, while the left path went down towards a river running next to the cottage. Jonathan took the left-hand path. It followed along the top of the riverbank for a few yards before taking a right turn down to the water. He scrambled down the short bank to a gravelly beach beside the river. The river was neither swift nor deep and only forty feet across at the point where he was standing. He supposed that it would be reasonably easy to wade from one side to the other.

Just a yard or two upstream, the hermit sat on a large boulder. He was fishing and throwing his catches, still live, into a large water-filled bucket. He turned to greet Jonathan. "Good morning. I'm catching us some supper. Have some breakfast—fish I cooked this morning before the sun rose. They're cold now, but still good. How are you feeling?"

"Better."

"Glad to hear it."

"Thanks for bringing me here," said Jonathan. "I'm surprised that you were able to carry me. I hope it wasn't far."

The hermit smiled. "I'm not as frail as I look— well preserved—that's all."

Jonathan gave him a curious stare and was about to ask a question but the hermit continued. "You should bathe your wound. Just downstream, the river deepens enough for swimming." He pointed, then added, "Leave your boots here, you can wade there."

Jonathan left his boots and sword on the beach, and after making his way carefully over the slippery rocks he found the pool the hermit had recommended. He placed the amulet on a nearby rock, but he kept his clothes on since they needed washing, too. Then, after swimming for a while, he removed them and let them dry on nearby boulders that had been heated by the mid-morning sun.

He enjoyed swimming, but soon he felt it was time to re-don his clothes, hang the amulet around his neck and gingerly wade back up stream. Yet just as he reached the spot where his boots were waiting, he slipped, and in his struggle to maintain his balance a sharp piece of driftwood bit into the bottom of his left foot.

"Ouch," he said in the hearing of the hermit.

Anastasis glanced up. "You've cut yourself," he pointed to the small trickle of red beside Jonathan's foot. The hermit approached carrying his rod. "Let's see it."

Jonathan sat on a boulder next to the water's edge, washed his foot and lifted it up for the hermit to look at.

But when the old man caught sight of the foot, he dropped his fishing rod and gasped.

"Is it that bad?" asked Jonathan.

Anastasis made no reply. He remained staring at the foot.

"Is it bad?" Jonathan repeated, examining it himself.

"Bad?" said the hermit, recovering. "No, no the cut isn't bad. A simple bandage will do." As he picked up his rod, he asked casually, "How long have you had that mark on the bottom of your foot?"

"Mark?" asked Jonathan. Then he remembered. He saw it so rarely that he usually forgot that a picture of the sun had been tattooed within the arch of his left foot.

"As long as I remember," he said. "Why?"

"You don't recall who gave it to you?"

"No. It must have been done when I was a very young child, and I don't remember much about my early childhood."

The hermit gave him an interested stare. "All right then," he said, turning and making his way back to his fishing rock. "I have a spare rag here. It will have to do as a bandage."

But Jonathan was curious now. "Have you seen this kind of tattoo before?" he asked.

"No, just heard about them. That's all."

"What did you hear?"

No response. The hermit paused for a moment,

thinking. He finally said, "We should talk about this over breakfast," And he bent down and tied the rag around Jonathan's foot. He pointed at a nearby boulder. "There, that stone will do nicely as a table. After breakfast we can go to the library."

*Library?* Jonathan had not realized that there was anything more to this place than the hut where he had slept.

Anastasis gave Jonathan two apples and some pre-cooked fish. Jonathan would have preferred that the fish had been freshly cooked, but he knew that campfire smoke could attract enemies.

He expected that over breakfast Anastasis would tell him the significance of the tattoo. Instead, the old man asked questions. "You said that you don't remember much of your childhood. What do you remember?"

Jonathan told him the brief scraps of information that he had told Ragnar. Then he gave him a run-down of the events leading up to their meeting in the cottage near the waterfall.

"And what has Ragnar said about all this?"

"Only that my uncle's family and my family, too, had supported the royal family. I mean the original royal family, not the usurpers, and because of this we were, and will probably remain, enemies of the current royal family."

"And that is all he said?"

"Yes." There was an uncomfortable silence, so Jonathan added. "He did say that there was more to the tale, but that it had better wait until I had met my uncle."

"Why did he say that?"

"He said that the less I knew, the less I would be

able to tell our enemies if I was captured."

"I suppose that would make sense to a certain way of thinking," said the hermit. "But that tattoo on your foot may change matters."

"Why?"

"If your enemies discovered it, then they would hardly have to torture you to learn more, would they? They'd know exactly who you are and who you were with."

Jonathan had no idea how to respond.

To Jonathan's annoyance, for a moment the hermit appeared to be speaking aloud to himself. "Unless . . . unless," he mused, "they didn't know any better. It could also be because those two particular soldiers didn't know specifically who you were. They probably just had orders to kill any strangers they met in the forest. Yes, that might actually be the case."

"What do you mean?" asked Jonathan.

"Your enemies might not have been informed about these tattoos and what they signify as fewer and fewer people are left that remember the old days. Nonetheless, we should not count on that. The best thing for you to do if you fall into the hands of the enemy is to keep your boots on. So I must concur with Ragnar's decision to wait until you're safely at your uncle's house."

Jonathan could have screamed in irritation. He had come so close to being told the whole story, and then at the last minute had his hopes dashed. Hearing this made him both very eager to meet his uncle, and eager to give his uncle a good solid wallop on the nose for sending all these people to look after him who refused to tell him anything. Why was everybody always so reluctant to discuss his past? And why did they always know more about it than he did?

The hermit must have sensed Jonathan's annoyance because when he said nothing, the hermit asked, "Why do you think those soldiers attacked us and left you for dead in the forest two days ago? And why did the Dragikoi follow us across to the island in the river?"

"I don't know. Why?"

"I wondered the same thing myself until I saw your foot. Now I believe that it was because you were there."

"Me? Why send soldiers after me?"

"Because you're a threat to the royal family. They will go to no end of effort to have you captured and killed, as they did with your parents."

This sobered Jonathan. He decided to leave the matter for now. If Ragnar and the hermit were so determined not to tell him the secret of his past then perhaps it was best if he spent his energies trying to get to his uncle.

"In any case, you will soon be leaving here and going on your way," said the hermit. "I want to give you something to help you before you go."

"That's not necessary. . ." began Jonathan, already embarrassed at needing the hermit's hospitality.

"Oh yes, it is. It will be very helpful for your uncle anyhow—and for you, too, I expect. It's too dangerous now for you to try to cross the open country to your uncle's house. We don't know how many of the king's soldiers are in the forest or how long they will stay here, but I expect that the king will soon have this district crawling with his troops. If that happens, then there would be great risk that you will be discovered. We will have to use a secret route for you to leave this area."

"And you know of a secret way out of here?"

"Yes," said the hermit. "Come with me."

Leaving the fish scraps for the magpies, they climbed the bank, but instead of going to his tree trunk hut, they walked towards a smaller creek running down to meet the river that Jonathan had bathed in. They followed this creek upstream as its valley rose around them and became a narrow canyon. Then after fifteen minutes of walking, Anastasis suddenly turned left and pushed his way into a stand of spruce trees.

"Come," he said, beckoning to Jonathan before he fully disappeared among the branches.

Jonathan pushed through after him, getting spruce sap on his hands. He was surprised when he passed the last branch and saw a cottage plus an attached barn to its right. Both were made of stone and had green tile roofs. Spruce trees surrounded them on three sides while a few feet behind them stood the canyon's wall. The hermit walked towards the cottage doorway and said, "This used to be a stopping off point for pilgrims on their way to the monastery between the waterfalls. But when the Verdorbens laid siege to the monastery, the flow of pilgrims dried up. Eventually the monks smuggled some of the monastery's library here. Enter. There's plenty of room."

Carefully ducking his head to avoid the cottage's low doorframe, Jonathan found himself in a room roughly fifteen feet wide and double that from end to end. The scent of old books assailed his nostrils. Bookshelves stood against all four walls as well as two shelves down the room's centre. Each bookshelf on an outside wall had a cutaway portion for the windows. A metal stove stood in the room near the cottage's centre. A desk holding a lamp sat near the stove.

From where he stood he saw three other equal-sized rooms in the cottage and an open door on his right leading to the barn. The barn and cottage also contained shelves full of books together with a disorganized clutter of scrolls, pens and bottles of ink.

Jonathan had seen the inside of the Mayor's house, and he knew that the mayor did not have nearly this size of a library. This whole place had a mysterious feel to it. Since Jonathan had only a limited exposure to the written word, he had always associated it with things magical and arcane.

The hermit walked into one of the nearby rooms. Then going over to a shelf, he gazed at it, obviously searching for something. Finally he selected a book and turned to Jonathan. "Sit down," he said.

Jonathan sat on a wooden bench underneath one of the shelves while the hermit paced back and forth, nervously passing his book from one hand to the other.

"Jonathan," he asked, pausing in mid-stride, "what do you know about Magelandorn and its history?"

"Just what Ragnar has told me. Not much."

"Tell me what you know."

Jonathan launched into the story of Morden, the man who founded Rindorn and on whose statue he had hung the mayor's trousers a few weeks before. But Anastasis interrupted with, "So much for Rindorn." Then catching himself, he added, "It's not as if it's unimportant. Morden was a brave man. Tell me, do you know anything about the first human settlements in Magelandorn?"

Jonathan did not respond. He had not realized that there had been a time when there were no human settlements in Magelandorn.

Anastasis sighed and sat down on a bench facing Jonathan. "Our human ancestors," he said, "didn't come from this land. Years ago they came from a faraway place."

"Why did they come?"

"Because they were persecuted by their enemies. So instead of facing continual warfare, they chose voluntary exile away from the land of their heritage. They arrived in large ships, founded this country and its cities and were very wise and skilled in arts and sciences that we no longer comprehend. We have lost much of their knowledge."

"How did we lose it?" asked Jonathan.

"Warfare mostly," said the hermit.

"What does warfare have to do with anything?"

"More than lives get destroyed in wars. Sometimes skills get lost, too. You see, after a time, our ancestors' enemies pursued them to this new land. Our people drove the attackers off, but there had been much destruction. And even though our ancestors had tried to hide away some books before the war to prevent them from being destroyed, much knowledge was still lost. In the meantime, our enemies had retreated to the north desert and begun the slow task of rebuilding themselves as well. Our enemies decided that, since they could not win the war in their own lifetime, they needed a leader to carry out their wishes when they were gone. And that is where the Black Wizard comes into the tale."

"Who is this Black Wizard anyhow?" Jonathan asked. "Does he never die?"

"We don't know if he is a creature who lives eternally, or a human who passes his leadership down from father to son or how exactly he exists. In any case, we know he moves, thinks and gives orders and has been around nearly forever."

"So the Black Wizard was originally from this far country too?" asked Jonathan.

"Perhaps. We don't know. But with the Black Wizard leading them, in time, attacks from the north were renewed and while they were never entirely successful, on occasion they have caused severe suffering. Fortunately, on our side we had the Knights of the White Rose. Many times heroic warriors from this order have sacrificed their own lives in order to defend us from almost certain disaster. And in addition to the knights, our ancestors brought six special items from their homeland."

"Do you mean the sacred gifts?"

"Yes, has Ragnar told you about them?"

"He did, but he told me that they were scattered. Surely if we could find them, there would be some people, even distant members of the old royal family, who could use them?"

"Yes," said the hermit. "And, actually, I have devoted the majority of my life to locating these objects. We are doomed unless our country uses them once again. One of these blessed gifts is located in the lowest level of Dorinon Castle. No one else, I believe, besides myself, the Duke and the King knows that it is there."

"How come you know where it is when no one

else does?"

"That's a long story, which I shall tell you some other time. In any case, what the Duke and the King do not realize is that there is a secret passage leading into the castle, and there is a second secret passage leading from the castle's lowest level to the outside world. Now, if you wish to escape this area and safely arrive at your uncle's house, it would be prudent for you to use these passages. While you are on your way, you might as well collect the sacred object to return it to the true royal family."

Jonathan nodded. "What should I be looking for?" he asked.

"A helmet."

"A helmet? Is that all?"

"What do you mean, 'Is that all'? It's one of the sacred gifts! Its name is Perikephalaia Soteriou—but yes, it looks just like an ordinary helmet, except that it has a crest on the front—a bird above a book above a sword. Ragnar can identify it."

"How will I find the secret passages that I need to break into the Duke's castle?"

"That's where this comes in." The old man held up the book he had been carrying. Then taking a key from around his neck, he inserted it into a keyhole on the book's cover. When the hermit opened the book, to his astonishment, Jonathan saw that there were no pages inside. It was a small chest made to look like a book. From within, Anastasis withdrew three small parchment scrolls.

"Here," he said, "I have in my hands both your path to freedom and a way to recover the sacred helmet."

As he unrolled one of the scrolls Jonathan

moved closer for a better look. It was a map. Jonathan had trouble figuring out which parts were land and which were seas until Anastasis pointed out the details on it. "This map can show you the route you have taken so far from Rindorn, as well as where you have to go to get to your uncle's house. I drew it myself by hand, which is why it looks a little rough."

After showing Jonathan the first map he took out a second. "This map is more immediately important. It shows the city of Dorinon. You can see that the castle is located at the centre. It's built on a hill of rock rising some two hundred feet above the level of the plain." The hermit stabbed a finger at an area of the city lying next to the river. "They call this The Cauldron."

"The Cauldron?"

"The thieves' quarter—not a safe place at night. Now there is a portion of this thieves' quarter that actually runs right up to the castle cliff. Below the cliff is an inn called the Castle and Crown. The secret passageway that goes into Dorinon Castle starts in cellars of this inn. I have seen it once myself—it's on the other side of a trapdoor in the wine cellar, but I don't even think the inn's owner knows it's there."

Anastasis put the second scroll away and unrolled the third. "This gives us more details of Dorinon Castle's interior. Once you are through the inn's trapdoor, you will climb a ladder and you will find yourself in the castle's outer keep. The sacred helmet is here"—again Anastasis pointed—"in the northwest corner of the cellars in the Duke's residence. Then, in the same room as the gift there is a door that leads to another passage, which in turn, leads away from Dorinon Castle to the sea—and to your uncle."

Anastasis then put the three scrolls aside and took out other maps to show his guest. Jonathan nodded, trying to appear wise, but secretly he hoped the hermit did not notice that he was not used to working with maps. Still, the map intrigued him. Their fancy lettering and pictures of mountains, trees and sea monsters spoke to him of mystery and enchantment beyond the realm of the everyday. Before this time he had really no concept of Magelandorn's extent or the distances between cities. Now he felt as if he had discovered a new power.

"Did you make these yourself?" he asked the hermit.

"I copied some of them, but none are my original drawings—except for the first three scrolls I showed you."

Then suddenly the hermit said, "Come, we must be going."

Anastasis followed Jonathan out the door. Soon they were squeezing their way through the spruce trees. After the cool stone cottage, the outside air felt uncomfortably warm. It was approaching noon and the sun was high.

They went down to the riverside again and kicked stones over the place where Anastasis had lit a fire that morning. Then, filling some buckets with water, they were preparing to return to the tree stump hut when they heard human voices. Anastasis was alarmed. "Hurry!" he said.

Ducking behind a thicket of young trees, they waited to see who approached—friend or foe?

# 12 DORINON

Jonathan's pulse raced as he strained to see the strangers through the trees. The footsteps and voices moved closer—then silence. Whoever it was had halted.

"Anastasis," said a hushed voice. It was Ragnar.

Breathing a sigh of relief, Jonathan gestured to Anastasis to emerge from his hiding place.

Jonathan climbed up the bank first. In addition to Ragnar, he saw Philip and all of his old friends. When Charissa saw Jonathan, she waved and smiled. His heart gave a leap. To him, the noon sunlight was nothing compared to the brilliance of that smile.

"My apologies for not greeting you," said the hermit as he approached. "One can never be too careful in these parts."

Since it was just past noon, Anastasis provided a repast of cheese, dried fruits and vegetables plus some of the leftover fish from breakfast. Jonathan sat by the stream to eat with the other travellers while the hermit headed out with Ragnar for a walk.

When they came back, they were deep in conversation, and they paused to talk for a moment just out of earshot of the rest of the party before re-joining them. Jonathan wondered if one of their topics of conversation was the tattoo on his foot. He was beginning to think that perhaps the reason no one wanted to tell him about his past was because there was something shameful about it. Maybe his father had been a crooked financier who had been forced to flee for his life. Or perhaps he, like Jonathan, had played a practical joke on the Verdorbens, and the usurpers had sworn vengeance on him and all his offspring for generations to come.

*Yes, that was probably it. My father was almost certainly a scoundrel just like me, and Ragnar and Anastasis think it is so shameful that they don't have the heart to tell me. Well, that's that!* He sighed. He had secretly been hoping that his heritage would have been more honourable, but he had to reconcile himself to the fact that it was not so. *Too bad it's not possible to change the past,* he thought.

Because Jonathan needed more time to heal his wounds, the travellers stayed that night with the hermit. Just before they departed the next morning they filled their water skins from the stream. They then set off on the path that followed the river upstream, gradually climbing in elevation until they reached the mountain plateau where Dorinon and Rindorn were located.

During rest breaks Anastasis took out the map of Dorinon and had them all study it. "You never know when knowledge of this city might come in handy," he said.

As the sun was setting they found a place to

camp. The night was warm with no sign of rain, allowing them to sleep beneath the stars. In the morning they continued on their way. Then two hours later Anastasis suddenly paused. "I have reached the eastern edge of my territory," he said. "Since I am known in Dorinon, it would be dangerous for you if I accompanied you any further. Follow this rivulet upstream until you approach the forest boundary. The rivulet won't be much more than a creek by then. Then, when you leave the forest, walk due east over a rise and across some fields until you arrive at the much larger Dorinon River."

"How long will that take?" asked Rannulf.

"By the time you get to Dorinon it will be sundown or close to it," he answered.

"And when do the city gates close?" asked the prudent Sonja.

"At sundown, but if you get there after dark you should be able to slip into the city unnoticed by way of the river outlet. The Dorinon River flows into the city from the north. If you circle around the city and slip into the stream after dark, you can float downriver into the city's centre. I have done so a few times myself when I needed to enter Dorinon unseen."

"Won't the river entrance be guarded?" asked Jonathan.

"Yes, but the chains across the river are designed to keep out boats rather than individual people. So you should be all right. Farewell."

Ragnar said. "We need to thank Anastasis for all that he has done for us. In addition to his help, he has also provided us with rations for the next two days."

The travellers individually said their thanks and

goodbyes to Anastasis and then watched him slip back into the forest. Just before he was out of sight, Jonathan waved once more. Even though he had only known the hermit for a few days, he felt that he had made himself a friend.

As they kept moving towards the town, the trees gave way to farm fields. They followed an old farm track meandering eastward, encountering only one peasant all that day. He, however, left the road and gave them a wide berth. Clearly strangers were not to be trusted in these parts.

As they got closer to the city, their farm track met the Dorinon River. Jonathan knew from the hermit's map that the river flowed into the city from the north, and then within the city it turned westward towards their present position. The road they were on skirted the river's southern bank.

When it was nearly sundown the road took them into a small patch of trees. "Jonathan," said Ragnar, "I don't think it would be wise for you to go in through the city gates."

"Why's that?" asked Jonathan.

"Dorinon isn't far from Rindorn and if any of Rindorn's soldiers have been brought in to help search for us, there's a good chance that you would be recognized."

"All right then," said Jonathan after a pause. "You think we should wait until dark and enter via the river?"

Before Ragnar could answer, Philip said, "Perhaps only those of us who run a risk of being discovered should enter via the river. I could take some of our belongings through the city gate and Charissa could come with me. No one will be on the lookout for the two of us."

Ragnar saw the sense in Philip's suggestion. "Here," he said, handing Philip a book. Jonathan recognized it as the same map container that the hermit had shown him two days earlier.

"Charissa and I can meet you at the church graveyard, and then afterwards go to the Inn of the Dancing Duck," said Philip, smiling. "It'll be an appropriate place to visit after a swim in the river."

Ragnar agreed. The group then emptied their packs and sorted the contents into three piles. One pile was mostly clothing that the swimmers would carry with them. Philip and Charissa were given as much of the rest as they could carry, plus most of the food. Sonja also gave Charissa her violin and Jonathan gave Philip his lute. Finally, they created a third pile, which they hid in the trees for Philip to come back and claim the following day. Ragnar stripped off his suit of chain mail and left it in this pile. "It would be difficult to swim with this," he said.

Once Philip and Charissa left, the rest sat down in a hidden spot to wait for darkness. Jonathan felt anxious. He disliked being parted from Charissa again. He had to admit to himself now that he had more than just a casual interest in her. Was there any possibility that she felt the same way? Or perhaps— and here a pang of worry gripped him—could she be taking an interest in one of his friends? He tried to dismiss that last idea and move onto another train of thought. Nothing came to mind, however.

Soon afterwards Ragnar said, "I'm going to creep closer to the city and look at the river walls, just to see what we are up against. In the meantime, wait here."

Jonathan sat with his back against a tree, glad of

the chance to rest. A while later he realized that someone was jogging his elbow. He had drifted off to sleep. "It's time," Rannulf said.

They ate some food as they walked. Now that it was dark, they felt more comfortable travelling around the outside of the city without attracting attention. Nevertheless, their trek across the fields was frustrating. The moon had not yet risen, and they could not always clearly see where to step. Jonathan kept tripping over stones and stepping into small holes. He still felt groggy after his nap.

The moon had risen though by the time they had reached their destination, the Dorinon River, a mile and a half upstream from the city. They slipped and slid their way down the bank and then began making their way south toward the city. Most of the time they were able to walk on the gravel bars right next to the water's edge, or jump from sandbar to sandbar, but in some places the river ran up against steep cliffs, and there they had to wade through water that was nearly waist-deep. Since it made him feel more alert, Jonathan actually welcomed the feel of cool water on his feet.

They still had half a mile to go when the river went round one of its many bends, and in the moonlight they could dimly see the city ahead. Ragnar crouched behind some brush that edged the river. Jonathan and his friends ducked down beside him.

The city fortifications overlooking the river extended north towards them on both sides, and at the furthest point of these extensions, towers rose up from the walls. Lights shone from the tower windows.

Ragnar pointed down the river. "You can't tell in

the dark, but the river starts to narrow as it approaches the city. The water gets deeper, but you should be able to touch bottom most of the time. Then just before it goes under the wall, the river is joined by a swift-flowing stream from the east, making it deeper yet. That's where we will have to float or swim. Remember to keep your body below the water, in case there are curious guards peering down from the wall.

"That's not so bad," said Olaf. "Chances are we should make it."

"Hopefully yes," said Ragnar, "but there is one last barrier that we have to pass. A net of chains hangs suspended between those two towers to keep out unwanted boats. It forms a fairly complete barrier except right where it joins the towers. Just at that point there are gaps. Try to float close to the left side where the chains meet the tower. We should be able to get through the hole there—if we're careful. Inside the walls there are docks along the river's left side for the city people's boats. We will use them to climb out of the river." Ragnar paused then added, "Oh, and one more thing. If we get separated, go to a park bordering the church graveyard. From there we'll go as a group to the Dancing Duck inn."

Jonathan was impressed that Ragnar had such detailed knowledge of this strange city. Ragnar made them all repeat his directions until he knew they understood and remembered what he had said. Then they tightened their packs, and crouching as low as they could to avoid being seen, they moved slowly and silently towards Dorinon.

Three hundred yards upstream from the city they met the creek. As Ragnar had predicted, from this point on the water became too deep to wade in. He urged them to all find logs or driftwood to hold while they swam downstream. Jonathan watched as the others went ahead. Rannulf nearly lost his sword and Olaf's driftwood left him behind and went bobbing down the river without him. Fortunately, he caught another log that came past and he was on his way again.

Jonathan went last. As he was floating, to distract himself from the cold water, he focused on the approaching towers. It appeared that the task of getting through the chains was proving more difficult than Ragnar had expected. Two members of their party were already struggling, and to give them more time Jonathan attempted to slow his own approach. With his feet he tried to catch something on the riverbed to anchor himself in place. He was helped by the weight of his sword that pulled him down so that occasionally he could touch bottom. Each time he did, he tried to get enough grip to stand still. However, the current was getting stronger by the moment and the water was even deeper than Ragnar had warned.

Finally, after several tries, his feet collided with a large rock. He had to let his driftwood go, but he was able to hook his toes underneath the rock and remain upright, even though the water formed a standing wave, pulling at him. As it parted around his torso, every muscle in his legs strained to resist the current.

Up ahead, one of his friends had now successfully climbed around the barrier, and seeing this, he prepared to leave. Just then he glanced up toward the towers. He almost wished that he had not. A city guard was leaning over the battlements and gazing down on the river below. Over the noise of the river, Jonathan thought he heard a shout from above. Had he been spotted?

But he was already drifting rapidly downstream, and in a few seconds the towers were overtop of him. Remembering Ragnar's advice, he tried to propel himself towards the left bank. Since the others had trouble climbing over the net of chains, he searched underneath it, straining his eyes in the darkness to figure out the appropriate time and place to dive.

There it was!

He could see why the others had encountered difficulties. Sticks, twigs, logs, and bits of slimy riverweed had collected against the chains, making them slippery and blocking all the holes. The water flowed underneath the blockage.

He inhaled deeply and plunged below the surface. A sharp pain exploded on the side of his head as something hard bumped into his skull. In his distress he nearly exhaled. He felt around to locate the object that he had run into and found that it was a piece of chain, but much thicker than he had expected. Then, to its left he discovered a hole.

Was it big enough? Grasping its edges, he started pulling himself through, but he got stuck. He struggled until he found the reason. His sword hilt had caught in the chain!

His lungs ached for air and he was starting to panic, but bending double he pushed himself backwards until he worked the hilt loose. Then pushing forward again he was through the hole.

When his head broke the surface, he gasped, relieved to breathe again. It took him a moment to orient himself. Brushing the water from his eyes, he looked up.

He was inside the town and the towers were behind him and receding rapidly. However, he could also see a group of people assembled on top of one of the towers. Suddenly he heard a splash behind him then another a second later.

Arrows! A third came, then a fourth. They were all near misses. Probably it was the speed of the current that had saved him. Taking a deep breath he dove under the surface again, the weight of his sword carrying him down.

Several more arrows splashed into the water. Then abruptly they stopped. He guessed that his foes could no longer see where he was.

He stayed down below until his lungs hurt. Then exhaling, he rose to the surface. Greedily he inhaled. Again the arrows streamed down. He dove again. Once he was under the water, the arrows ceased. When he rose, again they fell.

Fortunately, the river's current had now carried him around a bend to the west, and he was finally hidden from the tower. He was safe, at least for the moment. The docks were quite close now, looming on the river's left-hand shore as Ragnar had said. But in his flight, he had drifted towards the middle of the stream, and it took some effort to move himself back to the left bank.

A rope from one of the docks trailed into the river. Jonathan caught the end of it and, breathing a sigh of relief, pulled himself towards land. Safe at last!

On either side of him, two boats gently bumped against the posts to which they were secured. A hand reached down into the river to pull him to the dock. Eagerly he grasped it. The hand hoisted him upwards.

It felt good to have his feet on solid ground again.

But the hand holding him refused to let go. Rather it tightened its grip, moving around to pin him from behind. This puzzled Jonathan. With his other hand he brushed the wet hair from his face, and when he opened his eyes he understood.

Five city guardsmen faced him. He had been caught.

# 13 A SURPRISING EXIT

Jonathan struggled but they held him firmly. They yanked him off the dock and dragged him through the city streets. He decided to quit resisting. If they thought that he had given up trying to get away, they might relax their grip and he would have more chance to break away.

"What's your name, lad?" said the leader as they pulled him along.

"Cedrik," he replied. "Why are you arresting me?" But they gave him no answer.

A hot anger rose inside of him. He had been made a captive twice in the past month and he resolved that it would not happen again. Yet there were no apparent escape routes at the moment. Prison, it seemed, was inevitable.

On their way down the street a hooded and cloaked figure rose from one of the doorways in front of them and staggered over. "Excuuze me, shirs. Can you show me the way to the nearesht inn?"

The soldiers quickened their march, intent on

ignoring the stranger, but he persisted. They were just going past him when he suddenly tripped one of the guards gripping Jonathan. The soldier collapsed with the drunk on top of him. The grip of the remaining soldier holding Jonathan loosened. Seizing his opportunity, he slipped free!

"Shorry," gasped the drunken man as Jonathan fled down the street.

"Grab him!" yelled the captain.

Jonathan ran. Fortunately, having studied Anastasis' map, he was not completely lost. The guards, of course, knew the city better than he did, but the one factor he had in his favour was that he could outrun armour-clad soldiers. And he did.

As he ran, he hung onto his sword so that it would not trip him. At one point, he passed a lit lantern in a shop window, and looking back, he saw that the water dripping from him was leaving a clear trail on the cobblestones. *I need to find a place where my tracks aren't visible.*

Eventually he found a small park about fifty yards square. Thinking that the grass would conceal his water trail, he ran the length of the park and finally hid behind a tree. Standing there he tried to wring out his wet clothes. Then, seeing no immediate pursuit, he slipped into a darker alleyway, hoping that he was shedding less water than before. He did not want to continue running in case it attracted attention, and since he seemed to have lost his pursuers, he slowed to a walking pace. Carefully, creeping from shadow to shadow, he made his way to the rendezvous point.

The church graveyard lay within a large triangular-shaped depression about ten feet down from the street level. To get there, he had to hop over a gate and descend some stone steps onto a dirt path. Stone walls entirely surrounded the edge of the triangle, serving the dual purpose of protecting the graveyard and holding the cobblestones from the nearby streets in place. In some places tombs had been hollowed out of the wall, and he discovered Ragnar, Philip, Charissa and the rest of his companions waiting for him, in one of these hollowed-out caves, overshadowed by the street above. The relieved tone in their voices told him that they had been worried. He quickly described what had happened.

"We have to get to the Dancing Duck," said Ragnar when he had finished. "Fortunately it's run by a friend of mine, but there is no time to lose."

Following Ragnar the group moved through back alleys and deserted streets towards a large house identified by a lit lantern dangling from a duck-shaped sign over the roadway. They knocked once. No one answered. Ragnar, nervous about the noise made by knocking, tried the door instead. It was unlocked. Opening it, he led them in.

Inside the house everything was in darkness except for a fire in the next room. Ragnar searched the mantelpiece. A moment later he said, "I found a note. It reads: 'Be careful. Danger is close by. I'm going to get help—Lambert.' Lambert meant to meet us here," Ragnar said, "but we have to assume that he may not be back in time to aid us. I only hope that our coming here was not noticed by the watch. At least we arrived in darkness and likely then we will be safe enough here tonight."

Philip and Charissa found a couple of lanterns

and lit them. The others draped their wet clothes over nearby chairs, wrapped themselves in blankets and gathered in front of the fire. They were discussing where to sleep when a knock came at the door. No one moved. Jonathan had visions of the same city watchmen that he had escaped from earlier now standing impatiently outside.

The knock came again, louder this time.

"Jonathan," hissed Ragnar, "get down to the cellar." He waved his arm towards a room that Jonathan had not yet visited. His friends joined him in search of the cellar while Philip and Ragnar stayed above.

The first room they entered was a kitchen. Fortunately, Rannulf had thought to bring one of the lanterns, and its light revealed a trapdoor in the floor. When they opened it, they saw a ladder disappearing into the darkness. In a moment they had descended and were standing on a bare earthen floor, listening to the noises above—loud voices, then shouting and some brief laughter.

"Has the city watch arrived?" asked Rannulf. "Ragnar wouldn't sell us out, would he?" Footsteps boomed on the ceiling above their heads.

Jonathan looked for a place to hide. A stack of wooden crates stood in the corner, but he did not know if he had enough time to get behind them without making too much noise. He was just about to take his chances with the crates anyhow, when the trapdoor opened and a voice boomed, "Where is he? I want to see him myself." Slowly two legs descended the ladder, followed by a light grey cloak with a hood.

Jonathan was strongly tempted to rush forward and attack before the man could strike back. Yet something restrained him. At the very least, he decided, the stranger deserved a fair fight. It would be wrong to attack him until he had reached the floor.

Nonetheless, Jonathan drew his sword and his friends drew theirs. The stranger was on the ground now. He turned around. A tall but slightly overweight man in his late forties confronted them. His brown hair and beard were streaked with grey. A hawk-like nose underneath piercing blue eyes peered out from a face that Jonathan thought was commanding but kind.

But when Jonathan saw the man, he nearly dropped his sword in amazement. This was the drunk he had met on the street earlier that night, the man who had allowed him to escape. He was obviously drunk no longer, if he had ever been drunk at all. At the moment a smile creased his face from ear to ear.

Ragnar, who had followed the man down the ladder, also smiled. He took Jonathan by the shoulder and moved him towards the stranger. "This is the boy, your Lordship. Jonathan, I want to introduce you to your uncle, the Lord Gorwin, Duke of Eastmarch."

"Hello, Jonathan," said Gorwin. There was no slurring of words now. "It's nice to see you again."

"Hello," Jonathan stammered. This was a complete shock. He had not expected to see his uncle for a week or more yet. It was doubly shocking that the two of them had already met. He was at a total loss for words.

In the past two weeks it had seemed that the distance between him and his uncle could not be travelled fast enough, but now that they stood face to face, he did not feel ready for the encounter. He wished he would have had more time—time for what, he was not sure. Just time.

Gorwin gave Jonathan a huge bear hug, pinning his arms to his sides. Jonathan's sword fell clattering to the floor.

"At last!" said Gorwin. Then he put both hands on Jonathan's shoulders and looked him in the face. "Yes, yes. He has his mother's looks about him and his father's height, too. Or he will, I reckon. Ragnar, I am eternally in your debt. And you," said Gorwin, turning to Jonathan, "it's good to see you safe!"

"Uh . . . thanks," was all Jonathan could think to say.

Gorwin stepped back a pace while Jonathan bent to pick up his sword. "Ragnar has treated you well, I trust?" He shot a grin at the knight.

"Uh . . . very well."

"Good. I hear that these are friends of yours," he gestured towards Olaf, Charissa, Rannulf and Sonja.

"Uh . . . yes," said Jonathan. He felt a little tongue-tied and was uncomfortable with all the hugging. Still he managed to stammer out the names of his friends, who themselves looked sheepish and awkward.

"How was your trip here?"

Jonathan paused to reflect on the fact that he had never before in his life been shot at with arrows, put in prison twice, several times had to crawl underground, swim a river and been drugged by darts. "All right," was all he said.

"Good. Glad you made it. Well, boy, we have a lot of catching up to do and we will do it soon, but for now we have to look to our immediate concerns. Ragnar, you and I should allow these folks to get some sleep. We'll be on our way again as soon as possible."

Jonathan stood smiling and feeling foolish while Gorwin climbed the ladder. Ragnar followed.

Once his uncle was gone, he sat down heavily on a crate and exhaled loudly. Olaf, grinning broadly, shook his hand. "Congratulations! It looks as if you've finally met your family."

"Uh. . . I suppose . . ." said Jonathan.

The group of friends took their time before climbing the ladder to the kitchen. When he got to the top, Jonathan heard voices in a third room, which he had not yet entered. Curious, he stood in the doorway and saw not just Ragnar and Gorwin but a number of other strange men gathered there, too. Immediately he could see a difference between Gorwin and Ragnar. While Ragnar had always seemed intense and almost a bit gruff, Gorwin was clearly at ease and put others at ease. It seemed that at any moment he could burst into a laugh, but at the same time he had a commanding presence. Jonathan understood why people would want to follow him.

Gorwin turned, and spying Jonathan in the doorway, he smiled and introduced him to one of the strangers. "Jonathan, this is our host, Lambert."

"Thank you for your hospitality," said Jonathan.

"You are most welcome," said Lambert with a large smile. "Make yourselves at home. You are my only guests at the moment."

Gorwin then resumed his discussion with Lambert and the others, but although Jonathan tried to follow their speech, he found it difficult to concentrate. The fact that he had just met his uncle for the first time was making his head spin. So after exchanging pleasantries, he excused himself and wandered back to his place in front of the fire. Curled up inside a warm blanket, he eventually drifted into sleep.

When he woke, it was still dark outside, and he guessed that it must have been a noise that had wakened him. He lay quietly, listening for anything unusual. After a while he heard someone attempting to enter through the door at the corridor's far end.

For a moment he remained lying on his blankets then reached over and shook Olaf. "Are you asleep?" he whispered.

"Yes," came the response.

"There's someone trying to break in. What do we do?"

Olaf groaned and rolled over. "I guess we check it out."

The two of them rose, grabbed long sticks from the woodpile, and creeping silently to the end of the hallway, hid in a corner. When they saw the light from a lantern advancing towards them, they prepared to strike.

With a yell, Jonathan leapt forward, his stick raised above his head, and found himself facing a monk—or someone dressed as one in a brown cowl with its hood thrown back. The poor man was so startled by Jonathan's sudden jump that he almost dropped his lantern. Backing up to the nearest wall, he shielded his face with an arm.

"Who are you?" asked Olaf.

"Brother Richard," said the monk. "Is Gorwin here?"

They profusely apologized for startling him and escorted him upstairs to where Gorwin was sleeping.

"Richard!" exclaimed Gorwin when he had been wakened.

The two men then began conversing in a strange language. Jonathan found the sounds intriguing, and from time to time it seemed that he could understand some of the words being spoken, though certainly not all of them.

Most of the others in the house had now awakened, and Gorwin spoke in regular language. "Richard comes with bad news. St. Anselm's monastery has been attacked."

"What!?" exclaimed Jonathan, "how?"

"The Dragikoi," said Richard. "Their attack came a few days ago. Fortunately the damage was fairly light."

"What happened?" asked Ragnar.

"During the attack some of the Dragikoi lit torches and launched flaming arrows over top of the walls. A few thatched roofs caught fire," said Richard. "We extinguished most of these quickly, although two small huts did burn to the ground. Even so, it could have been a lot worse."

There was much discussion of Richard's news, but Gorwin eventually interrupted. "There's a lot of night left here, and we need our rest," he said. "I think we should all return to our blankets. We can talk more in the morning."

They followed his advice, but Jonathan found it difficult to get back to sleep. He stayed awake worrying about the monastery and about Hugh who had been left behind. He suspected that this attack had taken place because of him, and he vowed that if he ever had the personal means to compensate these monks, he would do so.

When he woke some hours later Jonathan could not remember where he was. Daylight peered in through the window shutters. He lifted his head from the wooden floor and saw Rannulf and Olaf sleeping in different corners of the room. Then he recalled the midnight swim, Gorwin, Lambert, and finally Brother Richard.

Getting up, he tiptoed into the kitchen, carefully closing the door behind him. Ragnar was already awake and making a fire in the fireplace. Jonathan helped him, handing him kindling as he needed it, and in a few minutes Lambert arrived to cook the morning meal.

During breakfast in the main dining hall Jonathan learned more about St. Anselm's from Brother Richard. It turned out that the three Dragikoi who had been wounded while attacking their own company and left on the road, had not been rescued by their Dragikoi companions. Instead Fredrick had found them a day later and brought them to the monastery where they were being nursed back to health.

"It was probably those three who saved us," said Richard. "During the worst part of the attack, one of the wounded Dragikoi showed his face over top of the battlements. Once his comrades saw him, they abruptly gave up their attack and left us alone."

This gave Jonathan a lot to think about. Apparently Fredrick's act of mercy on the road had not been wasted.

After breakfast Gorwin announced that they would rest there during the day and leave in the evening. He was worried that if they stayed much longer the city watch might find them.

Resting was fine with Jonathan, but the remainder of the day was one of the dullest that he had experienced since being out of prison. While his companions were put to work around the inn, because he had been spotted by the city guards, he was sent down to the cellar with one of Lambert's books. They did not want him to be seen.

"Go practise your lute or something," said Ragnar. "Relax."

"Relax? Music is my work," said Jonathan. "I don't do it to relax. I'll read the book."

He had taken some schooling in the Rindorn monastery as a child, but had never gone much beyond basic reading and simple arithmetic, so he welcomed any reading practice that he could get. Nevertheless, even with the book it seemed as if the day took forever to pass. Several times he found himself pacing around the room. He even tried practising the Dragikoi's attack patterns but found it difficult in the cellar's confined space. He tried playing his lute, but that too grew tiresome. He wished he could be involved in planning their next move. Where were they going next? Now that Gorwin had arrived, he also wondered if Charissa would be invited to come with them back to his castle. He hoped so. But if not, he hoped that he would have a chance to say goodbye to her before she left.

At last Olaf opened the trap door and descended into the cellar. "The kitchen's getting busy," he said, "and they need your help. I'll show you the secret way upstairs."

Jonathan followed Olaf through another exit from the cellar up a stairway and into a closed off area where he was put to work chopping vegetables with Rannulf and Sonja. In a corner of the room sat two of the men who had been with Gorwin the night before, and he thought he heard the men mention Charissa's name. Without appearing too obvious, he gradually moved his chopping board and vegetables to within earshot, but by then the conversation had shifted to discussing the local popular sport, pig-sticking. Then the men left.

The time passed swiftly in the kitchen and he was caught off guard when Olaf appeared a while later carrying a large tray. "Here's supper," he told the group. "Oh, and by the way, we'll be leaving in half an hour."

Jonathan bolted down his food then went downstairs to collect his few belongings, but it was another hour before he was summoned again. The regular patrons were gone and the two men at arms that Jonathan had seen in the kitchen were heading out into the night.

"What's happening?" he asked.

Philip answered his question. "Our escape route is blocked. Guards are doing house searches, standing at the city gates and throughout the countryside, but we will use the secret passage through the cellars of Dorinon Castle that the hermit told us about. We hope that this route will get us out of the city without being seen."

Philip talked about breaking into the castle as calmly as if he had suggested they go for an evening stroll. his concerned Jonathan. He knew that the castle-route would be dangerous, perhaps almost as dangerous as going across the country and hiding from the guards. Ragnar and Philip could be brave, but he hoped they were not just being foolhardy. "But won't the castle be guarded as well?" he asked.

Ragnar spoke, "We've learned that most of the castle guards have been taken off their regular duties in order to watch the gates and the country roads for us. They won't expect us to go this way. Yes, it will be risky, but it's probably our least risky option. If we had time, we could have come up with a cleverer plan—disguising ourselves perhaps and sneaking in. Yet, since time is short, it looks as if we'll need to take the hermit's advice. We'll just have to be careful."

"But do we know that this passage is still secret?" said Jonathan. "Won't the Duke have found out about it by now?"

"Not likely," said Philip, joining in. "The current Duke hasn't been in residence very long. In fact, we probably know more about it than he does."

"How's that?"

"We have our sources," said Philip in a tone of voice that discouraged further questions. Ragnar interrupted with instructions for Jonathan and Sonja. "Since we will be crawling underground, I'd advise you to leave your musical instruments here with Lambert. He'll bring them the next time he travels to Gorwin's castle."

Jonathan felt uneasy. Once more he was being thrown into a dangerous situation that he could not avoid. As a street kid in Rindorn, he might have been poor, but he had at least had some kind of control over his life. Yet it seemed that ever since that day at the inn when Vonich had awakened him, he had ceased to be free and instead become a pawn in a chess game moving at someone else's command.

After Philip paid Lambert for their stay and for

the transport of Sonja and Jonathan's instruments, they shouldered their packs and followed Gorwin out the stable door into the moonlit streets of Dorinon.

Jonathan was relieved to see Charissa travelling with them, and as they walked he fell into step beside her. "You're coming with us?" he whispered. "I thought you were going to be meeting your father's soldiers here in Dorinon."

"Gorwin thought that it would be too dangerous for me to meet my father's soldiers here in case they asked uncomfortable questions," she whispered back. "Everybody is searching for you right now, so it looks as if I'm along for a few more days yet."

"How are you going to get home then?" asked Jonathan.

"I'll probably take a boat back once we make it to your uncle's castle."

"But how . . ."

Ragnar turned and put a finger to his lips. This annoyed Jonathan, but his annoyance could not overshadow his happiness at being with Charissa once more.

Using dimly lit streets and hugging the shadows as much as possible, Gorwin led them through a confusing network of roads until they reached the rear of the Cathedral. As they paused there, sheltering in the shadows between two support buttresses, he beckoned them closer.

"That's Dorinon castle," he whispered, pointing. Jonathan glanced up. The castle stood on a giant stone hill in the middle of the city. If enemies were to attack it, they would not only have to climb the cliffs on which it was built, but at the top they would have to penetrate the three walls that surrounded it.

Gorwin spoke again: "The Castle and Crown is two furlongs hence, at the bottom of this cliff." He turned and walked down the street towards the inn.

When they arrived, Jonathan could tell just by looking at the place that it served a rougher sort of clientele, and he was not surprised when hostile looks greeted them as they entered. They sat at a table away from the regular crowd and waited to be approached by the serving staff. Jonathan leaned towards Gorwin. "How are we going to get down to the cellars?"

"I'm not sure, but I'll think of something," he said grinning back. "But you know, if a brawl happened to occur, perhaps we could slip downstairs unnoticed."

"I don't think you'll have to wait long for that here," said Jonathan as one of the customers gave him an especially dirty look.

Jonathan had started a number of brawls in his day, as he had found it an effective tactic for escaping detection by the Rindorn watch. He wondered if his expertise would have to be drawn upon tonight.

But he need not have worried. When he looked up, ten of the rougher-looking patrons were already swaggering over to their table. Some were brandishing knives and clubs.

# 14 THE CASTLE AND CROWN

It looked as if the group of regulars was going to demand that the travellers leave, but as they approached, an empty pewter drinking mug, which had been probably aimed at the newcomers, came flying across the room and nailed one of the locals in the head.

The injured man spun around. "Who threw that?" he bellowed. "Dick, was that you?" He strode rapidly back towards his suspect. Dick had no chance to answer though, as a similarly sized pewter mug was picked up and hurled in his general direction. Within moments a full-fledged brawl had erupted.

"Now's our chance," said Gorwin quietly. He rose and the travellers followed him without a word to the inn's kitchen. Fortunately the cook had abandoned his post to join in the melee, and there was enough firelight to see a narrow stairway descending into the cellars.

"Jonathan," said Gorwin, "you and Olaf stay here and monitor the confusion next door. If it subsides, warn us. The rest of you, follow me." From his pack Gorwin took a candle and lit it in the fireplace. Then he went down the stairs.

After the two friends watched the others disappear they poked their heads into the main dining room just in time to see one of the lanterns get knocked over. A small patch of oil began spreading onto the wooden floor before bursting into flame. The inn's owner, who had ducked behind the bar to avoid flying objects, came rushing out with a damp potato sack to beat out the flames. Jonathan and Olaf pulled back into the kitchen.

"That was close," said Olaf. "There better be a real exit from this cellar. Any more falling lanterns and things will be getting too hot for us—in more ways than one. We should let Gorwin know what's happening." He then went down the stairway. Jonathan followed. There was now enough noise and confusion above them that he figured that they didn't need to worry about being discovered for a while.

Gorwin had found a lantern and a torch in the cellar and when Jonathan and Olaf arrived, Ragnar was barking out instructions to look for trapdoors in the floor and hollow spaces behind walls.

For the next ten minutes they all tapped on the walls and moved aside wine barrels to search the floor but nothing of interest turned up. As the minutes passed with no success, their search became more frantic, and Jonathan started wondering if the hermit had misled them.

But at last he made a discovery. The cellar area contained a separate room, which they had already searched, but by chance, when he entered it one more time, he happened to glance upwards. The ceiling here, like most ceilings in the inn, was made of long thick planks of oak. Yet, in one corner the planks had been cut off, leaving smaller pieces, which formed a rough square, two feet by two feet on both sides. Perhaps the trapdoor they were looking for was in the ceiling, not the floor!

Jonathan grabbed Gorwin's arm and silently pointed.

"Philip, give me your staff," called Gorwin.

Gorwin took the staff from Philip and commenced tapping on the ceiling. When he tapped on the corner, the sound changed from a dull thud to a hollow boom.

"Quick, bring some barrels!" commanded Gorwin. Soon a stack of barrels reached almost to the ceiling and Philip and Olaf were standing at the very top, heaving upward on the trapdoor.

The part of the roof that they pushed started to move, shifting an inch or two. Yet no matter how hard they pushed, it would not move any further.

"There's a bolt or something locking it on the other side," said Olaf. "We'll need an axe."

Then Jonathan understood. The passage that they were attempting to enter had not been created as a secret entrance into the castle. Rather, it was an exit from the castle, an escape route for the Duke and his family.

Ragnar, who carried a hatchet that he used for making kindling, climbed up to replace Olaf and Philip at the top of the barrel stack. Jonathan, holding the lantern for him below as he worked away at the trapdoor, had to close his eyes so that they did not fill with wood slivers.

It was slow going. The oak planks were old and

hard and would not chip easily. An echoing boom also resounded throughout the cellar every time that Ragnar struck the boards.

"Let's hope they can't hear that upstairs," Ragnar muttered. He stopped chipping and listened. There seemed to be much less noise coming from above than there had been a few minutes before. "Jonathan," he said. "Check what's going on up there. The rest of you can help clean these wood chips— nothing like leaving a note telling them where we've gone."

Jonathan gave the lantern to Rannulf and carefully climbed back up to the kitchen. As he lifted his head above the floor, he could no longer hear fighting, but someone in the inn's main room was shouting orders. It sounded as if the watch had arrived. The situation for Jonathan and his friends was now worse.

*How will it be possible to continue chipping through the planks without attracting attention?* he wondered.

As if in answer to his own thought he saw a pile of candles lying on a nearby stool. A candle would not burn very much of the trap door, he realized, but it could burn some of it. If nothing else, the soot from the candles would partly disguise their hatchet marks.

When he re-joined his friends below, he told them what he had heard and explained his plan with the candles. Gorwin and Ragnar thought it would work better than he had imagined. While Jonathan had been upstairs, Ragnar had been whittling with his dagger and had punctured a small hole through the trapdoor to the opening above.

From then on they alternated between burning

and whittling, and within ten minutes there was enough space for Charissa's small hand to reach through to the other side and pull back the bolt that held the trapdoor secure. After that she could easily push it open.

"You'd better go first, Jonathan," said Gorwin. "And just in case, here's this." He handed Jonathan a rope from inside his satchel. Jonathan draped it over his shoulder and climbed up through the hole.

Once he was through the trapdoor, he tried to stand upright but his head struck something above. Charissa passed the lantern to him and its light reflected off her bright blue eyes. Once he had light he saw that he was in a small cave with rock walls, a wooden floor and a low ceiling. From one end of the cave, stairs angled upwards into the darkness.

The others climbing up after him soon filled the cramped room, and Jonathan volunteered to climb farther. After another twenty yards he arrived at a landing, and at this point the passage ran nearly straight upwards. Fortunately, metal rungs had been pounded into the wall to serve as a ladder, but it was difficult climbing and holding onto the lantern at the same time.

At the top Jonathan found himself on a second landing beneath a staircase that led to another trap door. He tied the rope onto the lantern's handle and gently lowered it to give light for the others behind him.

Philip now asked Sonja to climb the final stairway and listen at the trapdoor. She put her ear next to the wood and froze there motionless while the others stood by. "I hear voices in the distance," she said at last, "but they don't seem to be directly above us."

Then Sonja stepped down, allowing Gorwin to ascend the remaining stairs. After listening for a while, he pushed upwards. By chance the trapdoor opened freely. Gorwin lifted it a crack and looked around. Then in a move that made Jonathan wince, he raised it completely and climbed out of view.

His face reappeared at the top of the stairway a minute later. "It's fine," he whispered, beckoning them to follow. "Put out the lantern."

When they emerged, they discovered that they were standing within the base of a round tower. The door to the outside world stood open. Charissa poked her head out. "No guards in sight," she said quietly.

"They are probably all on the castle's outside wall," said Gorwin. "This tower is on the middle wall."

No one said anything. Ahead of them loomed a twenty-five-foot-high stone barrier, the castle's inner wall, which they had yet to climb.

The castle's middle set of walls and its inner walls were only fifty feet apart, and the travellers slipped across the courtyard one by one. Jonathan came last, and seeing that Gorwin was already feeling for handholds, he quickly moved to his side. "Let me do this," he whispered.

"Are you sure?" His uncle sounded surprised.

Jonathan nodded. "I've done this kind of thing before."

Gorwin tied the end of the rope onto Jonathan's belt. "Give it a try then," he said.

The moon had risen, but the section of the wall Gorwin had chosen was in the shadow of a tower, so Jonathan's task was made more difficult. He could not see well and had to go by feel, and in order to remain as silent as possible, he could not afford to slip or dislodge any stones.

Five agonizing minutes passed as he tested his hand and footholds, slowly climbing to the wall's crest. But once there, he secured the rope, and the others quickly ascended. From the top of the wall they looked out at the rest of the castle. As of yet, no one seemed to have spotted them.

In order to play the pranks that had made him infamous, Jonathan had snuck into most of the important buildings in Rindorn at one time or another, though he had never been inside a castle. But now, gazing down into the courtyard, he was almost disappointed. He had expected that the castle would be a building of special magnificence with marble flagstones and perhaps even a silver fountain or a wrought iron gate. Instead he looked down onto a very ordinary courtyard bounded by four walls and four towers with perhaps eighty yards between them. A post with a lit lantern stood next to a well, and by its light he could see several sheds and smaller buildings built beside the walls. Against the far wall, a larger stone building, fifty yards long, rose three storeys into the air. This had to be the Duke's residence, he thought.

They crouched behind the battlements while Gorwin searched for the best way down. Finding a route, he dropped the rope into the courtyard on the other side.

"I'll take the rear again," said Jonathan.

"Fine," said Gorwin, "but you'll need to untie the rope before descending. How are you at climbing *down* walls?"

Jonathan made no answer. Truthfully he did not know. Every wall was different. He watched as Gorwin and his friends used the rope to slither to the ground. Then it was his turn. Working quickly, he untied the rope and let it drop onto his waiting companions. Finally he began his descent.

It was easier than he expected. The castle walls had been built to protect from attack from the outside—not to keep people in. Consequently, the inner wall had a slight slant. Nevertheless, it was difficult to climb down while remaining quiet.

"Well done," whispered Philip as he reached the bottom.

He found the others huddled between the wall and two thatched sheds—probably stables by the smell of them. Ragnar had gone ahead to investigate. A moment later he returned and seeing that Jonathan had made the descent successfully, he signalled the group to follow him.

Nervously they hugged the shadows, working their way one by one toward the castle at the farthest end of the courtyard. The worst moment came when the door to one of the out buildings suddenly opened right in front of Philip, and two men-at-arms with lanterns stepped out. Philip fortunately kept his head and ducked into a nearby alcove. Hearts racing, the rest of the travellers froze in their places.

The soldiers laughed and talked as they walked towards an open archway in one of the towers. Jonathan watched as the lantern light disappeared up a wooden ladder inside and wondered if he had just witnessed the changing of the guard. Sure enough, a few minutes later, two different men-at-arms descended from the tower. They trudged back across the courtyard to the same building that the first guards had emerged from and went inside, shutting the door behind them. Once again there was silence.

After this scare no one was terribly eager to go on, but ahead they could see an open window on castle's the ground floor, and finally Sonja first made the first bold move, slowly tiptoeing toward it. This stirred the rest of them to action, and miraculously, they saw no more guards.

When they had all gathered near the window, Gorwin whispered, "I'll take you inside in pairs. If the alarm is raised, do not wait for us. Make your escape as best as you can." Gorwin took Rannulf and Sonja with him first. When he re-appeared at the window a few moments later, he looked less worried than before. "No guards to be seen," he said.

He departed with the rest of them two at a time until it was Jonathan's turn to sneak through the house behind Gorwin's silhouette. There was little light to guide them. Occasionally they would pass a blazing wall sconce, but in those areas they kept out of sight as much as possible. If not for his nervousness, Jonathan would have been quite interested in the surroundings. As opposed to the courtyard, the inside of the house was very ornate, and he wished he had the chance to examine it more.

Their only real scare came when they had to pass through the lighted dining hall. The meal had obviously recently finished, and moments after they entered, they heard a commotion beyond the archway at the room's far end. Gorwin had barely time to duck behind one of the doors. Jonathan crouched underneath one end of the table before a servant came in and began to clear the table. Then, spying a platter of mutton, the man put down his tray of dishes, checked to see that no one was looking and cut himself a knucklebone. Unfortunately, while doing this he overturned a wine jug and its contents started to drip through a crack in the table onto Jonathan's head. He was very tempted to move to avoid being dripped on, but he realized that if he did so, the sound of wine splashing onto the floor might alert the servant. Instead, Jonathan put out his hand to catch the droplets.

Much to their relief, the servant eventually left and Jonathan, still under the table, tried not to let his anxious breathing become too noisy.

Gorwin stepped forward. "Come," he whispered.

As quietly as he could, Jonathan got to his feet and followed his uncle out the door at the hall's northeast corner. This led them into a pantry, and immediately on their left a wooden stairway led down into the cellars. Jonathan followed as Gorwin vanished into the darkness below.

With only Gorwin's whispers to guide him, he felt his way downwards and forwards, wincing whenever a step creaked beneath his weight. Eventually his feet told him that they were on a solid stone floor. A glimmer of light ahead announced a single lit candle in a holder. Tired of running into things, as Jonathan passed it he grabbed it and took it with them.

They wound their way past cellars and dungeons, the light making it easier to travel but increasing the danger of discovery. Finally they entered a narrow corridor that ended in two doors, one on the right and the other directly in front of them. Gorwin knocked on the side door three times in a rhythmic pattern, and a moment later the door opened. There, within a small room, sat the rest of the travellers. They seemed relieved to see Gorwin and Jonathan and not the palace guards.

"Good," said Ragnar. "Shall we go then?"

Soundlessly the group got up and filed out into the narrow corridor. Ragnar opened one of his belt pouches and from within removed a single key that he inserted into the other door's keyhole.

"Where did you get that?" asked Jonathan, surprised that an outsider would be carrying keys to the Duke's house. But Ragnar only gestured for him to be silent and persisted with his work. For a few moments he struggled but at last with a squeak and a scraping sound the lock turned.

What happened next was quite different from anything Jonathan expected. When Ragnar opened the door, the corridor they stood in was flooded with a blinding white light. It came from the room in front of them.

"Quick," said Ragnar, practically shoving Philip inside. Like the rest of the group, Jonathan stumbled through the door and then stood shielding his eyes from the change in light. Gorwin shut the door behind them.

When his eyes had adjusted, Jonathan saw that he was in a room with a glowing white ceiling. Some of the walls and the floor panels glowed as well, though not with the intense brightness of the ceiling panels. In the room's centre stood a wooden desk and a chair. On the desk lay a book, a lantern, and a feather pen sticking into the top of an inkwell, although it looked as if the ink had long dried up. On one of the walls there hung a helmet with a small heraldic crest emblazoned on it—a bird above a book above a sword.

Finally, in one corner he could see a small doorway only two feet wide and four feet in height, but it was nearly indistinguishable from the walls around it since it, too, was made from the glowing white material. Jonathan had the same awestruck feeling that he had when they had visited the island library with its magically opening doors. Clearly there was a mystery here.

"Why is this room lit like this?" asked Jonathan.

"It is part of a much older building," said Gorwin. "The ancients once had a fortress here. Most of it was destroyed in the Founders' Wars. This is the only room left, and the Duke's palace was built around it."

Jonathan was silent for a moment as he tried to imagine how the rest of the fortress would have looked in the days before the Founders' Wars.

Meanwhile, Gorwin, Ragnar and Philip focussed on the tasks at hand. Ragnar and Philip began tapping the walls as if they were looking for hollow spots. Gorwin took the chair from behind the desk and moved it underneath the helmet. Then standing on the chair, he took out his dagger and cut at the leather straps holding the helmet to the wooden frame behind it.

"This at last will be returned to our ancestral house," he said when he had severed the straps. He gave the helmet to Jonathan and added, "Carry this safely until we reach my castle."

Jonathan handed his burning candle to Charissa and took the helmet from Gorwin's hands. Almost as soon as he had done so, they heard a sound from beyond the door through which they had entered. Ragnar made a wide gesture in the air with his arms, signalling for everyone to be quiet, but there was no need. They were all staring at the door apprehensively.

Then the door began to move. Like lightning Philip and Ragnar hurled themselves towards it. Philip reached it first and slammed his body into it, but he could not quite close it. A man's arm had reached around blocking it from being sealed. Philip tried again, and this time from behind the door there was a bellow of pain. The arm was withdrawn and Philip slammed the door shut. For a moment or two no sound came from the party behind the door, and Jonathan guessed that they had been surprised to find the room full of occupants.

"Apparently," said Gorwin, "this castle's inhabitants know more about this secret room than we had supposed. We need to barricade this entrance."

Taking advantage of the lull in action, Philip looked around for something to wedge against the door. "The chair!" he called out, gesturing with his head.

Olaf, who was nearest, quickly employed the chair as a doorstop. No sooner had he set it in place when those outside started trying to beat the door down. BOOM! BOOM! With every echoing thud Jonathan felt a chill of fear travel down his spine. He remembered all too clearly his room door being attacked on that disastrous day in Rindorn some weeks earlier. Quickly he set the ceremonial helmet down next to the wall and drew his sword.

Philip was trying to use the support from the

chair and the pressure from his body to keep the entrance sealed. Gorwin, Olaf and Sonya were busy dragging the desk over to act as an extra brace when Ragnar yelled to Jonathan. "The other door!"

For a split second Jonathan was confused. Then he understood that Ragnar was talking about the smaller doorway whose outline he had seen earlier—obviously a possible exit. He sheathed his sword and sprinted towards it, but there was a problem—no handle.

He tried pushing. No good. Then he searched for a way to pull on something, but he could not see how to do that either. Meanwhile the blows from outside grew more determined. The barrier, he knew, would not last much longer. In frustration he kicked at the exit door, which only hurt his foot. Then he had a thought. In tales, these kinds of portals always had some kind of secret catch or lever. Frantically he felt the nearby walls for loose panels or anything out of the ordinary. But nothing that he tried revealed any secrets.

A grinding and crashing from behind made him glance around. Their entry door had slid open a few inches, thrusting the desk and the chair back. Then with a crash it flew open. Nine guards leapt into the room!

# 15 A JOURNEY UNDERGROUND

Swords were drawn on all sides. Yet something was wrong. Their enemies were not pressing forward in the way that Jonathan might have expected. Then he realized that their eyes were getting used to the light as his own had earlier.

Ragnar shouted above the din, "Find an exit!"

Once more, Jonathan tried the various panels in and around the door, but it was not until he reached above the door that one of the wall panels gave way. Behind it he found a lever. He tried pulling, but it was stiff and would not budge. Then placing both hands on it, he used his full weight to pull it down. Wonder of wonders, the exit slid open.

Not a moment too soon. There was a sharp clang beside his ear as a sword came swinging towards his head, missing him and striking the wall. Olaf quickly engaged Jonathan's attacker, freeing him to investigate the other side of the doorway. Enough light from the room shone into the opening to show him that a staircase led down into a rough-hewn cave.

He glanced back towards the melee. Three of the enemy soldiers had already dropped out, their sword arms made useless by mild wounds.

He was amazed that there were not more casualties, but the fact that their enemies had been half blind at the fight's outset had certainly helped Jonathan's friends. It also seemed that his own side was parrying and not truly aiming to kill. Fortunately all of the travellers were unscathed.

Feeling left out of the combat, he drew his sword and rushed into the room trying to engage a man who had just stepped up to battle Sonja. But his attempt at chivalry was abruptly cut short by Ragnar's bellow from behind.

"Quick! The exit!"

Obediently, Sonja turned and disappeared through the door that Jonathan had just opened. Olaf also backed slowly towards that opening, all the while parrying his opponent's sword strokes. Out of the corner of his eye Jonathan could see Charissa vanish through the exit. Then not wanting to be left alone to fight a room full of enemies, he followed her.

But as he did so, he noticed that the helmet was still sitting where he had left it—up against the wall on the right—and he would have to advance into the thick of his enemies to retrieve it. Inwardly cursing himself for forgetting it, he re-joined the battle.

From behind Ragnar yelled, "Jonathan, what are you doing? This is no time for heroics!"

At the same moment a sharp pain in his left forearm distracted Jonathan's attention. One of their enemies had scored a hit. He was so shocked by the wound that he forgot to parry his opponent's next attack, and he felt the flat of his enemy's blade

222

bounce off his left shoulder. He was surprised only for an instant, however. Something happened inside him. The pain from the wound drove him mad. Pure rage coursed through him as he looked upon his foes.

He forgot about the exit behind him. He forgot all about his friends, about Ragnar and Gorwin. He forgot about Charissa. He forgot about the helmet that he had intended to retrieve. All of his hurts and frustrations from the last few weeks came spilling out and were directed towards the soldiers in front of him. His mind focussed on revenge.

*I'll make them pay, pay for my time in prison, pay for forcing me out of Rindorn, pay for the execution block that had been set up outside my prison window!* His sword blows fell faster and heavier.

In a couple of moves he broke past his opponent's defences and nicked his right shoulder with the point of his blade. Cursing, the man dropped his weapon and bolted for the door through which he had come.

Olaf's opponent had now moved in front of him. Jonathan continued to swing wildly, not caring about defence. Yet before the guard could take advantage of his vulnerability, Jonathan had managed to bring the flat of his own sword down with a loud smash on top of the man's helmet. The man staggered back onto one knee before falling over stunned. Another soldier immediately took his place, his sword raised in challenge and a twisted grin playing on his ugly face.

"Grin away," said Jonathan. "We'll see who's smiling when this is over."

They had only exchanged two sword strokes when Philip suddenly interposed himself between Jonathan and his adversary. The force of Philip's charge pushed his foe out of Jonathan's sword range. At the same moment Jonathan was tripped from behind, and a voice in his ear yelled, "You fool! Do you want to get us all killed?" Then someone started dragging him towards the exit door.

The pain from hitting the floor immediately cooled Jonathan's raging emotions, and he remembered the helmet against the wall. Kicking free from the grip on his heels, he struggled over to where he had last seen it. From out of nowhere a blow knocked him down again.

"The helmet!" he yelled, vainly trying to rise to his feet.

"We've got it!" It was Sonja's voice this time.

Finally he was able to stand, and he looked back towards Philip.

Amazingly Philip was now holding off three opponents, but as a result he was unable to retreat towards the rest of the party. Ragnar rushed in to help him, and together they gained the exit door. In a few seconds the travellers were all standing on the staircase leading down into the cave, and Philip slammed the door behind them.

Jonathan listened to the sounds of their enemies now beating on this second door. Meanwhile, a light slowly grew in the darkness. Rannulf had remembered to bring the lantern from the table and Charissa used Jonathan's candle to light it.

Gorwin pressed the helmet into Jonathan's hands. "Here, you'd better strap this on your head so you don't forget it again," he said.

He then urged them onwards. Jonathan fumbled with the helmet straps while slowly descending the stairway. He disliked the idea of going underground yet again and already felt cramped and suffocated. But clearly there was no other option. He knew that they had only a few moments to spare before their enemies discovered the same lever that he had found.

In the lantern's dim light he saw that they stood in a cave—and a large one by the sounds of their echoing footsteps. He could not quite see the roof but he could spot strange looking cones of rock, some rising from the floor and others dangling from the ceiling. From where he stood they looked like giant teeth waiting to devour him.

The paved stonework floor lasted for only a few yards beyond the staircase then it became rough un-hewn rock. They walked as quickly as they could without tripping on its surface, but they had only been travelling for two minutes when the banging behind them grew louder as if the soldiers had found a battering ram. Jonathan wondered why they had not pulled the lever.

The travellers quickened their pace, and soon they were loping across the floor, trying to avoid the holes, rock-cones, and other obstacles that appeared in front of them. It helped that they were going downhill, but at one point Jonathan tripped, fell and slammed his knee into something horribly hard. As he got up to limp after the others, he heard the last and loudest crashing sound of all. Light streamed into the rear of the cavern. Their enemies had broken through.

The travellers had a lead of several hundred yards and were not in immediate danger, but soon the light from ten or more torches dotted the darkness behind them. Reinforcements had arrived.

Since their foes had more light, Jonathan figured

that they would be able to move faster. No doubt as well, the alarm was being raised throughout the castle and perhaps the entire city of Dorinon. Additional soldiers would soon come. Meanwhile he was concerned that the ceiling was getting lower.

"How long will this cavern continue?" he asked aloud. "If it ends it will force us to turn and fight." No one answered him.

For a few moments it looked as if his fears might come true. Ragnar, who was leading, suddenly turned sharply to the left, towards the cavern wall. Then looking past him, Jonathan saw a boat sitting in a pool of water next to a gravel beach ten yards ahead. It was larger than most regular rowboats, and though its paint was flaking, it appeared to have once been white.

"To the boat," called Ragnar needlessly, since everyone was already headed there. As he got closer, Jonathan heard a gurgling sound. There was running water nearby!

Ragnar ran over to the rock projection to which the boat was tied and worked at the rope with his dagger. The others grabbed the paddles and lifted them off the seats, making room to sit down. As soon as Ragnar had the rope cut, they pushed off into deeper water and commenced paddling away from the shore.

They were no more than five boat lengths away when the first of their enemies arrived at the pool's edge. Their foe stopped to shout to those behind him, then, still holding his torch, he boldly strode into the water, attempting to catch Jonathan's friends.

It was a wasted effort. Since the travellers had swords he would have been more of a threat had he stayed on shore and shot at them with arrows. And this was exactly what the next two guards did. Their first shot ricocheted off the cavern wall. The next was closer, actually imbedding itself in the boat's wooden side. The third flew past Jonathan, and he heard a yell from Olaf. The arrow had grazed his arm.

Fortunately their enemies lacked the time to get off a fourth shot before the boat had caught the current of an underground river, and soon they were behind an outcropping that shielded them from further arrows.

But another challenge immediately presented itself. The channel they were in narrowed, causing the current to flow faster. The boat began to move so quickly there was serious danger it would crash into the rocks on either side. There was also a danger of the boat sinking. With all eight of them on board, it was sitting very low in the water. There was no bailing bucket to get rid of excess water, so Charissa and Rannulf scooped water that sloshed over the side of the boat with their hands.

As Philip tended Olaf's wound, Jonathan worked his way carefully to the bow and kept his paddle ready to push them away from threatening obstacles. It was difficult to see. "Light! Light!" he bellowed.

But as the lantern was passed to the front, Sonja, who was holding it at that moment, pointed and yelled, "Look!"

Jonathan momentarily forgot that he needed to watch for rocks and turned to see what she was pointing at. It was another boat, similar to their own, resting on another gravel beach. However, the current was moving too quickly for anyone to jump out and secure it. All they could do was hope that their pursuers would not find it.

Suddenly Jonathan was rudely reminded of his job by a loud thud as the boat struck a rock, nearly throwing him into the river. At the same moment the lantern fell out of Sonja's hands and rolled across the boat's floor, so that Jonathan found himself battling in near darkness to free the boat from the rock.

"Eyes to the front, Jonathan," came the needless reminder from behind him.

By some miracle the lantern had not gone out, and when it was righted, Jonathan was able to dislodge the boat from the rocky projection. Soon they were hurtling downstream again—down into the darkness.

Jonathan was now more alert, and kneeling in the bow of the boat he used the paddle to push off against obstacles as they loomed closer in the shadows. Yet despite his best efforts several times they slammed into rocks or into the canyon walls causing him to bang his shins into the boat's gunwales. At times they also encountered rapids that bounced the travellers around like balls, and once for a moment they flew through the air as they went over a five-foot-high waterfall. Luckily there was a still pool at the bottom, giving them a few moments to scoop water out of the boat before the current caught them again.

The underground river swept them onward through caves, caverns and channels, and in the lantern light Jonathan saw occasional side passages and imposing pillars of rock sparkling with luminous colours. Often they were soaked with water when they ran into boulders or ploughed through standing waves. Even so, the current eventually slowed, giving them more time and space to react to new obstacles, and collisions with rocks became less frequent. Thus far there seemed to be no sign of pursuit. They all relaxed just a little.

"Is your arm all right, Olaf?" asked Jonathan.

Olaf grunted affirmatively.

After that, silence reigned as they continued downstream. Jonathan realized how tired he felt. Eventually Sonja spoke, "Do you know where we are going, Gorwin?"

"Yes," he said. "I have been down here several times, though I've entered at different spots. I actually took this cave system to get to Dorinon from my castle, but I left the caves earlier and met the surface at a different point. Ragnar and Philip have travelled here too."

As they journeyed, Jonathan lost track of time. Every now and then there would be a gap in the cave ceiling and he would see moonlight up above. Once they pulled the boat to the side and ate some of the soggy food in their packs, and afterwards Jonathan dozed off while Olaf took over in the bow of the boat.

Some time later he was roused from slumber by Gorwin's voice. "Soon we'll come to an underground lake, and from there we can find a stairway leading to an exit."

"What about our enemies from Dorinon?" asked Rannulf.

"In case they follow us we'll need to find a good place to hide once we arrive at the lake. That shouldn't be difficult. It's large. You'll see once we get there."

Gorwin's prediction was accurate. The current

slowed as the narrow channel deepened, then without warning the rock walls on either side of them disappeared and they found themselves swept out into a large underground lake. Jonathan could tell by the echoes that this was the biggest cavern they had entered yet.

Gorwin immediately ordered them to paddle left along the shoreline. When they had gone far enough to satisfy him, he steered them towards the shore. Being in the bow again, it was Jonathan's job to hop out and pull the boat's prow onto the gravel beach.

When they disembarked, they discovered two side caverns, and Gorwin ordered them to hide the boat in one of these caves. The boat was large and heavy, and it took all of their efforts, but when at last it was stowed, Gorwin spoke again. "We'll have to wait here for dawn, so you might as well try to sleep. I will take the first watch, Philip will take the second, Ragnar, the third, Rannulf, the fourth, and Jonathan, the last one."

Most of the party fell asleep almost immediately, but Jonathan was no longer tired, and watched along with Gorwin for a while. The two of them sat behind one of the larger boulders on the beach.

"We don't want to attract attention with a light," said Gorwin as he turned down their lantern and covered its light with a hood. Jonathan saw the sense in his uncle's suggestion, though he found the nearly total darkness oppressive.

To distract himself from the darkness Jonathan thought he would get answers to some of his questions that had been puzzling him. "Gorwin," he asked, "Why did you come here to meet us?"

"Sorry, what do you mean?"

"I thought that we were going to meet you at your house, and instead you came all the way to Dorinon."

"Well, I heard that the pursuit was hot and I became concerned. That's all. And Lambert's inn is one that our people often stay at when we travel through Dorinon. A good thing I came though, otherwise you might be in some dungeon right now, correct?"

"Yes, thank you for that," said Jonathan. "You do a good job of pretending to be drunk."

Gorwin chuckled. "Am I supposed to take that as a compliment?"

"What about the Dragikoi," interrupted Jonathan, "the ones who stole the amulet from Rindorn?"

"We don't know what they are, or even if they are working for the Black Wizard."

"So you haven't heard of them before?"

"No, they're a new phenomenon as far as we can tell."

Jonathan reflected on this. For a few moments there was an awkward silence between them. He felt that he should say something, but he found it difficult to make small talk. Eventually Gorwin asked, "Jonathan, what do you remember of your childhood?"

Jonathan hesitated before answering. His old suspicious nature from growing up on the streets of Rindorn had resurfaced. Then he reminded himself that Gorwin had paid the ransom money that saved him from execution.

"I don't remember much of my life before Rindorn. The old widow who raised me once said that she found me after I'd wandered into town one day with a trading caravan. That was fourteen years ago and I'm guessing that I was between three and four years old at the time. I was hungry so she gave me some food and like a stray cat I kept coming back for more. In the end she sort of adopted me. She died a few years ago."

"Does she have any family left?" asked Gorwin.

"None that I know of."

"Hmm . . . Continue."

"There are two other memories that I have, which perhaps came from the time before I lived in Rindorn." He told Gorwin about the stables in the mountains and the man bending over him and telling him the name he should go by. Gorwin did not interrupt, but Jonathan had the sense that he was quite interested.

After Jonathan finished talking, there was a pause and then Gorwin said, "Is that it? Can you remember anything more?"

"No, that's all there is."

"What prompted you to use this name when you were about to be executed?"

"They asked me for my name," responded Jonathan truthfully, "so they could publicize it for the execution notice, and I figured that since I was about to die, I might as well die as the person I really was, and not under a name given to me by a woman who was not my real mother. So I gave them the name that the man in the stable had told me."

"That's not much to go on, is it?" said Gorwin finally, but Jonathan couldn't tell if he was talking to himself.

There was silence between them. Then Jonathan

said. "I'm curious. . ."

"Yes?"

"The helmet that we picked up yesterday, was it one of the sacred gifts?"

"Yes."

"What about the other sacred gifts? What are they? Where are they?"

"They are intended for use in combat, so naturally they match the various pieces of armour that a warrior carries into battle. There's the helmet, which we now have, and a shield, a sword, a belt, an armour-plated chest piece and some special shoes. Now the various gifts have various functions . . ." Then he suddenly stopped and grabbed Jonathan's arm tightly. "Sshh!" he said.

They peered over top of the rock. There, about three hundred yards away to their right, another boat was entering the cavern. Soldiers held lit torches in the boat's bow and stern.

Jonathan and Gorwin watched them for the next half hour. The soldiers made no attempt to turn right or left, but paddled straight out into the middle of the lake. Initially Jonathan wondered why they would have done this, but then it came to him that their enemies might not have realized that they were on a lake and thought that it was only a temporary widening of the river. After half an hour the soldiers veered to the right.

"They've probably found the other shore," said Gorwin.

Gorwin decided not to wake the others since there was no immediate threat of discovery. Instead the two of them watched silently for another couple hours. For a while the boat could still be seen as it followed the opposite shore, but each time they checked, the lights appeared more distant, and after a while they could not be seen at all.

Eventually Jonathan became concerned. He did not want the soldiers to find him, but he still felt slightly sorry for his enemies. The prospect that his foes would be trapped in an underground cave seemed to be a fate worse than death. "Are they going to be able to find their way out of here?" he asked.

"Yes, they will. Not far from where they are, the roof of the cavern disappears and the river emerges into the open air. If they continue to drift with the current, they'll eventually get there. There are other passages and routes to the surface, too. They'll certainly find them when light comes in the morning. In fact, there are so many openings that this cavern becomes fairly well lit in the daytime."

On hearing this, Jonathan felt better. He rejoined his sleeping friends and left the rest of the watching to Gorwin and Philip.

When he awoke, Rannulf was bending over him. "Good morning," he said. "It's your turn to watch."

Jonathan wandered out to the lakeshore. Enough light now shone through the holes in the cavern's roof to make lifting the hood on the lantern unnecessary. There was no trace of their enemies.

A short time later, the others began stirring, and seeing this Gorwin decided it was time to leave. After they had chewed down the remainder of their rations, Jonathan collected the helmet from where he had left it the night before. He was surprised that, given its obvious value, Ragnar and Gorwin seemed content to leave it in his possession rather than taking it themselves.

Abandoning the boat, they walked left along the shoreline—all the time glancing back to see whether or not there was any sign of their opponents. Fortunately there was none.

After three or four hundred yards, Gorwin led them away from the shore, and through a series of winding caves whose ceilings were only twenty feet in height. When they had gone a safe distance from the lake, they uncovered the lantern and in its light Jonathan noticed strange markings on the walls. Ragnar, Philip and Gorwin paid no attention to them, but Jonathan stopped to examine them and saw that they were symbols of some sort—perhaps letters from a foreign alphabet. Then, not wanting to be left behind in the dark, he hurried to catch up to the others.

They had reached a stone staircase that descended into the final cavern. Within it, two tooth-like cones of rock, one from the roof and one from the floor, had joined together to form a complete pillar, so that they appeared to be holding up the roof. This last cavern also contained more of these strange symbols, some of them forming patterns which reminded him of the hermit's maps that he had seen a few days earlier. He wanted to have a longer look at them, but Ragnar urged them towards the stairs.

"What are these drawings?" Jonathan asked as he hurried after his friends.

"Foreigners used to live down here," said Philip, "but they moved to the surface many years ago." The staircase descended about twenty-five feet before ending in a metal door. When Gorwin reached the bottom, he took another key from his pocket and fitted it into the lock. It turned with a snap and a click, and when he pushed the door open, daylight streamed into the staircase. Eagerly the travellers went forward into the sunlit world, all of them relieved to breathe fresh air again.

"This is strange," Jonathan said.

"What's strange?" asked Gorwin, pausing in the doorway to check behind for pursuing soldiers. Seeing none, he closed and locked the door.

"Well, we were underground, and normally when you're underground you have to go up to reach the surface. But we went down."

"Yes, but when you are inside a mountain," said Gorwin, "sometimes you have to descend to reach the outside world."

The travellers were standing in a shallow mountain cave with a wide opening about twenty feet ahead, and when they left the cave, they found themselves gazing west, into a valley between low mountains. Pines and cedars covered most of the valley's lower slopes and its upper reaches were covered by bright green grass dotted here and there with little white spots, which were probably sheep. Above them, mountain peaks resembling barren, black teeth contrasted sharply with the bright green grass and the blue sky. Jonathan also noticed an odd smell mingling with the pungent aroma of cedar trees. Much later he learned that this was the scent of the ocean.

They walked down into the western valley, the mountains climbing ever higher about them as they descended. After half a mile, another valley joined theirs from the north. Although a ridge of grassy hills blocked their view of the valley's end, the ridge was parted in the centre, releasing a creek that spilled down to meet the river in their own valley.

Gorwin now turned right to enter this northern valley, but to avoid walking in the creek, they climbed the ridge itself. When they got to the top, Jonathan saw that a line of spruce trees still shielded the valley's end from sight.

"Here we are," said Gorwin. "Home."

"What do you mean?" asked Jonathan. "I don't see anything."

His uncle beamed, "Precisely. You never can be too careful."

Jonathan felt confused. Ragnar had said that Gorwin lived in a castle. Was he being deceptive or only speaking figuratively? Were they going to be camping underneath the stars?

# 16 A JOURNEY UNDERGROUND

As they trudged up the valley, the ground gradually rose towards the heights of the mountains. When they entered the belt of spruce trees the going became even more difficult as there were no clear paths. Jonathan was also hungry. He hoped that they would soon break and make a fire for their noon meal, but neither Gorwin nor Ragnar seemed interested in stopping.

Then abruptly the spruces came to an end. They were a much thinner belt than Jonathan had expected, and with his view unimpaired by trees, he finally understood. The valley continued to climb gently for at least another three miles before it met its end in the sheer face of a towering mountain cliff. In front of the cliff stood a small castle with a high stone wall surrounding it.

"Incredible!" exclaimed Sonja, when she saw the castle in the distance. "I would never have guessed that this was here."

"Nor would have I," said Jonathan.

Gorwin beamed again. He seemed especially pleased that Jonathan had not anticipated finding anything in the valley. "Like I said, home," he stated. "Technically, we're outside the borders of Magelandorn, and very few people know of its existence—the fewer who know, the better, as far as I'm concerned. It was always fairly secret. It's an old smugglers' haven, which I have improved. The original inhabitants of this place called it Asiniwachis—which means mountain, in their language. We call it Caerathorn."

"We've only been here for about ten years," added Ragnar, "ever since Gorwin returned from exile."

"And it's not that much yet," continued Gorwin. "I have expansion plans, but at the moment I don't think it could really resist a determined attack by a large force of enemies."

"Not that much?" said Olaf. "What are you talking about? It's amazing!"

"Could we help you with those plans?" asked Rannulf.

"Quite possibly," said Gorwin.

While his friends chatted excitedly with Gorwin about the castle, Jonathan was lost in his thoughts. In the last few days whenever he had tried to imagine what Gorwin's castle looked like, he had wondered if it would strike some chord of recognition within him. Could he have visited it at an earlier period in his life? If he had, then it might actually prove that he was Gorwin's nephew. But as he gazed at it, he realized, with disappointment, that he could not recall ever seeing this place before. *Perhaps I am an imposter after all.*

Not long afterwards a trumpet sounded from the castle walls. Soon a horseman in chainmail rode towards them on a white charger. When he was within twenty yards, Gorwin motioned for their party to halt. The horseman saluted Gorwin and grinned. "Hail, m' lord," he called. "What tidings bring you from western lands?" He cast a curious glance toward Jonathan and his friends.

"I bring the boy and his companions," said Gorwin. "But enemies followed us underground at least as far as the lake."

The man nodded. "If your Lordship wishes, I will ask that suitable preparations be made."

"I do wish it." The man then turned and rode back to the castle.

The group was left to trudge the rest of the way on foot. And while it was only a half a mile, in their weary condition it seemed to take forever. Happily, a wagon from the castle eventually came and carried them the final distance.

On its approach, the road proceeded along several switchbacks, and as they drew nearer, Jonathan saw that the castle was perched upon the southernmost end of a half-mile-long arm of rock thrust out from the mountain to the north. From the base of the castle walls the ground fell steeply away to the valley floor on the southern and western sides, and less steeply on the northern side. The eastern side overlooked a precipice.

The castle, Jonathan realized, could only be attacked effectively from three of its four sides, as the cliff on the eastern side would prevent any attacks from that direction. On the northern side, where the slope away from the castle was the gentlest, the walls, which were otherwise twenty-five feet high, grew to an impressive forty feet.

Several square towers rose up from the walls, one on each of the castle's four corners and two smaller towers next to its gate, which was on the western side. From inside the walls a single tall rounded tower with a pointed top rose high above the others, and Jonathan was reminded of the pencil-like tower that he had seen at St. Swithun's monastery.

As soon as they arrived, Gorwin dispatched twelve soldiers to search the underground caves and see how closely they had been followed. Meanwhile, Jonathan and his friends were brought to the kitchen in the castle's inner keep and fed cold venison and shepherd's pie. Then they were sent off to have baths and a rest. A feast, he heard, would be prepared that evening to celebrate their successful return.

Before they left the kitchen, Gorwin pointed to the helmet that Jonathan was carrying. "I can put in a safe place if you want."

Jonathan was puzzled that his uncle would even bother to ask his permission about this, and not just take it, but he handed it over nonetheless. When he had finished his bath, he discovered new clothes waiting for him, and as he dressed, he decided that since they were now in a safe place, he would no longer keep St. Swithun's Amulet around his neck. Instead he placed it in his pants' pocket. Afterwards, a servant ushered him along a cramped stone corridor with a curved ceiling towards a staircase that led up to the bedchambers. Each of his friends, he was told, had been given separate rooms off the same corridor.

It was only as he walked up the staircase that the reality of his situation started to sink in. He was beginning a new episode in his life. His head was a whirl of nervousness, hope and wonder and once more the old doubts re-emerged. Did he really belong here? Would he fit in?

He reached out to touch one of the stones of the corridor wall. It seemed very strange that this castle, these stones, belonged to a family member. Just a few weeks ago he had been a penniless orphan waiting to be beheaded.

His bedchamber door was ajar, revealing a diminutive cell with stone walls, a carpet and a four-poster bed supporting green draperies. Two small windows with peaked tops peered at him from the far wall.

He did try to sleep that afternoon, but initially he was too excited. His suspicious nature would not be satisfied easily, and questions still kept him awake. *Why did Gorwin let me bring my friends along? Feeding one extra person is difficult enough, but three or four? He wouldn't just want to bring them along to keep me company, would he? He has to have some need for them. There has to be a catch somewhere. Of course, he could just be so filthy rich he doesn't care. He obviously can afford to have this castle, and he could afford to bail me out of prison. Maybe, just maybe, money is no hindrance to this man?*

Questions like these went through his head. But finally the exertions of the last few days took their toll. The next thing he knew he was being awakened by a knock on the door and one of the servants summoned him to the evening feast. The smell of damp grass filled his room. He glanced toward the window. The sky was grey and it was raining.

The servant led him down a narrow staircase to an oak-panelled hall. Just above the upper edge of the panelling, a row of shields boldly proclaimed their various heraldic devices, and an oak-beamed roof, coming sharply to a point, shielded them from the elements. Immediately below the roof, stained glass windows interrupted the bare stone walls. Candles set into iron candleholders as well as three large fireplaces lighted the hall. A long table filled with guests ran down the length of the hall. The shape of the room reminded Jonathan of a chapel, but there were no religious symbols in it.

For a few moments he did not recognize his friends as they had all bathed and were wearing much better clothing than he had seen them in before. Gorwin, too, looked different—he now had on a white tunic with a gold chain around his neck.

Despite the wonder of his surroundings, Jonathan could barely keep his eyes open during the feast. He sat next to Gorwin, and when Gorwin was not being interrupted by servants and other dinner guests, he was introducing Jonathan to the people nearby. Jonathan's mind soon was spinning with a confusion of names and faces.

Eventually, noticing that his nephew was nodding off, as the meal and entertainment drew to a close, Gorwin spoke into his ear. "I'll talk with you tomorrow, if time permits."

The next morning Jonathan was again awakened by a knock on the door, but for a moment he was confused as to where he was. When he realized he was in Gorwin's castle, relief flooded through him. Today for a change he had no fear of being hunted down, shot at or run through.

The door opened. Into the room popped the head of one of the servants. "The Lord Gorwin wishes to see you sometime after breakfast, sir. In the meantime, your friends are to go down to the stables for their first riding lesson."

Jonathan got up immediately, eager to discover if his strange childhood memories contained any substance, although at the same time, the prospect of learning about his past made him nervous. He was not absolutely sure he wanted to know the answers to all his questions.

Something else that the servant had said stuck with him. "Sir." The man had called him "sir." He had never been called that before. It felt uncomfortable. Living as Gorwin's nephew would take getting used to.

Jonathan dressed and walked down to the hall where they had dined the evening before, but this morning there were only his friends and six servants. The table, however, was set with platters of bread, butter, honey, cheese and tomatoes plus pitchers containing water and goat's milk. All of it looked appetizing, but his stomach was in knots.

"This is an amazing place," said Rannulf. "Half the time I walk around with my head craned up towards the ceiling. I've never seen a building so beautiful before."

"It is nice," said Jonathan, "although it's more of a fortress than a palace."

"Well," added Sonja, "unlike you, Jonathan, I haven't broken into the mayor's house to compare, so I agree with Rannulf."

"Yes," said Olaf, his loud voice echoing off the walls. "It's going to take a while to get used to the fact that I could actually call this place home."

"Speaking of which," said Sonja, "can we call it

home? I mean Ragnar invited us to come along, partly for your protection I think, Jonathan. But he didn't say what was going to happen when we got here. Can you find out from Gorwin what's next for us and where we might fit into his plans?"

"I can do that," said Jonathan, "and if I have anything to say about it, there will certainly be a place for everyone."

His friends finished their meal and went off to the stables. Charissa was the last to leave. When she and Jonathan were alone she said more quietly, "Can you also ask about me? Tell him that I'm in no particular hurry to get back home. I'll only be forced into a marriage with Baron Westerham's son when I do, and since I'd prefer to avoid that, any task around here is better."

"I'll do that too," said Jonathan. "Don't worry."

With that Charissa left to catch up with the others and Jonathan was alone with the servants. He sat waiting for a few minutes, but he quickly got bored. Seeing one of the servants rise from the table, Jonathan stopped him before he left. "Excuse me," he said. "Can you tell me where I can find the Lord Gorwin?"

The servant paused, pondering his question. "Actually," he said, "one doesn't usually go to find the Lord. One waits for him to send for you."

This made Jonathan even more anxious. The Gorwin he had met in Dorinon had not seemed terribly formal. Why the sudden change? He wanted to go exploring, but he figured that doing this would make it difficult for anyone to find him. So he simply returned to his quarters.

About twenty minutes passed before the servant

who had wakened him earlier summoned him to the castle study where the Lord Gorwin, as he put it, "is presently disposed to see you." The servant led him through some winding hallways and down half a flight of stairs, finally opening a door and ushering him inside. Then he closed the door and left.

Jonathan's mouth fell open in wonder. The study was one of the strangest rooms he had seen in his life. It was round and two storeys high, and the upper storey consisted chiefly of a single balcony that encircled the entire room. Two fireplaces were located on opposite sides of the room, their chimneys towering far above the glass-domed roof. Many windows on both storeys also ensured an abundance of natural light.

Strangest of all, everywhere he looked small trees and seedlings sprouted out of clay pots. He had never before seen such a thing—plants actually growing indoors. Moreover, on closer examination he saw that the plants were all unknown to him. In addition to the plants, several metal objects were scattered around the room. Jonathan puzzled over their purpose, because although they looked like sculptures, they were not in the shape of humans or animals—in fact, there was no recognizable shape to them at all. What kind of man would keep these things?

Just then, a door in the far wall opened and Gorwin entered. "Ah, Jonathan," he said, "how do you like my study?"

"It's very nice." Not willing to display his ignorance, he said nothing more.

"These metal structures are relics from the ancients."

"Relics?"

"That's right. They each had a purpose at one time, but we aren't sure what. And until we figure it out, they make great plant holders."

As Jonathan gazed at the strange contraptions with new wonder, his uncle pulled up a chair at one of the tables, sat down and gestured for Jonathan to do the same. "I'll skip the preliminaries," said Gorwin. "The reason I asked you here was to explain why I rescued you and brought you here to live, at least for a while."

With the words, "At least for a while," Jonathan's ears perked up. If he was only supposed to be here temporarily, then Gorwin must have other plans for him.

"But first, Ragnar informs me that he taught you something about the history of Magelandorn. Why don't you tell me what you know?"

Jonathan launched into what he knew of the kingdom's recent history, including his knowledge about the sacred gifts, the Black Wizard and the Verdorben family's rebellion against the rightful king.

"And what happened to the old king and his family?" asked Gorwin when Jonathan had finished.

"I don't know. Ragnar says that they weren't all killed off in the revolt, even though everyone thinks they were."

"That's very good," said Gorwin. "You have an adequate knowledge of recent events. Of course, there are people who know what happened to the old king's descendants. Naturally, they are very careful that this information doesn't fall into the wrong hands as there remain powerful people in Magelandorn who want to see the old king's family dead."

Jonathan nodded. This seemed logical.

Gorwin continued, "But you might be wrong on one thing."

"What's that?"

"You may also know, at least to some degree what may have happened to some of the old king's descendants."

"What do you mean?" said Jonathan, puzzled. "You think some of them might be living in Rindorn?"

"Yes," said Gorwin, "I think some of them might have been living in Rindorn, hiding out. It would be a natural place to hide, you know. It's out of the way, a border town."

Jonathan thought about various people he knew who might somehow be connected with the old king. He considered the girl he had first tried to impress by his stunt with the mayor's trousers. "Perhaps, you're right," he said. "There's this one girl I know there named Helena. She's certainly beautiful enough to be descended from royalty."

Gorwin looked at him curiously for a moment, but he made no comment.

Jonathan kept speaking, "What about this evil wizard? According to Ragnar, he isn't dead and he's plotting against us."

"For the moment," said Gorwin, "suffice it to say that our side is doing whatever we can to stop or slow the wizard down."

"Our side?" asked Jonathan.

"Yes, my family supported the royal side." Gorwin grinned, "That is why I'm living in a remote place like this castle. But this isn't exactly what we came here to talk about today. So . . ."

"Does the current royal family still wish the true king's supporters dead? Surely the old battles are long forgotten now."

"Ah, I was getting to that," said Gorwin. "To explain everything to you fully we'll have to go up a few flights of stairs. I've just been there to light a fire in the room."

Curious, Jonathan followed Gorwin across the carpet to a wooden door with a rounded top in the library's opposite wall. Gorwin opened it, revealing a narrow stone spiral staircase that both ascended and descended. It was barely wide enough for a single person, but Gorwin began climbing upwards and Jonathan eagerly followed. It was a long climb. Here and there they passed doors, which Gorwin ignored. Finally, after so many spirals that Jonathan's sense of direction was totally confused, they came to a small stone landing and another wooden door with a rounded top. Gorwin took out a key. After some struggle, he was able to push the door open and they found themselves standing in front of three crescent-shaped stone steps that ascended into the rest of the room.

Other than a tapestry of a hunting scene, the walls and floor were bare stone. Two windows plus several lit candles and a lantern illuminated the chamber. As Gorwin had said, a fire also burned merrily in the grate. Nevertheless, the room was still cold.

Jonathan mounted the steps. There was little furniture—only some bookshelves, a plain wooden table near the fireplace and two rough wooden chairs next to it. The helmet they had rescued from Dorinon Castle sat on one of the shelves, but what caught

Jonathan's attention was the golden ball on the table. It was about the size of a large apple and it glimmered in the firelight.

Gorwin locked the door behind them. Then he climbed the three stairs and pulled up one of the chairs, gesturing for Jonathan to do the same.

"Do you see this ball?" he asked. Indeed Jonathan could barely look at anything else. He did not think that he had seen such a beautiful thing before in his life.

"It is the most precious thing in this castle, worth more than this entire house and all the lands around," said Gorwin, "that's why I keep the door here locked at all times, even when I'm in this room. It is actually a child's toy, and once it belonged to the eldest son of your house, being passed down from generation to generation. In fact, you might have played with it as a child. Go ahead, pick it up."

Jonathan gazed at Gorwin to see if he was joking, but he seemed entirely in earnest. Rascal and truant that Jonathan occasionally had been, he had often got his hands onto things that he had no right to touch. Yet somehow, it felt improper for him to handle an object this splendid. He sat admiring its perfect shape. Gorwin urged him again, and so with hesitation, he reached out his hand and picked it up.

It was quite heavy. If it really was a child's toy, he wondered how any young child could have lifted it.

"If you stare into the centre of the ball," said Gorwin, "you may see that it has some interesting pictures."

Obliging him once more, Jonathan gazed intently at it.

"What do you see?" asked Gorwin.

The ball was completely blank. Jonathan could see nothing but the firelight shining off its golden surface. He shook his head in response to Gorwin's question. Then he stopped. His eye had caught something, not on the ball's surface, but deep inside.

"Wait a minute," he said. "There is something— yes, horses, I see horses galloping across a plain. And then, and then a ship—a small ship with a square sail, blown about on storm-tossed seas."

He put the ball down on the table, continuing to stare at it for a long moment before looking up.

Gorwin was smiling gently. "You see well," he said after a moment. Jonathan expected him to say something more, but instead there was an awkward silence. Then Gorwin slowly moved his chair back from the table.

"Jonathan, I need to tell you more about the royal family."

Jonathan felt slightly annoyed at this sudden change of topic.

"It was during the reign of the last king's father, King Edward, that rebels drove the royal family from the capital city and the usurper claimed the throne. Then after Edward lost his life through treachery, his son, Malclovis II, assumed the throne of Magelandorn, even though it was a throne in exile."

Gorwin stood up and began pacing. "The battle persisted for some time, but with superior odds against them, the king, queen and their children had to go into hiding. They posed as caretakers in a monastery where they lived under assumed names. Many of us who had remained loyal joined them there. After a while, however, the usurper discovered our location, and in a surprise attack, slaughtered all the monastery's occupants—all except myself—as I was away on a mission—and the king's youngest son who went missing in the attack. No one, neither our attackers nor I, ever discovered what happened to him. We have been searching ever since."

Suddenly he stopped and faced his nephew. "Jonathan, it's time for me to be frank with you. For a variety of reasons, we. . . I . . .think that you are that boy."

# 17 THE REVELATION

Jonathan was speechless. His lips moved but no sound emerged. Finally words came. "What?" he spluttered. "You can't be serious!"

"I am serious," replied Gorwin. "You are the lost son of the last true king of Magelandorn."

Jonathan pushed his chair back and stood up. "This is ridiculous!" His hands were up in front of his face as if to ward off a blow.

"No, it's not ridiculous."

"How could you possibly think it could be me?"

"We were not totally sure at first," said Gorwin after a brief pause. "But your name and your memories gave you away. The name that you remember your father telling you was the false name that the royal family used so that they wouldn't be discovered. There are very few people—if any—outside these castle walls, who would have recognized that name and to whom it belonged."

"So the name's not authentic?" asked Jonathan.

"That's right. It's not your real name."

"But why would you go to all the trouble of seeking me out? Aren't you now the heir to the throne?"

"No," said Gorwin. "I'm not of royal blood myself. I married the king's younger sister, Anna. She died in the attack before we could have any children of our own."

"Oh . . ." said Jonathan. "I am very sorry. . ."

"Yes, I'm sorry, too," said Gorwin, a grim expression on his face.

There was silence between them, but eventually Jonathan spoke. "You said you aren't absolutely sure of my ancestry. Don't you need to be certain before declaring me heir to the throne?"

"You're right. There is one last question I need to ask. According to the forest hermit, you have a tattoo on the bottom of your foot. Is that correct?"

"Yes."

"May I see it?"

Reluctantly Jonathan took off the leather slipper and woollen sock that he had been given the day before.

Gorwin looked at the foot and gasped. "God be thanked. It is true!" He sat down, slowly shaking his head. Then abruptly he stood again and gave Jonathan a bear-hug. "It's been a long time—a very long time," he said.

Jonathan sat and put his sock and shoe on again. The earlier news about being heir to the throne was beginning to sink in, and he felt quite uncomfortable with the idea, though he was not exactly sure why. After all, as a boy, he and his friends used to pretend to be princes and kings, and dreamed of one day becoming such, but discovering, as an adult, that he actually belonged to the royal family was different. He had come to Gorwin's castle hoping for a better life, and instead he had discovered that half of the soldiers in Magelandorn would kill him if they only knew his real name. He had, without giving his permission, suddenly become attached to a conflict with no real sense of exactly what it was about. Instead of being able to pursue his own ambitions, he now was the centre of other peoples' dreams and hopes. Suddenly he had a strong desire to run away and live in hiding, far from anyone who claimed to be his uncle, far away from the outside world.

Finally he summoned up the courage to ask. "Uh, are you sure you aren't making a mistake?"

"Yes, I'm sure," said Gorwin. "There aren't many people with a story like yours and the royal tattoo on their foot." He pointed to the golden ball on the table. "And only royals can see images in that ball. To the rest of us it's just a pretty object. It used to be passed down to each new generation partly as a way to determine who was a legitimate heir and who wasn't. No, it's pretty much guaranteed that you are my nephew and the rightful inheritor of the throne." Then sensing Jonathan's discomfort, Gorwin added, "Oh don't worry. You aren't king of anywhere yet and you might not be for a long while either. In fact, we may not regain the throne in your lifetime." He looked disappointed as he said this.

To Jonathan, however, this was news elating. Perhaps he could live the life of a minor noble after all.

As he stood up to leave, Gorwin said, "One more thing—if I was you, I wouldn't share this news with anyone, not even your friends—not quite yet.

You never know when someone will slip up and give you away."

Jonathan bristled. "My friends would never betray me. They'd give their lives for me, and I for them. And in the last few weeks they've tried to do so a few times already!"

"I don't mean to suggest that they'd ever deliberately do so," said Gorwin calmly. "I'm sure they're very loyal and brave, but torture or the threat of it can undo many a brave man—and drink can do worse things. I'm sorry, Jonathan. Unfortunately you'll have to start thinking of such things. If our enemies ever captured your friends it would be to their benefit not to know your true identity. No, we should keep this our secret. As for me, although Ragnar knows, we won't tell anyone else for now. It's not that I don't trust them, it's just that if word gets out that *the pretender* to the throne is living here, we can expect all kinds of trouble. The fewer people who know the better."

Jonathan nodded. He saw the sense in what Gorwin was saying. In fact, he rather liked the secrecy idea. Being the rightful heir to the throne would not be so bad if nobody else knew about it. If everyone treated him normally, then there might be a real chance that he could have a normal life.

"As far as we let anyone else know," continued Gorwin, "you are the son of my older sister, Leonora, not Jonathan Richard Arthur Malclovis, the heir of King Malclovis II."

"Fair enough," said Jonathan, feeling better all the time.

"And just to make sure that no one around here thinks that you're anyone special, we should perhaps assign you to stable duty for a while." Jonathan's heart sank when he heard this.

"From what I hear," said Gorwin, "it wouldn't hurt you to learn a little more about horses. If we are going to eventually retake the throne of Magelandorn, it will mean a lot of work of the ordinary kind, for all of us. In any case, they say that the best way to keep oneself sane is to have a mixture of intellectual and physical work."

Jonathan was unsure about this last bit.

"But the stables can wait until tomorrow," said Gorwin. "It's almost time for lunch."

"Before we go," said Jonathan, "what is to become of my friends and Charissa?"

"As long as they are willing to join in with the tasks like the rest of our community I'm happy to have your friends stay here," said Gorwin. "We could use a few extra hands around this place. I also expect them to learn to defend themselves—Charissa and Sonja too—living on the edge of the wild means that we have to be extra careful. As for Charissa, she can stay for now, but once word gets back to her father that she's here, we may eventually need to make some arrangement if we don't want him as our enemy. Yet that won't be necessary for a month or two."

"What sort of arrangement?" asked Jonathan.

"Likely he has received a pledge of some sort from this baron in return for promising his daughter in marriage. The two of them will probably need to be compensated if the engagement is to be nullified."

Jonathan shivered internally at the thought of arranged marriages among noble families. None of the lower classes that he knew followed this custom. He hoped that no one would try to arrange such a thing for him.

During the noon meal Jonathan found himself craving solitude in order to digest the news that Gorwin had told him, but he had no chance to slip away. While Gorwin had given Jonathan a day off from the stables he lost no time in starting him on his military training, and directly after the meal a servant arrived to tell Jonathan and his friends that it was time for archery practice.

Jonathan was surprised that the "man-at-arms" sent to teach them was not a man, but a young woman named Ingrid. Her long black hair was tied closely together so that it fell down her back in cord-like fashion. She wore a light brown leather vest over top of her red tunic. Instead of a skirt she wore dark green trousers over top of light brown boots. With her black hair and high cheekbones, her features reminded Jonathan somewhat of the Dragikoi, except that her irises were green instead of the Dragikoi's typical black colour.

Another local young woman named Erika also joined them in their training. Her face and dress were so similar to Ingrid's that Jonathan thought that she might be her younger sister.

Rannulf, Sonja and Olaf shot well. This did not surprise Jonathan. He and his friends had gone out into the woods near Ravenhall and Rindorn to practice archery and sword-fighting as children. Erika and Charissa had more trouble. Clearly they had not had as much experience.

Jonathan insisted that the others shoot their arrows first. This surprised Ingrid. She obviously expected that as Gorwin's nephew he would take the lead in all activities. But his mind was still reeling from his earlier discussion with Gorwin and he had a tough time concentrating on Ingrid's directions. In any case, his first shot did not even strike close to the target. It landed two yards to the right of it.

"Nice try, Jonathan," said Ingrid encouragingly, "a little closer next time."

Olaf, Rannulf and Sonja snorted in response. Still lost in his thoughts, however, Jonathan paid no heed.

Charissa and Erika's second shots were much improved over their first ones, and Rannulf, Olaf and Sonja got bull's-eyes. Jonathan's second shot flew over top of the target and out into the farmer's field beyond.

"Nice try, Jonathan, a little closer to the target next time," said Olaf mocking Ingrid's encouraging tone. "And try not to kill any peasants."

Jonathan grunted and waited for his next turn. Erika and Charissa landed their third shots on the target, while Jonathan, over compensating for his last shot, hit the ground well short of his goal.

"What's wrong, Jonathan?" asked Sonja. "You aren't usually this useless."

"Why thank you, Sonja," said Jonathan, sarcasm in his voice. "I'm still thinking about the chat I had with Gorwin, actually," he added in a more subdued voice.

"Did you discuss us?" asked Sonja.

"Yes, you all can stay, although in Charissa's case we may need to eventually work out some arrangement with her father," said Jonathan, "although we'll each have to learn how to defend ourselves and we'll each have jobs to do, including me. I'll start with stable duty."

"Oh, so it's good news then!" said Rannulf.

"Yes," said Jonathan sombrely.

"Aren't you happy to have us stay?" said Olaf, noticing his mood.

"Yes, I'm happy. It's not that. Gorwin told me more about my family background. It's not all good news. That's all."

"He must have said something really disturbing for you to shoot this badly," said Olaf. "It's a good thing we're not learning sword techniques this afternoon or you'd hurt yourself."

"Likely," said Jonathan.

The others seemed curious to hear more. Yet sensing that Jonathan was not in the mood to talk, and satisfied that their own situations were resolved they returned to shooting.

Jonathan's archery improved after this, and he even hit a few bull's-eyes. Then finally, after supper, he excused himself to go for a walk. If he could not talk to his friends about his discovery, he at least wanted space to think about this on his own, although he guessed that it would take him more than one evening to get used to the idea of being pretender to the throne. At the gatehouse he asked the guard to let him back in later that evening once the gate was shut for the night.

From the first moment he had seen the black mountains to the north of the castle he had been fascinated by them. He now realized that, since the castle was already at a high elevation, he would have only about four hundred feet to climb to reach the lower peaks. The easiest way up was to follow the arm of rock on which the castle was built back into the mountains. There was little vegetation on this route, but there was a lot of loose rock, as if recent avalanches had killed off most of the undergrowth.

Within a few minutes he was puffing and blowing with the exertion of the climb, but eventually he achieved the top of the ridge and gazed about. The drop-off on the other side of the ridge was steeper and deeper than the one he had just climbed—at least a thousand feet down to a short stretch of grass at the foot of the mountain, and from there not far to the sea. Further north yet, a number of black, mountainous islands dotted the water. To the south, bright green valleys interrupted the black mountains as far as the eye could see.

Seeing it from the ridge, he could appreciate the castle's strategic location. It was close enough to the ocean to allow an easy escape but it was hidden in a mountain valley, not visible from the sea or even from the surrounding land. It would be a difficult spot to locate even if one did know its general whereabouts.

Turning left, he followed a path west along the top of the ridge, a path so carefully designed that, while walking on it, he could stay out of sight of the beach below. As he walked he thought back over the last few days. Now that he knew that he was the true crown prince of Magelandorn, several things that had puzzled him before made more sense. The extra effort that their opponents had taken to track him was now understandable. And Ragnar's and the hermit's reluctance to tell him about his true identity made sense as well. How do you casually tell someone that there's a price on his head?

*Still it is sort of nice to be considered "a somebody" even if it means that I am an exiled, outlawed, and hated "somebody." And it is nice to know a little bit about who my parents were—or who they could have been.*

He wondered what his friends would think if they ever learned who he was. Would they be jealous? Or would they just think that he and Gorwin were crazy?

A sudden doubt hit him. *Maybe Gorwin is crazy. Maybe he intends well but is just deluded.* He had heard stories of half-insane nobles, living isolated lives in distant castles with just a few servants to tend to their needs. Jonathan toyed with this idea, and it did actually seem to have merits. Yet in the end, as with most of his other doubts, he had to dismiss it. From what he could see, Gorwin was not crazy. And even if he was, Jonathan had to admit that he, Jonathan, was benefiting fairly well from this craziness.

Jonathan continued his ponderings for a while, but when the sun started going down, and he turned and went back to the castle.

In the days that followed the pace of activities for Jonathan and his friends increased. They participated in the castle chores, working in the kitchens, milking cows or helping farmers with their livestock. Several times as well, they went with a cart to nearby groves of trees and got firewood.

At first it seemed to Jonathan that the days passed very slowly because there was so much to learn and to get used to. But after a few weeks he began to get a feel for the general rhythms of the community. As there was no village or town nearby, the local farmers came to the castle to get their tools fixed, their grain ground or their produce sold.

As Gorwin had promised, Jonathan soon found himself spending most of his time in the stables. Initially he did not enjoy the work but it grew on him after a while. In a week or two he became much more comfortable around the horses than he had been before. He also learned how to take better care of saddles, straps and harnesses. The other stable hands teased him that he obviously had done something to annoy his uncle if he was working with them. In response he just smiled. There was little that he could say.

In the evenings after the day's work, members of Gorwin's household took turns teaching him and his friends battle skills. Jonathan enjoyed these times the most. They learned about the shooting and making of arrows, horseback riding, lance work, sailing and sword fighting. To Jonathan's surprise, Rannulf appeared to be the most serious about their martial training, often staying to practise or ask their trainer questions after the rest of the friends had departed.

In a short period of time Jonathan's shooting improved tremendously. He had owned a sword in Rindorn and he thought that he knew how to use it, but learning sword fighting from a master was very different from the hack and slash style that he and his friends had done before. Gorwin also insisted that Sonja and Charissa accompany them to these lessons so that their skills too would improve.

One morning when Jonathan was working in the field to the south of the castle, he noticed three strangers riding towards him. One was dressed as a knight, but the second and third men wore robes, not the usual tunic and trousers common to Gorwin's people. Jonathan thought about raising the alarm. Then he reconsidered. Three people could not be much of a threat.

As the figures approached Jonathan gradually

saw that the first man was Hugh, returned from the monastery! He did not recognize the second person. The third was an old man. In fact, as he moved closer Jonathan saw that it was Anastasis!

"It's good to see you, Jonathan," called the hermit when he was within speaking distance.

Jonathan grinned. "It's good to see you too. And Hugh, it's great to see you on your feet again! What brings you to these parts?"

"Hugh is returning home and I have pressing business with your uncle," said Anastasis.

"What sort of business?" asked Jonathan. He eyed the second man, the man he did not recognize, curiously.

The hermit smiled. "That will be my secret for the moment. Oh, I also brought your lute and Sonja's violin. Since you are busy working now, I'll take them to the castle."

"By the way," said Hugh waving towards the stranger, "I should introduce you. This is Hung-Tai. He is one of the Dragikoi who has spent the last few months at St. Anselm's monastery with me. We have gotten to know him quite well and he is now a trusted friend. He wishes to see his own people freed from domination by the Black Wizard." Hung-Tai bowed and the three men rode on and through the open castle gate. Jonathan gazed after them as they went. Hugh likely had good judgment, but Jonathan wondered if Gorwin would agree with Hugh's assessment of Hung-Tai.

Jonathan was looking forward to the chance to talk with Anastasis. Ever since Gorwin had told him about his ancestry, he had craved a private conversation with the old man. Clearly the hermit had suspected something when he had first seen that tattoo on his foot. Perhaps it would be safe to tell him that Gorwin thought that he was the pretender to the throne and then to get his advice on the subject. For the next two weeks, however, Jonathan was able to find neither Anastasis nor Gorwin. When he inquired, he was told that they had gone on a trip and that Ragnar had been left in charge. No one knew of their whereabouts or when they would return.

Frustrated with his attempts to find the hermit, Jonathan decided to do more exploring. Gorwin had earlier assigned one of the servants the task of showing Jonathan around the castle grounds, but there were several towers that the two of them had not entered. According to the servant these were used as weaponries and storage for animal fodder.

Jonathan decided to investigate one of these. The base of it turned out to be much as the servant had described. Quivers of arrows hung on pegs and two racks of spears stood next to several stacked barrels of oil and one large pile of hay.

Then on a whim, Jonathan proceeded up the ladder to the tower's second level. When he stuck his head through the trapdoor he was amazed. The second floor occupied the complete width of the round tower, but floors above it were only partial, stretching shelf-like across the tower's upper levels. This left the resulting chamber with an extremely high ceiling. In addition, a number of ropes dangled down towards the ground, some longer than others.

What was even more amazing was what his friends were doing inside the tower. Philip was busy climbing one of the ropes while Hugh climbed the walls.

Jonathan did not say anything. He thought that he would merely observe what the men did next. From where he stood he could see into the partial floor above, which appeared to be filled with strange statues and equipment. As he was trying to guess what these were for, he saw Philip begin swinging the rope back and forth across the tower's width. Eventually, he swung far enough to be over top of the loft. Jonathan then saw him drop from the rope, land on the floor, and dive out of the way of a bag attached to a rope that had somehow started moving towards him. After this Philip grabbed a pole and thrust it towards the retreating bag before beginning an elaborate attack on a rough statue made from a tree stump. Abruptly stopping, he next did a somersault, and in mid-roll he withdrew a dagger from his boot and threw it at a target behind him.

Standing up he glanced back at his target, giving a cry of delight when he saw that he had hit it. He looked down to where Hugh was continuing his climb. "Three for me," he shouted.

"Don't brag," said Hugh.

Philip was about to retort when he saw Jonathan.

"Oh, hello, Jonathan," he said cheerfully. "Did you want to try climbing the rope?"

"What is this place?" asked Jonathan, not answering his question.

"It's where we send people who haven't done enough stable duty," grunted Hugh from the wall, thirty feet up.

"No," laughed Philip, "it's the exercise room. If you ever get to the school for the Knights of the White Rose, you'll see one very similar to this."

"Oh," said Jonathan, not knowing what else to

say.

"Come on," said Philip, gesturing towards him. "There's a ladder that leads up here. You don't have to climb a rope."

Jonathan took the offer and was soon standing in the loft next to the strange contraptions. Philip had quit throwing daggers and was trying to jab another set of moving targets with his sword point. Jonathan stared fascinated. There were several targets in pairs stacked on top of one another from the floor to a height of seven feet. No sooner had Philip driven back one target when another would pop forward.

Hugh meanwhile had ceased climbing and had begun moving sideways along the wall towards where Jonathan and Philip now stood. He arrived just about the time that Philip finished his sword-thrusting exercise.

"This is very interesting," said Jonathan. "It reminds me of the strange activities that the Dragikoi did while I was their prisoner. Since Gorwin appears to be assured of Hung-Tai's loyalty, I wonder if we could ask him to train us in the Dragikoi manner? Has Hung-Tai taught you any of those yet, Hugh?"

"No," said Hugh, "but they sound interesting. What do you think, Philip? If Hung-Tai is willing to teach us, would you be interested in changing our regular training routine?"

"I think you are just trying to keep me from besting you at dagger throwing," laughed Philip again. "Just when I start to win, Hugh changes the rules. But actually, a bit of variety wouldn't hurt. As long as it's all right with Ragnar, I'm willing to try something new."

And so it was that only a few days later Jonathan

found himself, together with Hugh, Philip and Ragnar, in the Great Hall following Hung-Tai's orders.

Hugh grimaced as he went down for a stretch, "I don't know if these stretches are supposed to be helpful, or if they are just Hung-Tai's clever revenge for all the bad food at the monastery."

"Just revenge for your singing Hugh," said Hung-Tai.

"Yes, the monks had us do plenty of that," said Hugh, wincing again at another stretching pose.

When it came to performing the Dragikoi moves, the three knights had an advantage over Jonathan in their speed, strength and agility. Nevertheless, since Jonathan had been practising some of the moves earlier, overall he found them easier to learn than the knights. Despite his best efforts to convince them though, none of Jonathan's other friends were interested in the classes.

The first two days of the third week after Anastasis' arrival were holidays and no chores and instruction were offered on holidays. Markus, one of the guardsmen, was teaching Jonathan and his friends how to play chess in the dining hall. Charissa excused herself early and went for a hike.

The rest of them played for the remainder of the morning, but in the early afternoon Jonathan tired of the game and suggested they follow Charissa. They used the same lookout path just below the top of the ridge that Jonathan had taken on the day when Gorwin had told him about his ancestry. They were in no particular hurry and they stopped several times to savour the view.

After a while Olaf left the group, wandering fifty

yards off the path and to the top of the ridge. There he paused to look north towards the ocean, but a moment later he turned and threw stones in their direction. Curious, Jonathan looked back. Olaf was gesturing wildly for them to join him. When they had jogged over, he said, "Don't make any loud noises. Go to the edge and look down."

They did as he suggested. There on the beach were several hundred soldiers, marching in two columns.

# 18 THE ATTACK

From the height of the ridge Jonathan and his friends could not tell where these soldiers came from. He did not recognize either their uniforms or their insignias.

"Should we tell Ragnar or Gorwin?" asked Olaf.

"Would they care? They're probably our soldiers," responded Rannulf.

"They don't look like Gorwin's soldiers," said Sonja.

"Can we ask one of the lookouts up here?" said Olaf.

Jonathan shook his head. "Gorwin's mountain lookouts are usually posted further east above the castle harbour."

They were silent for a moment as the soldiers climbed a small hill beneath them.

"I wonder where Charissa got to?" asked Jonathan.

"Maybe she hiked down into the valley," said Sonja. "She likes visiting the farms there."

"She's probably already back at the castle," added Rannulf.

"There's something very odd about a strange group of warriors marching in formation out here, don't you think?" asked Olaf.

"What if they are enemies? Or what if they're looking for us?" said Sonja.

"Why would anyone want to be looking for us?" asked Rannulf. Then in answer to his own question, everyone, as if on cue, turned and gazed at Jonathan.

"Don't ask me," he said. "I didn't invite them. Yet maybe Olaf is right. I haven't seen Gorwin lately. Perhaps we should return and find Ragnar, just in case they aren't our troops."

Since they were still staring at him, Jonathan took charge. "Rannulf, how about you running to warn the guard at the other lookout. He's on the same path as we are, just further east." Jonathan pointed. "In the meantime, Olaf, do you want to watch these soldiers and see where they go? Sonja and I will go down to the castle."

The friends went their separate ways. Sonja and Jonathan left the ridge and jogged southwards. What with the steep drops and loose rock, it was difficult to go at any speed. It took them half an hour to get back inside the castle walls and locate Ragnar who had just come in through the gate.

"Soldiers?" he said, "where?"

"On the north beach," said Sonja. "Are they Gorwin's by any chance?"

"No, they're not ours unless Gorwin recruited people that he hasn't told me about. But I doubt it. Show them to me."

Before they left, Ragnar dispatched some men to

make sure that none of the castle's boats were in the strangers' path. Privately, Jonathan wondered if these men would arrive at the ocean too late to save the boats, but he did not think that Ragnar wanted to hear his concern mentioned at that moment. Then Ragnar departed with Jonathan to see the soldiers himself. Sonja stayed behind this time. "I'll go and find Charissa," she said.

"There's an easier way up," said Ragnar as they left the front gates. Intrigued, Jonathan allowed Ragnar to lead him behind some bushes towards a barely visible stairway cut into a crack in the cliff face.

The two of them climbed towards the highest part of the ridge, then lying down near its northern edge, they peered down onto the beach below. The cold rock sent a chill into Jonathan's bones, but now there was nobody to be seen below, no soldiers, no invaders, nothing. Jonathan felt foolish. It looked as if he had brought Ragnar all that way as a prank. He watched as the wind blew about a tuft of grass growing out of a crack in a nearby rock. A gull flew overhead.

Still nothing.

"Why don't we try and find Olaf?" he suggested. Ragnar agreed. They left their spot and walked further west. Within fifteen minutes they met Olaf and Rannulf together, returning in their direction.

"Where are the soldiers?" asked Jonathan.

"We saw them last about five minutes ago, marching along the beach eastwards towards the harbour," said Rannulf. "But they've since disappeared behind a mountain."

"Let's wait here and see if they reappear," said Ragnar.

They watched for another ten minutes. Jonathan was about to suggest that they go back to the castle when Olaf gave a start. "There they are," he said.

A column of soldiers had reappeared on the beach, just rounding the base of the mountain to their left. They were further away than when Jonathan had first seen them, but he was sure it was the same group.

Ragnar sat up and stared with intense interest. Then, suddenly remembering, he said, "The boats! Did our people have time to hide the boats?"

Keeping low to the ground and out of sight of the soldiers below, he ran a hundred yards to the east and gazed down at the sea. The three friends followed him.

"Yes, it looks like they managed to hide them," said Ragnar, relief showing on his face. "But it's time we reported back to the castle. Someone will need to run down. The rest of us should keep an eye on these strangers."

Olaf volunteered to go down this time, and they watched him gradually shrink in the distance as he jogged along the ridge towards a place where he could descend.

Shortly afterwards, they observed the soldiers beneath them inexplicably halt. A moment later they turned and began marching back westward in the direction from which they had come. "What are they doing?" asked Jonathan.

"It's tough to tell," said Ragnar. "But they probably had orders to patrol the beach up to a certain point, and now that they have reached the end of their patrol boundary they are returning home. We do the same thing with our troops."

They watched for another fifteen minutes, but the soldiers persisted in the new direction and showed no sign of turning back towards the castle or its boats. Finally Ragnar spoke, "Jonathan, by now Gorwin will have returned. You had better go tell him that the soldiers have changed course."

Jonathan raced down the stairway that Ragnar had shown him. When he got back to the castle, he discovered that the news about possible enemy soldiers had already spread, and Gorwin was waiting near the gates to hear his report.

Jonathan quickly told him what he had seen, and without pausing for thought Gorwin barked out commands. "Markus, Wilhelm, Robert, Patrick, Edmund, get some rations and join Ragnar on the mountain. We may need to follow those soldiers for a few days. From time to time send a report on their progress."

Gorwin sounded serious when he gave these orders. But on the whole Jonathan thought that he looked relieved. Strange soldiers this close to his castle were obviously a concern, but at least it appeared that he would not have to fight off an immediate assault.

Jonathan walked down to the gatehouse to watch the soldiers depart. Shortly afterwards Sonja found him. She looked anxious. "Jonathan, there's been no sign of Charissa."

"Has anyone seen her anywhere?"

"No," she said.

"I'm sure she's fine," said Jonathan, more to reassure Sonja than because he was certain about what he was saying. "I've never known her to go for walks on the mountains. She usually visits the farmers in the valleys."

"Let's hope so," said Sonja.

As the afternoon wore on, one by one, Jonathan's friends drifted down from the ridge. Each of them came with news about the intruders' progress. It seemed that the soldiers were doing just what Ragnar had predicted—moving westward and eventually northward along the coastline.

By late afternoon all of Jonathan's companions had returned—all except Charissa. Supper came and went, and there was no sign of her. The sun edged behind the mountains, and the shadows grew across the valley, and still she did not appear.

Jonathan was getting worried. What if she had encountered the soldiers below? He went down to the gates in the hope of getting news. No one there knew anything about her. Then as he stood chatting with the gatekeepers, Ragnar returned from his patrol. Jonathan asked if he had seen anything of Charissa.

"No," he said, "and I'd advise you to wait until daylight to track her down. In this darkness you can't see anything out there anyhow."

Reluctantly Jonathan took his advice. He returned to his room and after some tossing and turning he managed to get to sleep. Not for long. It was still dark when he woke. He had been dreaming that he had been out searching for Charissa, but in the dream, as soon as he had found her she had turned into an inhuman monster.

Panic gripped him. He knew that it was just a dream, but he was so anxious now that he realized he would not be able to sleep. He went down to the gate tower for news.

The guard had been changed an hour earlier, and

Jonathan recognized the new guard. "Nathan," he called, "have you seen Charissa?"

"Who?"

"Charissa, blond hair, about seventeen or eighteen." Jonathan paused for a moment. How old was she? He realized he did not actually know. "She came with Ragnar and the rest of us from Dorinon."

"Oh. . . I know who you mean. No, I haven't seen her all night."

"She went for a walk this morning and no one has seen her since."

"Hmm."

"You wouldn't be able to let me out to look for her, would you?"

"Uh . . . I . . . uh, you know I'm not supposed to open the gates after dark unless it's exceptional."

"This is exceptional," protested Jonathan. "She's out there all alone and there are strange soldiers wandering about."

"Don't you think that morning would be a better time to look for her?"

"But she might need help now. She could be lost."

The soldier thought for a minute. "Well, I'll open the gate but you have to promise me something."

"What's that?"

"If you don't find her within two hours, you will return to the castle and wait until morning. I have to tell you this, you see, because my neck will be on the block if you don't come back."

"Good enough. We have a deal."

Jonathan climbed down from the top of the wall where the sentry stood, snatched up a lantern from the gatehouse, and lit it from a nearby candle. Soon the gates were open just enough for him to get through. He slipped out into the night and the gates shut behind him.

From where he stood, Nathan could see a light bobbing up and down in the darkness as Jonathan moved away from the castle and towards the mountain staircase.

Eventually Jonathan reached the top of the stairs and commenced walking westwards along the lookout path. He had no clear destination in mind, and now the sheer size of the mountain and the near hopelessness of his task started to sink in. Charissa could be anywhere. Furthermore, he knew that if the enemy soldiers were about, his lantern might attract their attention, too. Nevertheless he kept going and soon he passed the valley in which Gorwin's castle stood and was approaching another mountain valley on his left.

After more than an hour, he caught the strong scent of wood smoke and saw a crofter's hut thirty yards below the ridge. He had seen the hut several times before in the daylight, though he had never entered it. What attracted his attention now was the light coming from the windows. He wondered why any farmer would be up at this time of night. Still, he was cold, and he welcomed the thought of a warm fire. As well, perhaps the farmer might have seen Charissa earlier and be able to tell him which way she had gone.

Trying not to stumble or slide in the dark, he moved down the hill towards the cottage. As he drew near, he noticed that the light from within was unusually bright. Only a really large fire would make that kind of light.

Carefully covering his lantern, he set it down on the ground and looked inside. The window was partially fogged with moisture, but he could see most of the interior.

It was furnished as any other crofter's hut would be, but everything else about it was extremely odd. To begin with, several people sat on the floor with their backs against the wall. Their hands and legs were tied with ropes. Jonathan recognized one of the prisoners: a young shepherd boy named Adam whom he had seen around the castle on occasion.

Two more figures with their backs to him were bending over the fireplace. A moment later they stood up, and one of them, still with his back to Jonathan, moved towards the people seated on the floor.

Jonathan then saw that he held a red-hot poker in his hand. He waved it in each of the prisoners' faces in turn, but seemed to pay particular attention to a young blond-haired woman. Jonathan could not see who it was, but a moment later she screamed. Instantly he recognized the voice. Charissa!

He drew his sword and burst into the hut.

His initial concern was to distract or disable the man, so that he would not hurt Charissa, but his first sword blow bounced harmlessly off the man's goatskin armour. Startled, his opponent snarled and spun around, waving the poker within inches of Jonathan's face.

Jonathan, all his attention on the poker in front of him, parried it once, driving it to his left. Then instinctively he felt his sword arm moving into the figure eight attack pattern that Ragnar had shown him. It worked. His opponent collapsed on the floor.

A bellow erupted from across the hut as the man's partner, also brandishing a poker, launched himself towards Jonathan. Jonathan, meanwhile, intended to stare his opponent down to show him that he was not intimidated, but when he caught sight of the man's face, he nearly dropped his sword.

His enemy was not a man. At least he did not resemble any human that Jonathan had seen. Though he was roughly man-sized in shape with regular hands and feet, his nose curled into a pig-like snout and two fangs protruded from his open mouth. And what Jonathan had thought was goatskin armour was actually the creature's own natural hide.

What made it more terrifying was the fact that he had actually heard of creatures like this before. Every young child in Rindorn had been frightened into good behaviour by stories of the Black Wizard's evil minions who had snout-like noses and tusks growing out of their mouths—creatures who ate human flesh. They were called mrothgars and were all but invincible.

The mrothgar must have sensed his shock because with a yell he jumped up and brought his poker crashing down towards Jonathan's head. Jonathan barely blocked the blow in time. Then, feeling weak at the knees, it was all he could do to parry the next few strokes, retreating step by step before the mrothgar's fierce onslaught. Once he was not quick enough and the fire-poker slammed into his right thigh. He hollered in pain, but as a result he parried it immediately with extra force and the poker spun about and landed on his opponent's right shoulder. This time his enemy howled, and there was a stench of burning hair. Somehow this encouraged

Jonathan. The mrothgar's own weapon had been used against him. He had weaknesses, after all.

Returning to the attack, Jonathan used Ragnar's figure eight attack pattern for a second time. Again he succeeded, pricking his enemy's right shoulder. The mrothgar was not moving nearly as quickly now, but suddenly he jumped backwards and with his left hand he pulled a sword from his belt. Jonathan now faced two weapons.

Once more the mrothgar attacked and the air in front of Jonathan's face was a blur of moving steel. He did the best he could to parry but it seemed that whenever he managed to block the sword, the poker struck his body. In addition to his right thigh, he now had burns on his left thigh, right calf and left side. He could feel his reactions slowing. Ragnar had not trained him to deal with two weapons. He did not know how much longer he could manage to survive.

But just when it seemed as if all would be lost, an old man who was tied up nearby thrust his feet out and tried to trip the monster. The mrothgar retained his balance, but his attention was distracted for a second. Jonathan dove forward though his foe's defences and his opponent went down.

The prisoners cheered. He would have liked to share their celebration, but he was unable. Suddenly sick to the stomach, he rushed out of the hut and vomited into a bush.

A minute later he staggered back inside. Jonathan severed the old man's bonds, and the old man, in turn, aided the other prisoners to cut their bonds with the downed mrothgar's sword. Jonathan tried to continue helping with this, but his stomach lurched once more. Leaving his dagger with Charissa, he stumbled out onto a bench outside. The cool air felt better than the oppressive heat of the cottage.

It was a few moments before he could stand. *This is humiliating. None of the heroes in old tales ever threw-up after their battles. I wonder what Charissa thinks?*

But he need not have worried. A moment later she stepped out of the hut and put her hand on his shoulder. "Thank you," she said.

"Don't mention it," he gulped.

The old man who had tripped the mrothgar came out just after her. "We made sure that the mrothgars were dead," he said to Jonathan, "but let's see those burns." He disappeared for a moment and returned with a bucket of cold water, which he used to bathe Jonathan's wounds.

"Are there any more of those creatures about?" asked Jonathan, gasping with the pain.

"There were more when we were captured," said the old man. "And there might yet be more around. Still, we haven't seen any except these two for some hours now."

As the prisoners left the hut, Jonathan asked, "Is anyone badly hurt?" In addition to Charissa and the old man, there were five other prisoners: a young boy, eleven or twelve years old, two older women, and two shepherd girls.

"No," said the man, "Fortunately you came by before they could do anything worse."

"Why didn't they just kill you?"

"I think they wanted information and they planned to torture us in order to get it."

"Come, we must get you all back to the castle." But as Jonathan said this, he suddenly felt the burns on his legs. Perhaps returning to the castle would be more difficult than he had thought.

Because of the risk of encountering more mrothgars, they did not dare use Jonathan's lantern. Instead, they managed as best as they could to climb the hillside in the darkness. Luckily just before they reached the lookout path, the first glimmers of dawn appeared. By now Jonathan's legs ached with every step and he hobbled along behind the others. Noticing, Charissa turned back to support him. Normally Jonathan would have found her touch elating, but at that moment all he could think about was the pain of his burns and how embarrassed he was to have to depend on someone else for help.

Shortly after they reached the path, they met Gorwin's morning guards coming out to take their posts. From the rear of the group Jonathan could see the old man and Joshua, the foremost guard, rapidly conversing. Then Joshua began urgently gesturing them towards the castle.

Jonathan kept hobbling as fast as he could, yet even with Charissa's help, he fell further behind, and eventually the rest of the group stopped to wait. One of the young shepherd girls named Carmen ran back to see if she could help.

"Tell your friends to keep going," Jonathan told her. "The sentries are up here now so I should be fine. But I want you to run to the castle and tell them what's happened."

Carmen carried Jonathan's message back to the former prisoners, then as Jonathan had asked, she ran ahead and down to the castle. After the group had departed, Jonathan and Charissa walked until they found a fallen tree trunk to sit on. Though trees were rare on the mountain ridge, this one had grown in a crevice between two rocks and had received shelter from the wind.

There was an awkward silence after they sat down. Now that the threat of immediate attack was over, Jonathan was exhausted. He did not think he could walk all the way back to the castle.

Charissa broke the silence, "You know . . ."

"What is it?" said Jonathan.

When she did not say anything more he looked at her with concern. Even though she had been up all night and soot streaked her face, he still thought that she looked beautiful.

"I don't think I really thanked you properly for rescuing me," she said at last.

"Oh that was nothing," said Jonathan. "You don't need . . ."

He did not get a chance to finish. Charissa threw her arms around his neck and kissed him on the lips. Despite the cold morning wind, Jonathan suddenly felt warm inside. He had been hoping for some sign of affection from Charissa for days but he had not expected this. He tried to think of something to say.

"Perhaps, you won't have to go home to Janzilar anytime soon," he finally stammered.

"Perhaps you're right," she said.

And this time he kissed her.

They rested there with his arm around her for a few more minutes, while Jonathan reflected on all the bizarre adventures that they had experienced together. Soon she stood up. "We must get back to the castle," she said. "There might be more mrothgars nearby."

The two of them stumbled on again for another half mile as an ocean mist gradually blew in, shrouding the mountainside.

"You're very quiet," she said.

Jonathan's head was spinning as he dealt with the fact that Charissa was returning his affections, and he struggled to find something to say. "I'm still grappling with the fact that I've just been fighting actual mrothgars. Real ones," he finally ventured. It was the only thing that came to mind.

"And you find that strange?" asked Charissa, pulling closer.

"Yes. I mean, I believed in mrothgars as a child, but when I got older I just assumed that they were legends. But since the wizard actually exists, I suppose I could have figured out that his warriors weren't fireside tales either. I guess I hadn't been thinking that far ahead. Now I don't have to. I've seen them in the flesh."

"I don't know much about them, do you?"

"According to the stories, mrothgars are the Black Wizard's crack warriors—half human, half beast with human intelligence and beast-like ferocity. Supposedly their ancestors were humans, but over time, by craft and cunning, the wizard bred them into a race of invincible soldiers—especially cruel and malicious. They are humans no more. They no longer have the capacity to be merciful. Oh, and they can see in the dark."

"But at least we've just seen that they aren't invincible," said Charissa. "I wonder how much of the rest is true?"

"I don't know. I hope we don't have to find out."

Their conversation ended as Jonathan searched for the mountain stairway that would take them down to the castle. He had just found it when a shadowy figure loomed out of the mist.

"Who's there?" asked Jonathan.

"Is that you, Jonathan?" It was Philip's voice.

"Yes."

"I'm here to help you down the mountain. They told me you'd been hurt."

"I guess so, yes."

"Come," said Philip. "There's an easier way over here."

Jonathan wondered how many more secrets this castle contained that he was still unaware of. Following Philip, he and Charissa went about fifty feet up the mountain instead of down, and there, behind the shelter of some cedar trees, was a door.

Philip took out a key. "This is a secret route and it is not to be talked about, do you understand?"

They nodded and together stepped through the doorway. Philip helped Jonathan down a few more painful steps until they came to a landing where they met Ragnar, Gorwin and two servants with a chair. The servants carried Jonathan the rest of the way down the stairs, which ended in a long, smoothly paved passageway.

"Where are we going?" asked Jonathan.

"This takes us underground to the castle," said Gorwin.

"Did you dig this?" asked Jonathan, amazed.

"No. The smugglers did long ago, but it does come in handy on occasion."

They lifted Jonathan onto a cart and rolled him to the end of the passage, which brought them to the castle infirmary. After his burns were treated, he fell into an uneasy sleep.

# 19 THE MROTHGARS' REVENGE

All the next day Jonathan rested in the castle infirmary, but though he had been badly burned, he found it difficult to remain idle. His mind would not stop going over the events of the last twenty-four hours—especially Charissa's newly expressed affection for him. He did not see her for the next two days, as she apparently came by when he was sleeping.

He was awake, however, when Ragnar and Anastasis came to visit him the second morning after his adventure. Jonathan smiled when he saw them. "Give me the news, Ragnar. Have there been any more encounters with mrothgars?"

"No," said the knight. "But Gorwin has ordered more patrols. Honestly, we don't know what to expect next. Perhaps that attack that you interrupted was a mere raid, or perhaps the start of an invasion. Initially everyone had been relieved when the soldiers that Olaf had sighted turned around and marched north and west. No longer, your adventure made it clear that the mrothgars hadn't really left the district."

"What do you think?" asked Jonathan.

"I'm wondering," said Ragnar, "why the soldiers that Olaf spotted a few days ago retreated. If they really wanted to invade us, why didn't they just keep coming?"

"Perhaps their retreat was a feint to draw off our defenders so that they wouldn't be around to protect us during the real invasion," said Jonathan.

"I am thinking the same thing," said Ragnar. "Still, Gorwin is thankful that you rescued those peasants. Not only did it save their lives, it also let us know that our enemies are plotting something. You see, up until then, Gorwin thought that the Black Wizard didn't know about this castle's existence. Things are different now."

"What's Gorwin going to do?"

"Prepare for an invasion, just in case there is one. He doesn't have much choice. Luckily, most of the farmers nearby are shepherds and not grain growers."

"Why is that lucky?"

"Sheep can be moved, but if an attack comes, crops will get burned in the fields. Gorwin has already advised the shepherds either to come to the castle or to flee with their flocks eastward—further from the Wizard's territory. He's also continuing his wall project."

"What's that?" asked Jonathan.

"Some weeks before you arrived, Gorwin started extending one of the castle walls. He wanted to create more space for livestock if an invasion ever happened. Now that one could be imminent, he's ordered that every spare hand be used to finish the wall."

Anastasis smiled. "Yes, you're fortunate to be in

here, otherwise you'd be put to work, too."

Jonathan grinned. "Given the choice between work and burns, I'd probably rather not have burns." Then becoming serious, he turned to the hermit, "Tell me about the mrothgars. Where did they come from? Are the legends about them true?"

Anastasis sighed. "They first appeared about six hundred years after the initial war with Magelandorn's enemies. Despite what the legends say, we don't actually know where they're from. We only assume that the Black Wizard created them or warped them from our original human enemies, and somehow he made them stronger than humans."

"I used to think that mrothgars were a myth," said Jonathan. "It's just very odd for us Rindornites to discover that supposed fairy tales are actually true."

Anastasis smiled, "When you truly commit to work on the side of good and get involved fighting the Black Wizard, you often find that both the good and the evil creatures that you once believed to be mere fantasy, are more real than you think."

"I suppose you might be right," said Jonathan. "I've seen more legends come to life in the last few weeks than I would have thought possible. Surely though, in addition to the things that we think are legendary and later turn out to be true, there are also things that are nothing more than stories and hoaxes."

"Yes, there are many hoaxes," answered the hermit, "but somewhere in the midst of these there are the things that are true as well. It is wise to remember this, since it was this vision that created Magelandorn in the first place."

"So how do you determine what is true from

what is a hoax?"

"What is tried and true for many years is often the truth, whereas the hoaxes generally offer us cheap pleasures, reduced personal responsibility or an easy way out. And when you stop and think about it, to be offered an easy way out is really an insult. It is equivalent to saying that you aren't capable of doing any better. Truth and love do us the compliment of expecting the best from us and asking the highest that we can offer, because truth knows that each of us is capable of things that are truly remarkable."

Jonathan shook his head. "I don't feel capable of doing anything remarkable."

"Neither do any of us. But when the time comes, I'm sure you will rise to the challenge." He stood up. "Now I think we've kept you talking longer than we should have. You need rest." With that Ragnar and the hermit departed to perform their morning duties and Jonathan was left to ponder their conversation.

After three days of bed rest the pain of his burns began to diminish. Feeling frustrated with inactivity, Jonathan hobbled out to help the fletcher make arrows. It was a job he could do sitting down which did not cause much discomfort.

Three evenings later, he had been asleep for only a while in his own room, when he was awakened by loud shouts and noises from the courtyard outside. Drowsily he wondered how long it would take the drunken peasant to be restrained by the night watchmen.

Then there came a banging on his door, "Jonathan, get your sword on. We're under attack!"

Within minutes he was dressed, had splashed cold water on his face, strapped on his weapons, and was stumbling down the stairs.

Chaos confronted him in hallway below. He had to press himself against the wall almost immediately in order to avoid being flattened by a servant barrelling up the stairway calling, "Water, water, we need water!"

Just then Ragnar stepped through the door. Catching sight of Jonathan he yelled, "Jonathan, get out here!"

Dodging two more servants, Jonathan made it to the door. Ragnar pointed at the wall, "Grab a bow and some arrows and cover that section—quickly."

Jonathan hobbled over to the archery shed, scooped up a quiver and bow, then going to the nearest tower, he climbed to the place that Ragnar had indicated. It was the wall's southern portion, the left hand side as he faced west.

Everywhere he looked the castle was surrounded by foes. Although the darkness made it tough to count the exact number, he could see their shadowy forms outlined by the occasional lit torch or campfire. There seemed to be a larger cluster of enemies on the northern and western approaches. Jonathan guessed that this was because the ground sloped away from the castle at a gentler angle on those sides.

Anxiety gripped him. Of all the threats that he and his friends had faced in the last few weeks, this seemed to be the greatest. His heart went out to the crofters who were not inside the castle walls. He only hoped that they had received timely warning and fled to safety.

Something whizzed past his ear. Quickly he ducked behind one of the battlements as a volley of arrows flew overhead, one of them ricocheting off the wall behind him and landing at his feet. As soon as the volley subsided, he risked looking out beyond his shelter to the valley below. The mob of invaders outside had swelled closer now.

There came a clattering sound from the wall beneath him. Staring down, he saw that a ladder had been raised by his foes, and as Jonathan watched, a shadowy form scurried up the rungs. He should throw the ladder down, he knew, but there were arrows flying, and he wanted to wait until his adversary had climbed a little higher first. Glancing around, he saw four more upraised ladders to his left, and he wondered who was supposed to be covering that section of the wall.

Suddenly he realized that he did not have the luxury of finding out. Despite the risks, he had to act. Bounding to his feet, he braved the arrows and heaved the nearest ladder away from the wall. He grabbed the next three of them in time, but he was too late with the fourth. A man had already climbed it and was standing on the wall!

"Enemies on the wall! Enemies on the wall!" cried Jonathan as he charged. He hoped that someone else would come to help him soon. There was no way that he could successfully repel all the ladders on this section while actively fighting an enemy at the same time. Still he would try.

He drew his sword as he ran. In surprise his foe moved back a couple steps, which was exactly what Jonathan wanted. With his right foot he caught the edge of his opponent's ladder, kicked it out away from the wall, and he heard a yell from the next invader climbing it. Then Jonathan faced his adversary, a man both taller and stronger than he was.

His opponent had his sword out now, and with a smooth stroke he brought it swiftly down towards Jonathan's neck. Jonathan countered with his own sword. Metal struck metal. More strokes were exchanged. Right then a volley of flaming arrows passed over their heads, which made them both duck. Most of these landed on stone or bare earth, but a few found their marks. A nearby thatched stable roof caught fire, illuminating the area around Jonathan in its red glow, and for the first time he could see his adversary clearly. Fangs hung down from his mouth—another mrothgar. Jonathan felt the same panic and nausea that he had a few nights earlier. It had been tough enough to beat those first two mrothgars. Could he manage a third?

Then out of the corner of his eye he noticed two more ladders being lifted. If he did not dispatch this creature soon, there would be more foes to handle. Just at that moment he was saved by pure luck. One of the mrothgar arrows, intended for the castle courtyard, flew through the air a little too low and struck his enemy. With a cry, the creature fell backwards over the wall.

Jonathan rushed towards the other ladders, quickly knocking them down. Wiping the sweat from his brow, he breathed a sigh of relief. There were no more ladders being raised, but gazing out over the wall, he spied something further to his left. When he ran over to it, he discovered one of Gorwin's soldiers, pierced by three arrows and already dead. That was why he had no help on his section.

He wanted to call for more aid, but he was sure that with the amount of noise around him his voice would go unheard, and of course, he could not abandon the wall himself to recruit more assistance. Three new ladders had just then appeared. Risking the arrows, he tossed them down as quickly as he could.

After this he paused to catch his breath. He was worried. If his foes were smart, they would concentrate all their offensive efforts on him since he was the only defender on his side. How long would it take them to figure this out? There had to be a way to stall them until more help arrived.

In desperation he grabbed his bow and started shooting down in the general direction of his enemies, and this seemed to have the desired effect. No more ladders were lifted while he was shooting arrows. The problem was he could not tell if he was hitting anyone. He was also running out of ammunition and was soon forced to gather up stray mrothgar arrows. They were longer and heavier than his, but still usable. Yet even these too eventually ran out.

"May I be of assistance?" said a voice behind him.

Jonathan jumped in surprise. Spinning around he spotted Philip in the half-light. "Assistance?" said Jonathan, exasperation in his voice. "Absolutely! I'm the only one on this part of the wall. Recruit some help or help me yourself."

At that moment Jonathan spotted five new ladders. Leaving Philip, he ran down the wall pushing out two of them. Philip in turn pushed out three others. Then the two of them crouched behind a battlement while Jonathan caught his breath.

"You know," added Jonathan, between gasps, "something else I could use would be a stick with a fork at the end. A halberd of some kind would do. If I could reach down with that and push each ladder away, it would be a lot easier than having to grab them by hand."

"For now I've brought you something else," said Philip, as another volley of arrows whizzed above their heads.

"You know, this isn't exactly the best time for food or gifts."

"It's the helmet from Dorinon," said Philip, and this time Jonathan sensed annoyance in his voice. "Helmets are somewhat useful in battle, I would think. But I will get help."

"Thanks," said Jonathan, feeling ashamed at the tone of his earlier comment. "What exactly is it supposed to do anyhow?"

Philip, however, had already disappeared, but not before he had set the helmet down at Jonathan's feet. Jonathan was about to put it on when he noticed several new ladders resting on the wall's edge. Chiding himself for forgetting his proper job, he left the helmet and dashed off, dislodging each of the ladders just in time. Then taking cover behind one of the battlements, he glanced back towards the castle courtyard. A few fires were still burning, but servants with buckets and wet sacks had smothered most of them. Moment by moment more guards issued forth from the main keep's doorway. It seemed that as they belatedly woke, Gorwin's soldiers were joining in the defence.

"Nice holiday, isn't this?" Then he recognized Rannulf's voice. Relief flooded through him. It was also the first time that he had seen his friend since his adventures a few nights before.

"Holiday? I suppose so. If I was planning it, I would have chosen a different activity," said

Jonathan.

Rannulf crouched beside him. "So, did Ragnar and Gorwin arrange this for our entertainment or is this part of the training?"

Despite the rain of arrows, Jonathan chuckled. "It may be training," he replied, "but I don't think they arranged it."

"You know, when we first arrived, I wondered how Olaf, Sonja and I would be able to contribute in Gorwin's community. But I think I've figured that out."

"How's that?"

Rannulf laughed and waved his arm outside the wall, "With this!"

Jonathan was glad that Rannulf could maintain such a positive attitude in the face of battle. "Does that bother you?" he asked more seriously.

"No. I've always wanted to be a knight. Now it appears that I'll get the chance." He laughed again.

"We have to win this battle first."

"I brought a couple halberds. Philip sent them."

"Good. Do you have arrows? It seems that firing them delays our foes from tossing up ladders."

"No, I don't. We could throw other stuff at them. There must be loose stones up here. Or how about this?" Rannulf groped in the darkness around him. "An old helmet." He raised it above his head, ready to toss it down.

"Wait!" shouted Jonathan. "That's the Dorinon helmet!"

"The family heirloom?"

"Yeah."

"What's it doing up here?"

"Philip wanted me to wear it. I forgot."

"You better put it on then. Look, there're more ladders."

The two of them rushed along the wall knocking the ladders down sideways with their halberds. As soon as he could spare a moment Jonathan strapped on the heirloom.

"If you want to get more arrows," said Jonathan. "I can hold out for just a bit longer."

Although Rannulf was gone only a couple of minutes, Jonathan was hard pressed during his absence. Yet at the same time, something now felt different. Once, he had an unexplainable urge to move away from the battlement where he had been sheltering. No sooner had he done so when a large stone hurled by a catapult crushed that section. It would have killed him had he remained. Another time he obeyed a compelling urge to flatten himself on the top of the wall. A moment later a volley of arrows landed where he had been standing. *Is it my imagination or is this helmet actually helping me dodge missiles?*

Nevertheless, despite these coincidences, if that's what they were, he was exhausted when Rannulf returned. "This is insane," he said. "Aren't there more people who can help up here?"

"Philip was trying to recruit a few. But I think that most of the men are already involved in the defence. It might be just you and me."

Despite Rannulf's pessimistic prediction, four other men-at-arms did eventually show up. Jonathan had only met two of them before, Patrick and Edmund. Yet even with the extra hands, the friends found themselves almost as busy as before. It seemed that their enemies had increased the frequency of their attacks.

"Perhaps they've finally figured out that this section had the fewest defenders," said Rannulf.

During a particularly vigorous assault, one of the mrothgars did manage to climb a ladder. But he had the misfortune of arriving between Rannulf and Jonathan. He was no match for the two of them attacking from the front and the rear simultaneously.

"Someone told me that you had met up with mrothgars," said Rannulf, wiping the sweat off his forehead after they had finished their melee. "I didn't believe it."

"Sorry to disappoint you," said Jonathan, "it's true. Yet as you can see, at least they're not invincible."

"I've noticed. Still, it's pretty unnerving."

"I know how you feel. Meeting them for the first time a few nights ago unnerved me too."

Together they toiled for over an hour to keep the wall free from enemies. They succeeded, but at a cost. Edmund, standing on Jonathan's right, was killed by an arrow. Finally, Nathan, the soldier who had been on gate duty several nights before, arrived to help in the defence.

Jonathan asked him if he had seen any of his friends recently. "Sonja is shooting a crossbow from one of the towers," said Nathan. "Anastasis is involved in a bucket chain, and I think Olaf may be putting out fires."

"Where's Charissa?" he asked.

"I don't really know," he replied. "She might be with Sonja or be part of a bucket chain."

The thought that she might be in danger bothered Jonathan.

"She'll be all right," said Nathan, sensing his

concern. "Or she will be if we can keep these folks off our walls."

The half moon was veiled now by thick clouds, and in the darkness they had no idea how many foes were below. Unless the mrothgars climbed ladders, they could not tell where they were at any particular moment. Jonathan realized that most of their side's arrows were being wasted.

Someone else on the castle's western wall must have been troubled by the same thought because not long afterwards he saw lit torches being thrown down into the midst of their foes. The torches went out shortly after hitting the ground, but they gave Gorwin's people a momentary target to shoot at. Nevertheless, defending themselves against these determined enemies seemed nearly hopeless.

After a particularly fierce assault, out of the corner of his eye Jonathan spotted some mrothgars running along the top of the wall towards one of the towers on his left. A ladder or two had obviously escaped the defenders' attention.

Jonathan chased these foes and arrived at the tower to find its bottom door forced open. Charging up the stairs he discovered a torch-lit room at its summit and Sonja, Charissa and Olaf. They would normally have been shooting crossbows bolts through the tower's arrow slits, but right now they were battling three mrothgars.

With his typical bravado, Olaf was whirling around like a madman, attempting to defeat all three opponents at once. And to Jonathan's surprise it appeared to be working. Jonathan was tempted to laugh at the expressions of fear on the faces of these supposedly fearsome monsters.

But the smile died on his lips. Just as he was about to enter the fray, he saw Olaf leap in front of a blow that had been aimed at Sonja. He yelled in pain as the blade sunk into his flesh. Anger and fear for his friend swept through Jonathan like a wave. Shaken, he barely had the presence of mind to strike at the creature that had attacked Olaf. Fortunately, he dispatched it from behind, but an instant later the second mrothgar whirled around to face him, leaving the third monster to battle Sonja and Charissa together.

Jonathan cursed his luck. He was below the mrothgar on the curved stairway leading towards the tower's summit. The tower had been designed to favour the defenders, who in normal circumstances would have been standing above their assailants, and so the stairs curved clockwise, making it more difficult for the soldiers from below to use their sword arms.

The two assailants exchanged blow after blow. Jonathan found himself using his shield more than his sword. Consequently, the fight was only tiring him out without actually damaging his foe. In the meantime he could see that Charissa and Sonja were having difficulty defending themselves against their enemy. Olaf groaned in a corner.

Then disaster struck. With a savage blow, his opponent slashed downwards onto Jonathan's sword, knocking it clean out of his hand. He was weaponless and facing a superior enemy. He still had his shield, which he now used twice as much as before, but it was only a matter of time before the mrothgar's sword struck home.

Then an idea came to him. He thought of the

Dragikoi's ability to use the very force of their enemies' blows to knock them off balance. Moving toward his opponent, he deliberately allowed his left side to go unshielded. The mrothgar fell for the ruse and drove forward with all his might towards the vulnerable spot. Anticipating this, Jonathan slipped back to the side, causing his enemy to miss him completely. Over-reaching himself, the mrothgar stumbled forwards, passing Jonathan on the stairway. Jonathan then spun around and kicked the monster's back with his right foot, causing the creature to fall on his face. Then quickly grabbing his sword and dispatching his foe, Jonathan leapt upwards to assist his friends above.

The three friends quickly dealt with their remaining opponent before attending to Olaf's wounds. Just in time. He was barely conscious.

"We'll get him to the infirmary if there's a break in the battle," said Sonja. "In the meantime this is as safe a place as any."

"Take care of him" said Jonathan, "I need to get back to my wall. Once I've left, you can bar the tower door behind me. It's nice to know that I have friendly archers covering my back."

"Wait," said Sonja, "I saw you drop your sword, and yet you survived?"

"Dragikoi techniques. Luckily, they worked."

"Lucky? I think not. I should learn them," said Sonja.

"There's room in Hung-Tai's class," said Jonathan. He waved at Charissa and left the tower.

The assault persisted unabated for another half hour. Then, immediately after Patrick was wounded, their enemies inexplicably ceased the attack. No more arrows flew over their heads and no more ladders threatened the ramparts.

Rannulf and another soldier took advantage of the break and carried Patrick off the wall. Jonathan remained to guard the battlements. As he watched, the moon re-emerged from behind a cloud. In its light he could see the entire valley clearly including the mrothgar host. They were retreating from the wall and already out of bowshot range.

Jonathan picked up his bow and fired a couple of shots at those still lingering nearby.

"How are you making out?" said a voice from behind him.

Once more Jonathan started in surprise, nearly stumbling forward towards the wall's edge. He recognized the hermit's voice. "You surprised me," he said, "but I'm doing fine. It seems like the mrothgars are leaving." Jonathan sat down, taking advantage of the lull in activity to rest his legs.

"No. They're just getting out of the range of our arrows while the moon is shining. They'll be back with reinforcements once it goes behind some clouds." He pointed and Jonathan's eyes were drawn further along the valley. A fire had been started about a mile away. The mrothgars were burning down the spruce trees that had stretched across the valley floor and concealed Gorwin's castle from view. In the light of the distant fire, Jonathan could see a second host arriving to swell their foes' ranks. "That's why I've come up here," the hermit continued. "There's something I need to tell you about your parents."

"You knew my parents?" asked Jonathan.

"I did. I knew your mother quite well. Your father, too, though not so well."

"How did you get to know them?"

"That's what I came to tell you. We don't know how the battle is going to end tonight, and you have a right to know. Jonathan," said the hermit, looking squarely at him, "I am your mother's father."

"Her father?" He rose to his feet in surprise.

"Yes. I didn't want either of us to die without you knowing that."

"So then you are my . . . my . . ." began Jonathan, unable to say the word.

"Your grandfather? It would appear so."

"Then . . . uh . . ." His mind was spinning, trying to absorb the information. He had no idea what to say.

The hermit chuckled. "I was a nobleman once— the Duke of Dorinon actually—one of Morden's descendants, which is why I know my way around my old castle so well. Of course, being the king's father-in-law, I lost the duchy when the Verbordens took power. But I don't worry about Dorinon as much as I do about you. It's good to know that you're alive."

"It's good to be alive," said Jonathan. "It's been an exciting few weeks."

"It has been," said Anastasis, "but that's enough talk for today. We need to make sure that you stay in good form and the rest of us, too. I'm going to find you more arrows."

The hermit departed, leaving Jonathan lost in thought. He almost wished he could have heard this information at another time, because despite the advancing army, he now found it difficult to concentrate on the task at hand. His thoughts kept going back to what Anastasis had said.

Rannulf returned a few moments later. "I saw

Olaf in the infirmary."

"I'm glad they got him there," said Jonathan. "How is he doing?"

"It was tough to tell in the light," said Rannulf.

Worry, like a dagger, stabbed into Jonathan. Yet he resolved not to let his anxieties overwhelm him but to take out his vengeance upon the source of Olaf's malady—their foes. To get his mind off both Anastasis and Olaf, he moved over to listen to a conversation that Rannulf had struck up with a newly arrived soldier named Karl.

"The hermit person gave me these to bring to you folks," said Karl, placing five quivers of arrows down on the top of the wall.

"Thanks," said Rannulf, "Say, uh . . . you know there are mrothgars down there, do you?"

"Yup," said Karl. He did not seem terribly surprised or worried. "People around here haven't forgotten about the Wizard or his soldiers like folks down south."

"Do you often fight mrothgars?" asked Jonathan.

"Yup. Aren't many humans in the Wizard's army. Just mrothgars and a few human slaves. Least so far as we've seen. We often see them. Not around here but on our patrols to the northeast."

"So are the old tales true in other ways, too? We heard that they eat human flesh," asked Rannulf.

"Not sure about that," said Karl. "They do eat raw flesh of various kinds. So, p'raps yes, they might eat human flesh, though I've never seen it."

"We heard growing up that they were invincible," said Rannulf.

"Obviously not, there's dead mrothgars all over the place down there," he replied. "But are they cruel and tough? Yeah. I'd rather be fighting human warriors any day. It looks as if you'll get a chance to find out for yourself. They're coming back."

He was right. The moon disappeared behind clouds again and the swollen horde approached. The defenders gathered all the unbroken arrows they could find and marshalled the remaining troops to the castle walls.

The next hour was the most strenuous yet. The freshly arrived troops launched their assault with animal ferocity. Gorwin's people shot volleys of arrows, but in the darkness they shot blindly and without any real accuracy.

Ten ladders were thrown onto Jonathan's section of the wall as volley after volley of mrothgar arrows flew over their heads. Then from the western side, Jonathan heard the shout, "Enemies on the wall! Enemies on the wall!" The castle bell rang out in warning.

He looked west. A thick crowd of mrothgars were battling with the defenders both on top of the wall and in the courtyard below. Their opponents had broken through!

Seeing the confusion, Karl rushed over to the western wall to prevent any more enemies from entering. Jonathan, Rannulf, Nathan and Hillary were left to defend the southern wall by themselves. Jonathan wished he could be in two places at once, helping the defenders in the courtyard also, but he was busy enough keeping all the ladders off their own section. They had to hope that Karl and the others on the western side would prevail.

Gradually the situation on the western wall appeared to stabilize. No more mrothgars entered that way, but some who had already gained access were still in the castle courtyard.

During a brief lull in the fighting, Jonathan, glanced down and saw Ragnar and Philip both bravely battling two enemies each. Observing the duels, Jonathan said, "If only we can get rid of the ones on the inside we'd be fine. If not, who knows what kind of damage they'll do?"

"The only good thing about having mrothgars in the courtyard is that there aren't as many arrows coming in over our heads," replied Rannulf. "They don't want to shoot their own comrades." It was true. There had been fewer overhead arrows since the attack on the west wall.

Jonathan was about to make another comment, but a single soldier in the courtyard distracted his attention again. The man, wielding a sword in each hand, suddenly launched himself into the midst of the crowd of invaders. Weaving, almost dancing between his opponents, he occasionally spun a full circle to strike or parry a blow. Jonathan wondered about the identity of this talented soldier. Then the man briefly looked up and the light of a burning roof reflected on his face. It was Hugh, making up for all his time convalescing in the monastery by taking on numerous foes at once.

Jonathan was brought back to his own task by more ladders being raised. He and Rannulf had no opportunity to worry about the courtyard for a while. Again and again, the mrothgars came on. Again and again they were pushed back, but despite the humans' best efforts, the ferocious attacks continued.

The defenders were becoming exhausted, and even with the superior sword skills of people like

Ragnar, Philip and Hugh, Jonathan began to doubt whether they could actually win. There were only so many servants and men-at-arms inside the castle, and their enemies showed no signs of weariness. Also, if legend was correct about the mrothgars' superior night-vision, the humans would be an easy target for their opponents. It was only a matter of time, he thought, before the defence was finally swept away.

And yet, just when he was most tempted to despair, his attention was distracted by something in the pocket next to his right leg. At first it merely felt warm, but soon it grew hotter to the point where the skin beneath the pocket started to hurt. This was annoying. The middle of a battle was not the best time for a new and perplexing problem.

*What's wrong with my leg?*

Then he remembered. That right hand pocket was the place where he had recently been keeping St. Swithun's Amulet—the amulet the Dragikoi had stolen from Rindorn. He had almost forgotten about it.

For a moment he did not know what to do until he realized he had to get it out of the pocket before it burned him. He grasped it, but it nearly scorched his palm. Reacting to the pain he yanked it out and dropped it onto his foot. From there it rolled onto the stone pathway on top of the wall where it lay radiating a white light of such intensity that his eyes ached with looking at it.

No one was more surprised than he to see it glowing at his feet. The amulet that he had made fun of so often in the past had suddenly shown itself to be more than it appeared. He rubbed his eyes to be sure that he was not seeing things. But it was still visible.

From behind him Rannulf said, "What in the world is that?"

"St. Swithun's Amulet."

"You're not serious! What's it doing?" asked Rannulf.

"I have no idea. It was in my pocket as usual and then it started getting really hot. So I took it out."

"Can you touch it?" said Rannulf.

"I can try." Jonathan bent down to grasp it but the blast of heat coming from the rock stopped him from actually picking it up.

"So I suppose you couldn't put it around your neck then," said Rannulf.

"Why do you say that?"

"It's an amulet, right? You're supposed to wear it. That's its proper use."

"Is it?" said Jonathan, "perhaps this one is different."

Meanwhile, the rock glowed ever brighter until it became difficult to gaze at any part of the wall nearby.

"What are we supposed to do with this thing?" asked Jonathan.

"I have no idea. What use could it have?"

Jonathan thought for a moment. He recalled how the mrothgars had retreated out of bowshot range when the moon came out from behind the clouds.

"I have a plan," he said. "Can you get me a rope?"

"I'll try," said Rannulf, and in a few minutes he returned with a length of heavy cord.

The amulet was now far too hot to touch, but Jonathan bent down and felt towards its chain. Then carefully he ran the end of the rope through it. The amulet now dangled beneath the rope.

Then together, while shielding their eyes, Rannulf and Jonathan lifted both ends of the rope and carried the amulet to the centre of the western wall where they draped the rope around one of the battlements. The amulet was now suspended over top of the gate, where it bathed the whole of the field in front of the castle in its powerful light.

The defenders could now easily see and shoot at the mrothgar host beneath them. The mrothgars stood helplessly, shielding their eyes from the rock's powerful brilliance. When they tried to move forward with ladders, arrows found them.

All this time, the other guards on the wall had been casting curious glances at the amulet.

"What is that!?" one of them finally asked, when he had a break from defending the wall.

"St. Swithun's Amulet," said Rannulf.

"St. What?" asked Karl, joining in. "What's it doing?"

"Don't know," said Jonathan, attempting to keep the conversation short. "But it's working. That's good enough for me."

When at last the mrothgars discerned that they had lost the advantage on the castle's western side, many of them fled to the northern and southern sides where they attempted to continue their attack. Rannulf and Jonathan followed with the amulet. At times, though, Jonathan wondered how much of an advantage the rock actually gave them as most of the soldiers on the wall were so awed by it that he had to keep reminding them to do their work.

Nevertheless, the assault soon turned into a rout. The invaders—both inside and outside the castle courtyard—were either driven off or killed. Mrothgar bodies lay strewn all over the fields surrounding the walls. A short time later the attack ceased altogether.

"So do you still think that the amulet is merely a 'lump of rock,' Jonathan." asked Rannulf as they waited to see if the mrothgars would try again.

"Fine, rub it in. No, I don't—obviously."

"Have you figured out how it works?"

"No idea," said Jonathan. "It's too bad we can't ask St. Swithun."

As their foes withdrew, Ragnar and Gorwin emerged from one of the towers and stood on the southern wall near Jonathan. From there they surveyed the rapidly changing battle.

"Should we pursue them?" asked Gorwin.

"Perhaps," said Ragnar, "yet this retreat could be just a trick—an attempt to draw defence away from the castle."

"Of course, but if we don't pursue them, will they just regroup farther down the valley and ravage more of the nearby farms?"

"Possibly."

"Then we must send mounted soldiers. Since dawn isn't far off, even with some troops away on sortie, we will be better able to defend ourselves than we were when they attacked us in darkness." Then seeing Jonathan nearby, Gorwin added, "That was very clever of you to bring out the light for us, Jonathan. How did you manage it?"

"I didn't," said Jonathan. "And I wish I could tell you how we did, but I really have no idea."

"It was St. Swithun's Amulet," said Rannulf.

"St. Who?" asked Gorwin.

"Swithun," repeated Rannulf, "the patron saint

of Rindorn."

"And how did you get his amulet?"

"The Dragikoi stole it, but Jonathan got it back when he escaped."

"We're lucky you did," said Gorwin. "Thank goodness those Dragikoi took you prisoner, Jonathan. We might have lost this battle if they hadn't."

"I don't know if I'd use the words 'thank goodness'," said Jonathan. "I didn't exactly enjoy the experience."

"Why not use those words?" said Gorwin. "It's worked out for the best. And rumour has it you found a fair maid at the same time, too?"

"Well, I . . ." Jonathan blushed.

Ragnar and Gorwin left the wall. Moments later Jonathan heard a trumpet call echo throughout the castle, and a company of soldiers on horseback departed to pursue their foes. The friends were not asked to take part in the pursuit. Jonathan guessed that this was because Ragnar did not think they could ride well enough. For once Jonathan was relieved to be left out. He felt exhausted. No one told them to stop guarding the wall, though. It was as if they had been forgotten.

While he and Rannulf remained guarding the wall's eastern section, Jonathan's mind kept going back to the news that Anastasis had given him earlier. I have living relatives! he exulted.

An hour after the sortie departed, Jonathan looked over at his friend. Even with the chill morning air Rannulf was yawning constantly. "Why don't you get some sleep? I'm not tired now," Jonathan lied. "I can stay until we're relieved."

"Thanks," muttered Rannulf. Then supporting

himself with one hand against the battlements, he turned and slouched off towards bed. Rannulf had not sounded terribly thankful, but Jonathan knew that he had meant it.

Jonathan stood on the wall until the eastern sky grew light. To his surprise the amulet gradually faded as dawn drew near. Eventually two other guards arrived to relieve him from duty and he, too, returned to his room. Then the last thing he did before falling asleep was to place the helmet in a hidden corner underneath his bed. The amulet still dangled from its rope in front of the castle where they had left it. Gorwin had ordered that it be guarded and not removed.

When he awoke he learned that soldiers pursuing the mrothgars had cornered them in a wooded valley and reinforcements had been called for, but again, Rannulf and Jonathan were not asked to go. Instead Philip assigned Jonathan to sentry duty.

Compared to the action of the previous evening, Jonathan found his late afternoon on the wall rather dull. He saw no enemies and the biggest excitement he had was watching birds fly overhead. The monotony was relieved when the hermit joined him.

Anastasis hailed him with, "I'm glad to see you survived!"

Jonathan waved back. Although he was dying to find out more about his parents, he found himself less than comfortable with the subject. He was still working through the fact that the hermit, whom he had always understood to be a friend, was now someone with whom he had a much closer relationship. He was not used to having family members. What was it all supposed to mean? "It's good to see you in one piece too," he responded, smiling. "And I'm glad you've come. I've had a few eye openers since I saw you last and there are things I wanted to ask you."

"Like what?" said the hermit.

"The helmet for starters, it could have been my imagination, but I think it really helped me avoid some of those enemy attacks."

"I'm not surprised. Your father's family kept it around for a reason. Keep using it, and in time you'll know more about it than I do."

"How does it work?"

"I've never used it. But I do know that the more sacred gifts you have the greater power each individual gift has. We'll have to work on getting you the other gifts."

"Like the amulet?" said Jonathan.

"Yes, I heard about that. No, the amulet, though special on its own, is not one of the sacred gifts."

Jonathan thought for a moment. "You know, I used to make fun of the amulet, just as I used to make fun of everything else in Rindorn: the mayor, the upper classes. And I can understand why. The city nobles used to make such a huge, pompous fuss over the thing—dragging it about for fairs and special events. Now it turns out that all the legends are true."

"And that makes you uncomfortable?" asked the hermit.

"Frankly . . . yes," he said.

Anastasis paused before answering. "Over the years I've learned that it isn't wise to despise things or people," he eventually said. "If you do, it tends to come back and haunt you. You might find yourself one day walking in the shoes of the people whom you used to despise. You said that you used to make fun of Rindorn's nobility, for instance?"

"Uh, yes. They were an easy target."

"And now you find that you are part of these same noble classes yourself?"

Jonathan was silent. He had not thought of things that way before. It suddenly dawned on him that if Anastasis was descended from Duke Morden, then he, Jonathan, had hung the mayor's trousers off a statue of one of his own family members. He laughed. "I guess the joke is on me now, isn't it? Perhaps someday someone will publicly hang my trousers off a statue."

"A most likely possibility," said the hermit with a smile. "But actually, in a sense you were correct in your disdain of noble titles and classes."

"How's that?"

"Being part of the royal family is more of a job than a privilege. Yet it is the kind of job that involves more than just winning a war or defeating the Black Wizard or guarding our family's sacred duties and treasures. It's about trying to do something better and reach for something higher. It's about being a purer and nobler kind of person, striving for things that elevate the human spirit. And doing this not for the sake of vaunting oneself above others, but in order to be of service to others and being an example of what all people can and should be—even if no one notices you for doing it. Doing that is real nobility, and it's the kind of nobility that anyone can reach for, regardless of who their parents are."

Jonathan tried to absorb what the hermit had said. Finally he added, "And the amulet too, I had always thought it was merely ceremonial."

Anastasis chuckled then sat down on the top of the wall. Jonathan copied him. "I understand the shock of discovering that something is real when one had always thought it to be legendary," he said. "I had the same shock myself when I was about your age. But I've learned that such things don't need to make you feel uncomfortable. Provided that you are striving in truth to do what is right, you can often count on Providence to help you. That at least was the view that your parents had—and your grandparents. Now I need to catch up on my rest. I'm not quite as young as I once was. We'll chat again."

Jonathan was too absorbed in thought to respond, so he just nodded and watched Anastasis descend the stairs, cross the courtyard, and go back into the castle.

Sometime after sunset he turned to see Charissa walking towards him. "Hello," he said.

"I couldn't sleep," she said. "I wanted to know how you were."

"Fine," said Jonathan. "Have you seen Olaf? They've kept me up here all day and I haven't had a chance to visit him."

"I've just been down to check on him. He's resting."

"Is he hurt badly?"

"Nothing that won't heal, I think."

They remained on the wall together until another guard came to relieve Jonathan. He said farewell to Charissa on the stairway outside the dining hall and then exhausted, he locked the door to his room and quickly drifted into sleep.

# 20 THE FEAST

Salvage, repair and cleaning occupied all the inhabitants of the castle for the next few days. In addition to the collecting and sorting of weapons and armour, straw and sticks were gathered to repair the thatched roofs that had burned.

Gorwin had taken the amulet from the wall and moved it to a safe place inside the castle. Jonathan guessed that this was the same room where the helmet and the golden ball were kept. They also heard that the sortie had succeeded in their battle against the mrothgars. All but a handful of their enemies had either surrendered or been killed. The others had escaped into the mountains to the northeast. Miraculously, none of Gorwin's people had perished in this last defensive action.

Meanwhile, the peasants set to work burning the bodies of the fallen mrothgars before disease could spread. Since this job was nearly completed by the time that Jonathan and Rannulf were sent to help, they were told to gather abandoned armour and weapons. These would be taken to the blacksmith later and refashioned into horseshoes, tools or other needed farm implements.

A few days after the battle Jonathan's classes with Hung-Tai resumed. This time, with Sonja's encouragement, his friends joined in as well.

Despite the sobering events of the past few days and the hard work involved in cleaning up the aftermath, for Jonathan this period had turned into one of the happiest times of his life. The fact that the woman he had come to love also loved him made all the hard work seem like a brief moment. They found what time they could to walk together in the valley— Charissa wanted to avoid the mountains—but mostly they sought out quiet corners in Gorwin's library when he was not there.

Other people noticed the new relationship. Three mornings after the battle, Sonja joined Jonathan in his work. "I hear that you and Charissa have paired up," she said.

Jonathan was a little uncomfortable that she had already discovered his secret. "How did you hear this?" he asked.

"Oh, the usual sources."

There was no point in denying it. "Yes I suppose we have . . . paired up—if you want to call it that. Do I have your permission?" he added with a touch of sarcasm in his voice.

"Permission? Of course. As long as it's not too ap*par*ent every time I see the two of you." She smiled at her own pun. "I'm sure it will be just fine."

Jonathan tried to grin in response. But at that moment he found the fact that his private life was public knowledge rather disconcerting. He had not anticipated this side to romance.

As the afternoon wore on he started to feel better. He realized that in all likelihood people would soon tire of this topic and find something else to focus on. Besides, he was too happy to care. In fact, he could not remember feeling this happy in years. Each day he looked forward to the chance to spend more time with Charissa once his work was done.

A week after the battle, Gorwin presided over a magnificent feast with exquisite entertainment. Olaf had recovered enough to attend, although he excused himself early. In addition to the usual mutton, there were seaweed salads, local vegetables, venison, salmon and roast squid spread out upon the tables.

Finally, near the end of the banquet, Gorwin stood up to speak. "I am very aware that I am standing in front of a room full of heroes. I personally witnessed many acts of bravery, and since the battle I have heard many other stories of tremendous courage."

He then began to tell them about some of the feats which had been performed. After he had finished each story, he asked the person or people in question to stand for public recognition. Among other stories, Philip and Hugh's defence of the castle courtyard was mentioned. Jonathan noticed that Hugh's arm was in a sling.

Gorwin returned to telling stories of the battle, but most of the time Jonathan found it difficult to pay attention to Gorwin's recollections, his own memories of the evening were too vivid. Then suddenly he got a sharp nudge in the ribs from Rannulf on his right. "Jonathan," he hissed, "he's talking about us." Abruptly Jonathan's attention was drawn back to the present.

"A short time ago, a few friends arrived here from a distant city," said Gorwin. "To be honest, when I first met them, I and some of the other soldiers wondered if they had it within them to face the kinds of foes we meet here. But two nights ago showed me what they were made of. In addition to the other feats of courage we've heard about this evening, we owe these two heroes a debt of gratitude as well. During a lengthy portion of the attack they defended the eastern wall by themselves without the aid of others. They also figured out a way to harness St. Swithun's Amulet, the light source that allowed us to repel our enemies, and suspend it over the wall in order to illuminate the mrothgar hosts. It's good to have you on our side."

As he briefly rose to his feet and noticed the beaming faces and clapping hands, Jonathan blushed. His clearest memory of that moment was the smile on the face of Charissa as he and Rannulf acknowledged the applause.

"All of this goes to show," continued Gorwin, "that when right is on their side, a relatively small group of dedicated individuals can overcome superior odds to win the day and advance their cause. Let this be a lesson to all of us. What we have done here tonight, we can do again. Though the enemy appear strong, we can and will overcome. The Verdorbens and their Wizard ally will be defeated and goodness and safety will once more return to the Kingdom of Magelandorn!"

There was a burst of applause as Jonathan, his friends, and the entire hall rose to their feet.

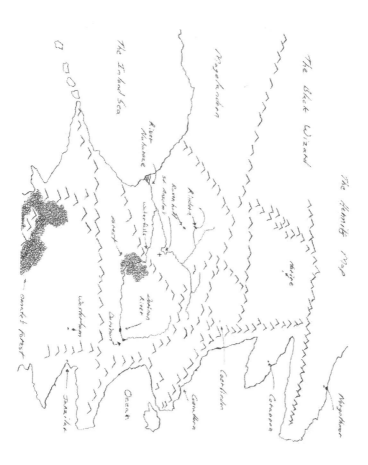

The Hennifty Map

# ABOUT THE AUTHOR

Bart Eriksson was born and grew up in Camrose, Alberta, Canada and lives with his family in Cochrane, Alberta. His hobbies he enjoys hiking, music, skiing and history.

Made in the USA
Charleston, SC
22 December 2015